In the Devil's Own Words

Cathedral Chronicles
E.M.G Wixley

Cover Design: E.M.G Wixley

This book is a work of fiction, and any resemblance to persons, living or dead, or events is purely coincidental. The characters are products of the author's imagination and are used fictitiously.

Dedication

I would like to dedicate this book to all those who have helped me through the process of writing: my partner Phil and my two sons, Thomas and Richard, for having such patience.

Chapter One

Isobel Miller sat in the passenger seat next to her mother as they drove into the picturesque village of Langham. The sun was shining, and the sky was sparkling blue without a single cloud. All the car windows were open, and the sweet sound of birdsong floated in on a soft breeze.

The vehicle turned down into the thick green tunnel of trees of Hollow End Street; their ultimate destination lay further down the road. Golden spikes pierced through the gaps in the canopy onto a mass of brightly coloured flowers that grew profusely on the bank beneath the tangled hedgerow. Running parallel to them on their right was the castle wall, behind which towered tall, dark pines, standing guard in their tranquil grounds of dappled light and shade, emitting a pleasant fragrance.

The scene would have been one of perfection to anyone other than Isobel, who hated it all with a passion. To the truculent teenager, it felt like she was being dragged into alien territory. She knew how it would all pan out; they would stay with her mother's parents, John and Daisy, for a while, and then Isobel and her parents would move to another featureless box that her witch of a mother would attempt to brighten up with a lick of paint and new furniture. It would be house number fifteen; she had worked it out in her head, averaging it at one house for each year of her life.

Isobel glanced over and saw her mother's hands trembling on the steering wheel. *It's coming up to her drinking time,* she thought to herself. The pattern was always the same—a bottle of red wine with dinner, and when the last drop was consumed, she would begin weeping for her absent husband, Major Jacob Miller.

The teenager was suddenly drawn from her thoughts by her mother's voice. Isobel looked up at Jean's wrinkled lips as she momentarily paused to suck on a cigarette. Then, the quivering voice continued.

'It was your grandfather that told me about the skeletons. They were only discovered a week or so ago under the floor in the Black Horse pub.' Jean paused for another drag on the cancer stick. 'You know, the one that is situated next to that eleventh-century church. The landlord and some of his friends, including Gramps, were moving one of those old inglenook fireplaces to carry out some repairs. In the process, they damaged the flagstone floor and decided to level it all out and start again. It was quite a surprise when they found the skeletons. They had to call the police in case it was a murder.'

'Ok, great, why are you telling me this random crap? It won't make me want to live in this dump,' Isobel replied, knowing her mother had thrown out the piece of information in an attempt to appease and distract her from her dark mood.

'Well, isn't that interesting?'

'Mum, just don't bother. Leave the storytelling to Gramps - he's much better at it than you.'

Isobel lifted her legs up to place her hiking boots on the edge of the seat and began to suck her thumb in deep contemplation.

'Oh, take that out,' her mother scolded. 'You're fifteen now and far too old for that. And look what you're doing to the seat with those filthy boots,' she added in an exasperated tone.

'Why should I when you smoke? That's way worse, and you're pregnant,' Isobel snapped back but then complied. They both fell into a wounded silence. The teenager didn't want to hurt her mother, but she despised the fake persona Jean wore for everyone except maybe her father.

Just lately, they'd grown apart; her mother had become like a compassionless, empty shell, living in a cloud of Valium calm, whose only desires seemed to be materialistic. All this was in direct opposition to her interests, as she cared nothing for the mundane and frivolous. She hankered for something wild and reckless and was interested in the arts, history and music, but everything she introduced to her mother was received with shock and expressions of repulsion.

However, Isobel was able to remember a time when she had worshipped her mother when she had thought her beautiful with her long rust-coloured hair and dazzling smile.

She looked over at the frail-looking middle-aged woman with her swollen belly who scrutinised her face in the rear-view mirror and adjusted her now short hair.

'Mum, you should really stop dieting now that you're pregnant,' she spoke up, genuinely worried by her emaciated appearance.

'Oh darling, you can never be too thin. You could do with losing a few pounds.'

'Look, they still don't have any street lights. I hate this place... it's so lame, like time has been turned back,' Isobel stated anxiously and fixed her gaze on the passing scenery beyond the car window.

She knew her mother was tactically ignoring her comment, not wanting to have the subject of all her daughter's anxieties dragged out into the open. The whole family were aware of her genuine fear of the dark, and now she was being moved to a place where, in the winter, she wouldn't be able to see her way home from school.

'I sneaked into the grounds of Avernous castle when I was young with a boyfriend, but Lord Langley's father chased us away.'

'Oh, my god, Mum, you tell me that story every time we pass. I know you love this place, but I think it's creepy. When I last visited the bungalow, there was no one to hang around with, and they were all backward country bumpkins. 'Deliverance', kids,' Isobel ranted, wildly waving her arms about to express her frustration.

'Darling, I know it is difficult for you with all this constant change, but your father plans to leave the army in a year's time, and this would be a good place to settle. Also, I would like to have Granny at my side when your brother or sister is born. Please give it a go, it will be more fun than you think,' Jean pleaded.

'Mum, I've got nooo bloody friends - don't you understand?'

Isobel's mother didn't reply as she was too busy trying to get another cigarette out of the packet with one hand.

'You never listen,' the girl muttered to herself.

Isobel knew that her new home was situated on the Pilgrims Way to Canterbury as her grandparents had lived there for as long as she could remember, but she had rarely visited them because her parents were always on the move. Her father had been in the army for over ten years and had, of late, been discussing with Isobel's mother his desire to lay down roots in the country. Previously, Jean's elderly parents had travelled to their son-in-law's various homes, but now they were finding the long journeys increasingly tricky. Also, this time, it was different as Isobel's mother was having a baby and required extra help.

That was another thing that riled Isobel—the thought of a baby. She was too old for a whinging brother or sister, and she loathed the whole idea. She turned her head and looked out of the window as tears of frustration tumbled down her cheeks. The moving air was like a furnace and dried her face instantly, leaving no evidence for any dramatic effect.

At last, the agonising journey was over. The line of trees petered out, and to her left was an oasis of brightness and colour where petals from a blossoming tree were falling lightly onto the gravel driveway, carpeting it with a delicate pink. The car crunched its way down towards one of two large bungalows that sat side by side, surrounded by beautiful gardens. At the far end was a glistening stream, behind which stood the tall, slender, silver frames of a poplar wood, and in the distance, soft rolling hills could just be seen.

Isobel hardly had time to settle into her new bedroom when the adults announced that they were all going to the pub in the village for a meal. As they walked along the country road in the fading evening light, Isobel's granddad started one of his spooky tales. John Bridges loved nothing more than a good ghost story. His various myths and legends had provided her with much-needed entertainment and the attention she had craved during her early childhood. She had always been grateful for the oasis of peace that his presence granted and had often wondered how her mother could have been the spawn of such gentle people.

They strolled along side by side. Isobel felt sheltered and warmed by her granddad's tall, stooping frame, and she listened eagerly even though, from the first word, she felt the shivers run up and down her spine.

'Of course, it all happened hundreds of years ago in medieval times, when Raymond Langley was the Lord of the old Castle, as the manor house hadn't been built at that time.' John paused, and once sure he had his granddaughter's attention, he continued with relish. 'What you have to understand, Isobel, is that in those days, everyone believed in God and knew if they committed a sin, they would go straight to hell. Jane Lacy was one of those God-fearing folks. Everyone at the time liked the girl as she was pretty and a devout Christian who attended the village church every Sunday.'

'You mean your church?' Isobel enquired.

'Yes, the one by the pub. Anyway, Lord Langley employed her as a cook, and she was praised far and wide for her skills in the kitchen. Old Raymond liked her very much, but being a lady of good virtue, she shunned his advances.' He stopped speaking and stroked his beard as though in deep thought. 'Issy, I'm not sure this story is really suitable for you, especially with your fear of the dark.'

'Gramps, I will be fine. You can't stop now.'

'Okay, but don't do your wandering-around-the-house-at-night thing.'

'I won't, and that was years ago.'

'Well, after some time, Raymond got bored—or perhaps it was to make Jane jealous. Anyway, he invited a distant female relative to stay, and soon Jane's life became harder as she was expected to cook for the new special guest and a whole host of others who joined Raymond at night. The beer and wine flowed continually, and the parties went on for weeks.

'At first, the ungodly behaviour scared Jane, as she feared for their souls. Then she became angry and one night decided that it was her duty to put an end to all the debauchery.'

'What did she do?'

'She put poison in the meals of Raymond and his special guest, who was now his lover. The next day, a group of knights who had been at the party found the couple dead and instantly blamed Jane.'

'Gramps, that doesn't mean she poisoned them—they could have died for other reasons.'

'Well, these men decided they would enforce their own form of justice. Jane tried to run and escaped through a small door in the castle wall, but they caught her.'

'Well, what happened?'

'I don't think I should tell you that bit.'

'Please,' Isobel begged, desperately needing to know the end and hated being treated like such a child.

'Some of the men held her while the others dug a hole by the wall. They threw her in and lay rocks and old flagstones on her body until she was slowly crushed to death.'

'Ha, that's so cool.'

'Issy, it's just an old tale. I don't suppose any of it's true.'

'So, did she become a ghost?'

'Yes, she was buried not far from the bungalow. She has been seen many times on Hollow End Street crying and looking lost. Tourists have even gone up to her to offer help.'

'Have you seen her?'

'No, no, of course not,' stated Isobel's granddad, but his tone of voice was unconvincing.

After their meal, they all walked home in the dark with John holding their one small torch. Isobel wondered how she would ever feel comfortable in a place that was so different from the warmly illuminated streets of the towns she had found so familiar. Secretly, she felt terrified as they walked through the dark throat of trees where the occasional shot of moonlight punched down onto twisted branches and the inexplicable shapes that moved in the undergrowth.

Chapter Two

Peter Archer could not free himself from the technologically chaotic black hole of his attic bedroom. He was an only child. The books, pens, and an array of broken electrical items, which lay scattered over every surface, were like substitute companions. There were his many unfinished attempts to build the ultimate robot and numerous other projects. In the roof at the centre of the space was the oversized skylight his father Bill had made for him with the sole purpose of providing a home for his pride and joy, the most powerful home telescope they could find.

After finishing a sandwich his father had prepared for his lunch, Peter lay on his bed listening to music as the sun lanced through a smaller window that overlooked the front garden.

Peter was an observer. He preferred to sit back and watch others rather than be at the centre of things. He chuckled to himself as he looked over at his kitten, who was trying to climb up the checked curtain, pulling out threads as he slipped on the shiny surface. It was the summer holidays, so he could stay frozen in place for as long as he wished—until it was dark, and he could look up into the night sky he preferred until the dark turned into light.

Beds were very familiar to the teenager, as he was bed-bound for much of his early years, which had been spent patiently waiting to get well to recover from one of his asthma attacks or other illnesses. In those days, he had resigned himself to his desperate situation and used books to escape from the pains of reality.

It was during that period of his life that he discovered the enticing magic of the celestial utopia. Soon, his passion for the immensity and finite details of the unfolding universe was all-consuming. He loved its clarity and cleanness, and there was no need for him to be a robust, healthy hero or a blood-and-guts fighter like his friend Oswald. The cosmos was the perfect mystery and something of value in which he could become engrossed.

Most of all, he enjoyed baffling less-knowledgeable adults with his unanswerable questions. He remembered how he used to badger his father over and over with one particular problem. One time, when he was about six, and they were safely away from his mother, working on the vegetable patch, he had asked.

'Dad, what's at the end of the universe?'

His father had stood up straight, brushed the mud off his hands and looked at his son quizzically. 'Wow, that's a big question. Well, let's see. Peter, I believe there is no end.'

'But there must be. Everything ends.'

'Space is curved. Think of it like an orange: you start at one point, and if you keep walking, you arrive back at the beginning. Here's another thought for you: if you could travel at the speed of light, you would be home before you left.' Bill chuckled to himself.

'Yes, but what's the orange in?'

'Well, I don't quite see what you mean, but I suppose it's in nothing.'

'What do you mean nothing? It can't be nothing.' Peter had shouted with exasperation.

'Peter, I'm not sure I can answer that one.'

'Ok, where did the orange come from?'

'Oh, I know the answer to that. First, there was emptiness, and then in that space, there was a very dense particle that held huge amounts of energy. Well, it exploded, with a big bang and spread out. Over time, our solar system was formed and the whole universe. Although, don't tell your mother I said that—you know how upset she gets by all this stuff.' Satisfied with his answers to his son's enquiry, Bill returned to his planting.

'Dad, what was there before the 'big bang'?'

'Son, that's enough. I'm busy. It would take a whole lifetime or more to figure that one out. Now look at these plants—doesn't their perfection say it all? Everything is amazing. The fact that any of us exist at all is enough for me.'

Peter loved hearing his father's voice. He was a quiet, shy man and seemed nervous about expressing his views in front of his wife. He worked hard as a Landscape Gardener and spent most of his spare time tending to his own plants and speaking to John over the hedge.

However, Peter had learnt a long time ago not to ask his mother Emily anything, as she was deeply religious and mortified by any suggestions that God may not exist—at least not in the form that she understood. Now, as a teenager, he resented the way she believed absurd stories and would visibly flinch from anything that failed to fit into her view of existence. She was fanatical about her faith, and every Sunday, without fail, she would stride up the hill to the church and would be burdened with guilt if she failed to attend due to her son's sickness or for any other reason. This caused a gulf between him and his mother as he cared equally vehemently in his belief that the truth lay in incontrovertible facts. The only common ground on which they occasionally met was with her love of horses, two of which she owned and kept in the stables on the last farm before the road petered out into a track that led over the downs.

Emily's real and frightening state of craziness had all started with the animals. One night not long ago, he had caught his father with a worried expression on his face, listening to one of Emily's stories while they were cooking in the kitchen.

'Bill, it was so frightening. The horses were uncontrollable, breaking free from their stables and running wild. We couldn't get them back in; they were kicking out and rearing up. There was nothing any of us could do to calm them.'

Peter stood concealed behind the frame of the open door, concerned that if he revealed himself, they would fall silent. Periodically, he peered around the edge to see what was going on, but they were so engrossed in the dramatic events they remained unaware of his presence.

'It was the birds,' she whispered, and Peter saw tears coursing down her cheeks. 'There was a huge black cloud of starlings and crows swooping down, blinding the poor creatures and pecking at them until they bled. We put coats on and anything over our heads to prevent them from pecking our eyes out. Look, look at my hands.' Peter poked his head out and saw her outstretched hands covered in blood.

A week later, Peter came home from school and, on passing his parent's bedroom, found his mother sitting on the bed sobbing, with her face buried in her hands. He sat down close and put his arm around her shoulder.

'What's up, Mum?'

'All the fruit trees are dying, and your father's spring vegetables have all withered.'

'Don't get upset about that, Mum. You know Dad will sort it. These things happen,' he said sympathetically, wanting to cajole her out of her misery.

Then, without warning, she venomously hissed, 'It's all your fault.'

'No, it isn't, how's it my fault!' he shouted, so shocked he immediately pulled away and stood up. 'Are you crazy? Have you gone loony tunes or something?'

'You're infected with evil,' she burst out. Her hands were wringing in her lap, and an ugly, tortured expression crumpled her face. 'Your mad ideas. People like you have driven God away.'

'Mum! Mum! You can't believe that crap,' Peter screamed as the tears brimmed in his eyes. He was desperate and torn apart by her unbelievable accusation.

The door slammed, and Bill walked in on them, both screaming at each other hysterically.

'You're no son of mine. Soon, there will be nothing but a never-ending night, and it's your fault.'

'Whatever, you stupid cow, I wouldn't want to be your son; you're crazy.'

Shaking, Peter ran from his mother and speedily climbed the ladder to his room, slammed the door, put his headphones on and listened to his music as loud as it would go while he lay weeping into his pillow. Occasionally, he heard distant shouting; as far beneath him, he could just make out the sounds of his parents arguing.

The next day, his father gently explained to him that his mother had scalded herself while cooking and that she'd gone to the hospital. He also tried to reassure him that she hadn't meant any of the harsh words that she had spat out at him. Peter chose not to listen—nothing his father said could take away his torment. He had actively blanked his father out and continued to play with the Night Sky app on his iPhone. Peter knew what his father really meant was that his mother had finally cracked and been carted off to the insane asylum.

It was a good thing that Emily had not been home, as a day later, Peter had drawn back his curtains to see a thick plague of toads covering the whole of his view of Hollow End Street. Obviously, it was some kind of natural phenomenon, but his mother would have read the toads' appearance as a sign of impending doom. The strange thing was that he had also seen the figure of a small man in a black cloak picking them up and putting them in a bag. However, when he mentioned it to his father, he claimed not to have seen the creatures or the stranger.

That was over a week ago, and since then, Peter had retreated into the predictable world of science and facts.

The loud ticking of the clock was annoying him. It was dark, and at last, he could go and see if the 'Seven Sisters', which was the name he had given to a peculiar-looking group of stars, were still there. Peter had first spotted them on the night after the skeletons had been found in the pub. He had never seen them before and had been unable to discover their identity. It was exciting, but he was unsure who to tell and what reaction he would receive.

He went to the small window, looked out, and thought of John and Daisy's granddaughter, who had recently moved in with them. The last time he had seen Isobel, she had been about seven, smaller than most of her age, thin with long autumnal hair and fabulous, soft brown eyes. They had never played together, as he was usually going through a bout of illness, but he had enjoyed watching her rollerblading along the road in her isolated little world. Once, she had looked up and smiled, and the sweetness of her face had never left his mind. However, when he saw her arriving a few days ago, he had been shocked—her hair had been cut short and dyed a bright red. Isobel wore a kind of cap, huge boots, tight jeans and a baggy t-shirt. She looked like some goddamn emo. What a transformation! Since Isobel's arrival, his father had been prompting him to go and call on the girl, but he hadn't been able to summon up the courage.

Chapter Three

Oswald Hunt never reflected deeply on anything, as it was always too painful. He knew that his father, George, viewed him as the diabolical child who had killed his mother on the day of his birth sixteen years ago. The hatred was intense and mutual, and everyone who knew them recognised that they were both damaged humans. No one had ever tried to intervene in his or his sister Ariel's plight. They were dismissed as eccentrics, just another facet of Lord Langley's household.

Anyone would think that it would be wonderful to live on the grounds of such a beautiful estate, complete with a large fortified house and a ruined castle keep but it was far from a perfect life for Oswald and Ariel. The three of them lived in a dilapidated old farmer's cottage within the perimeter of the castle grounds and had free run of the place. Their father was also the present Lord Langley's Game Keeper, so more and more frequently, Oswald was made responsible for the birds in the falconry. Ariel was expected to carry out most of the household duties.

Oswald was a fearless fighter and had been excluded from school more times than he could remember, either for protecting his sister or Peter, his classmate and his one and only friend. The only reason he was permitted to enter the sixth form was because of his high exam results. The other children saw him as a challenge; the outsider was not welcome in their pack. He was grimy, someone to be driven away like a wounded animal. Oswald was preyed on from all sides.

Although quite handsome with a tall, lean frame and dark gipsy looks, he appeared uncared for, his trousers were often too short; his dirt-grey school shirt was always half tucked in his trousers and half hanging out. His thick black hair was rarely cut, never combed, and on close inspection, was often flecked with sawdust from cleaning out the birds. Also, he was hyper-vigilant and always ready to pounce. He had boundless energy and was only ever calm when he was with animals. His wildness and energetic need for attention annoyed people in authority more than anything. However, within the village, he was tolerated.

Lately, Oswald found himself bored with the drudgery and futility of life, and he found himself wishing for a war or some catastrophe to liven things up. He wouldn't have cared if the whole world were exterminated, except for three things: Ariel, Sir Lancelot, his golden eagle, and his friend Peter.

His sister was only one year older than himself, but from as far back as he could remember, she delighted him. Like a bird protecting its chicks, he had a desire to keep her safe under his wing. She was the one person who had always been there to soothe away his troubles. He loved to watch her doing her pop star routine as she jumped around on her bed singing to her favourite music. She had an impressive voice, and he firmly believed that one day, she would be a star. Together, they spent much of their time fantasising about how they would spend their vast riches. He would be her manager, and they would travel the world in a colossal campervan. She would be loved by everyone who set their eyes on her symmetrical face and her dark, seductive eyes. Oswald thought of her as his caged bird of paradise that one day he hoped to see fly free.

Oswald stood in front of the rows of cages. Each bird would have to be fed, one by one, and then taken out to be exercised. He was looking at the snowy owl sitting on its perch, blinking at him. He was there, as usual, to keep out of the way of his father.

'Ill-tempered, vindictive scum. I hope he rots in hell,' he grumbled to the creature that just regarded him dumbly. He was aware of his rumbling gut, but the moment he had smelt the reek of booze on his father's breath, he had lost his appetite for breakfast. The whole situation seemed insoluble, and the older he became, the stronger the desire to escape grew. 'Oh God, why can't someone or something save us?' Oswald pleaded to the empty sky.

Oswald heard a faint rustling behind him and thought that his sister must have come to find him as her biggest fear in life was that her brother would become so frustrated with his father's temper that he would run away and abandon her to the monster. Slowly, he turned around and found himself face-to-face with a beautiful young girl. She wore a long white dress that was mostly covered by a thick cotton apron, which did little to conceal a pregnant belly. She smiled tenderly, but her eyes were sad, and her beseeching white lips were trying to move.

'I put a curse on them all for their cruelty, but alas, we no more remain. It be your task to finish this, my lad,' she whispered in a piteous voice.

Oswald wanted to look away, but he was somehow dazzled by her presence. She reached out her hand and touched his shoulder. Instantly, all his anger decayed as calm was transferred through her fingertips into his anguished soul, and he felt still. Then, one by one, the quality and details of her loveliness began to fade.

The teenager was not left quivering or traumatised by the strange event—instead, he felt serene, as though his burdens had finally been lifted. He returned to his task of feeding the birds, and as he bent down to fill up a feeding bowl, he noticed blood dripping onto the ground. *Oh no, not another nosebleed,* he thought to himself as he desperately searched his pocket for a tissue. Finding nothing, Oswald pressed his shirtsleeve against the flood and hurried back to the cottage.

Chapter Four

'Are we going shopping tomorrow, Mum? I want to see if they have got any good shops in this dump.'

'Isobel, don't be so rude. They have the same shops that you would find anywhere.'

'I don't want those crap chain stores. I mean my kind of shops.'

'Please don't talk like that in front of your grandparents,' Jean scolded.

They were all sitting around the kitchen table having supper before bed. Isobel glanced at her grandparents' embarrassed faces as they enthusiastically dunked biscuits into their drinking chocolate.

'Well, are we going? I am fed up hanging around on my own. It's supposed to be my holiday.' Issy whined.

'I am afraid we can't tomorrow, your gran and I are going to go to the hospital to have the baby's progress checked.'

'You cow, you promised me.'

'I know, dear, but I am very busy at the moment, and you are old enough now to look after yourself. Granddad will be home but don't go too far, stay near the house. I don't want to have to worry about anyone else.'

Lazy bitch, she never cared about anyone else other than herself and the stupid baby, Isobel thought. She felt stung by her mother's words, betrayed and more resentful than ever towards the precious baby who seemed to be taking up everyone's attention before it was even born.

THE MOMENT THE SUN rose the next day, Isobel was jolted awake by a loud banging that sounded like it had cracked open the sky, coming from the woods at the bottom of her garden. Isobel recognised the sound from the shooting ranges from when they were living on an army base. Without further thought, she jumped out of bed, rapidly dressed and rushed down the corridor to the kitchen. There, she found her grandfather, John, sitting at the wooden table, calmly reading the paper. With his reading glasses balanced on the end of his nose, he looked over them as she approached and saw her obviously startled white face.

'What's the matter, Issy?' he said as he stroked his grey beard and took off his glasses.

'Did you hear that banging? It sounded like some people are having a gunfight in the woods.'

'Oh, don't worry about that. It's just some folk shooting rabbits in the backfield. You will soon get used to the country ways.'

'I thought it was some mad person come to kill us all.'

'No,' he laughed. 'What would you like for breakfast? I am not great at cooking, but I do good bacon and eggs," he said, standing up and unhooking the frying pan off the wall and placing it on the Arga. 'Will that suit you, or I can do cereal?' He was such a tall man compared to the rest of the family, who were all quite petite.

'Bacon and eggs would be fine, thanks.' Isobel sat down, and then something caught her eyes on the front of the local newspaper—a picture of a magnificently ornate gold box, like a small treasure chest. She dragged the paper in front of her and began to read.

'Gramps, it says the bones they found were ancient, very, very old.'

'Yes, I have been reading the article, and it is exciting. Look what they say about the box they found.'

Isobel silently read on and was amazed by what she discovered.

'A mysterious box and bones have been discovered in a local public house, buried under layers of lead which took a long time to remove. Scientists with Geiger counters had been called because the pub owner, Mr. Leonard Parker, feared that the contents might have been concealed in such a way because they were radioactive. Eventually, the box was taken to the Museum in Canterbury. At first, it could not be opened as there was no apparent lock, but finally, the curator managed to find a trigger, and inside, they discovered a very large book.'

Isobel looked up. 'Hey, Granddad, they are saying that they found a book bound in human skin.'

'How do they know that Issy?' John replied as he busily attended to his cooking.

'The pores of human skin are different from those of pigs and cows. Also, they say the skin has a strange waxy odour.'

'What else does it say?'

'There are symbols embossed in gold on the front cover of a dragon biting its tail and five gold rings. Gramps, this is so cool I will have to look it up on the net.'

John ambled over to the table, slid the fried breakfast onto a plate and then sat down beside his granddaughter.

'The pages of the book are made of a so-far unidentifiable material. Each page has been highly decorated with illuminations, detailed drawings and symbols.' Isobel read aloud, only pausing to take a mouthful of food.

'You eat your breakfast. I will tell you what it says.' John took the paper, placed it in front of him, and continued to read to himself.

'Go on, Granddad.'

'It says the book could be ancient —perhaps pre-dating Christianity.' He then recited that *the book has another odd feature in that some of the text appears to have been written in some kind of blood. We are hoping that we might be able to extract some DNA samples. Unfortunately, we are so far unable to decipher the main body of the text as it is mostly written in an unknown language.* It also says the Archbishop Sir Philip Wighard has claimed that he recognised the symbols as being of an ancient religious code and has made a request to examine the book further, along with another knowledgeable clergy in the Cathedral.'

Full up, Isobel pushed her plate away, 'Is that it, gramps? Is that all it says?'

'Well, yes, other than to say that the two skeletons would be buried in the church's graveyard.'

'Oh, my God, Gramps, that is awesome! A real mystery.' Isobel squealed, hardly able to contain her excitement.

'Well, we have all been saying that the pub is haunted; strange things have been happening there for years. Perhaps that's why.'

'Have you seen any ghosts in there?'

'Well, one Sunday afternoon, after I had been fishing, I popped in the Black Horse for a drink. There was no one in there except me, the landlord and a strange-looking chap who sat by the fire. I just glanced at him and thought nothing of it. The barman went into another room to get some stock, and I was left on my own. I had my back to the dark figure but felt uneasy. So, I turned for a second look and, as I did so, saw him fade away. When I mentioned it to Leonard, the landlord, he said he hadn't seen anyone. However, some of my friends have seen him; they call him 'the monk' on account of his strange clothes.' John smiled to himself and went on about his various tasks.

Isobel had just finished her breakfast when the doorbell rang, which her grandfather answered.

'Isobel! There is someone to see you,' the old man called out.

She pushed her plate away and went to the door. There stood a skinny boy with hair as white as snow. His bright blue eyes peered at her through the thick lenses of his wire-rimmed glasses. *Obviously, a nerd.* Isobel thought.

'Hello, I am Peter. I live next door. I thought you might want to hang out. I could show you the place.' Isobel was surprised by the encounter but smiled and nodded her approval at the idea.

'I am off out, gramps,' she called out to John, who had disappeared back into the kitchen. Then she grabbed her cap and mobile from her bedroom.

'I will be working on the vegetable patch if you need me.' Isobel felt a pang of deep love in her heart for the gentle old man who seemed to understand her better than anyone, then she stepped into the light.

Once outside, Peter felt he had to make the situation clear. 'I am only here because you are new here, and someone should show you around the dump.'

'Well, I am fine by myself. I don't need a guide. I am not blind. This place is so fucking dry. What does anyone do for fun around here?' she said, scared he was going to suggest something that she would find boring—like football.

'Well, I am gonna visit my mate over there.' He pointed over the road towards the castle wall. 'If Lord Langley caught us, we would get into real pigs' shit. He owns the castle, all the land, and even parts of the village. And he hates trespassers.'

Isobel followed his gaze and felt a thrill of excitement as she looked into the shade of the pines.

'You mean you go in there?'

'Yes, that's where my mate lives. Come on then,' he said, walking ahead.

As they approached the boundary, Isobel noticed a sickly stench, which grew stronger with each step.

'What the hell is that smell?'

'It's the wild boar. They won't hurt you, they're fenced off.'

Each branch they climbed took them higher until they reached the very top. Isobel swung a leg over, sat astride of the wall for a moment, conscious of the sharp surface of the stone digging through her jeans, and looked over to a distant hill that appeared different to all the others.

'What's that weird-looking hill?'

'It's an old long barrow. It's where the early people, probably the Iron Age, buried their leaders. You know, like our version of the pyramids.'

'Yeh, I know that. History is one of my main subjects. Have you been up there?'

'Yes, we sneak out there at night since it's by the water mill, have a few drinks and chill.' Peter was starting to warm to Isobel. She was different to the girls at school, with her shocking bright red hair and a piercing he noticed on the side of her nose. She was definitely more interesting than Ozzy's tiresome sister, who fancied herself to be some kind of pop singer.

Then, they both turned into the shadows of the trees and simultaneously jumped down onto the soft ground. Peter was already whistling while Isobel was still dusting the leaf mulch off her hands. Then she heard squealing, looked to her right and jumped as her eyes alighted on the monstrous black shapes of the wild boars, with their beady eyes and sharp tusks.

'Honestly, they won't hurt you,' Peter reassured.

She averted her eyes, and as she looked through the trees, the figure of another boy soon appeared with a large falcon perched on one of his arms. Finally, he was standing in front of them, the huge bird clinging to an oversized leather glove.

'This is my mate, Oswald Hunt— Ozzy for short. He's the falconer's son,' Peter explained.

'Hiya, who are you?' Oswald interjected before Peter could talk.

'I'm Issy, Peter's new next-door neighbour.' Isobel looked at the boy for some time. He was long-legged with a straight, chiselled nose and dark, lively eyes. Ozzy was obviously older at about sixteen and looked masterful beyond his years with the intimidating bird on his arm. He had an overall look of scruffiness that she found exciting.

'What kind of bird is that?'

'It's a golden eagle. Called Sir Lancelot—Lance, for short. Do you want to hold him?' Oswald smiled keenly.

Issy glanced down at its dragon-like talons and wasn't so sure that taking the eagle was a good idea, but she was now desperate to be part of this group, so she said yes.

The three of them pushed their way through the trees until they came upon a clearing of bright green grass. Far away up a slope, there were terraced gardens and crystal blue fountains. Towering up on the horizon was a grand fortified house, and to the left of this was the ruins of a much older keep of a real castle.

Ozzy had immediately noticed Isobel's large, beautiful, hazel eyes that gazed remotely, full of meaning, and knew if he looked at her face, he would become clumsy and lost for words. Therefore, he deliberately glanced down, arranged the girl's limbs, and suggested that she stood straight and confident. She waited patiently with her right arm stretched out with the heavy glove on her hand. Then he re-adjusted the bird's position, holding it on a tether, and walked some distance away.

The apprentice falconer spoke to the bird, gesticulated some signal with his left hand, and the coppery-gold creature swooped up into the air. Before Issy could think, Lance was plunging towards her hand, where a piece of meat had been buried between her fingers. One minute, she heard the beating of its wings, and then in the next there, it was—a majestic beast, its talons embedded in the leather glove. She wanted to take a closer look at the bird—it was so beautiful, its hooked beak opened as it squawked, revealing a pointed red tongue. Its shape and demeanour was one of a proud, noble predator.

'She is ok, your neighbour,' Ozzy stated as he approached Peter. 'Real, cool. Even my sister won't hold him.' He took the bird back and instructed it to rocket high into the sky. They all stood watching it circle above on the thermals, floating like a kite, then it soared up to the distant decorative chimney pots and perched, watching every movement in the grass below.

'Aren't you afraid he will fly off?' Issy asked.

'No, he always returns because I have the food,' he replied, shaking a small bag that was attached to his leather belt.

One happy hour moulded into the next as Ozzy and Lance performed all their best tricks. Then they strolled through the woods. Oswald allowed his bird to follow them freely while he and Issy climbed various trees, challenging each other to rise higher. Peter tried to follow but was soon struggling for breath.

'Bloody asthma,' he moaned, sucking at his inhaler.

Then, the peace was shattered as loud, sharp shouting punctured the air. They all looked in the direction of the commotion and saw a blustering, rotund, red-faced man marching their way angrily.

'Where are you hiding, boy?'

Without even turning to say goodbye, Ozzy hurtled back up the hill towards the house. Issy turned to Peter.

'What's happening? Who is that?'

'That is mad, George, Ozzy's father. He's a right wanker, a drunk. He beats him for no reason. Anyway, we had better go, too.'

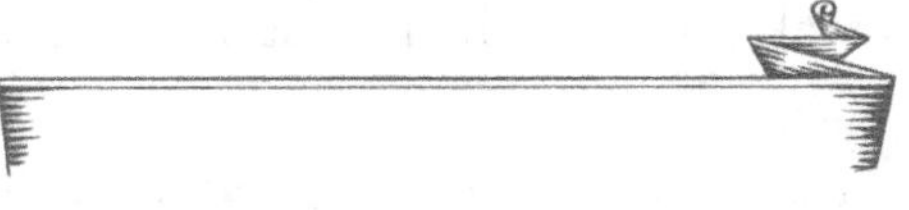

Chapter Five

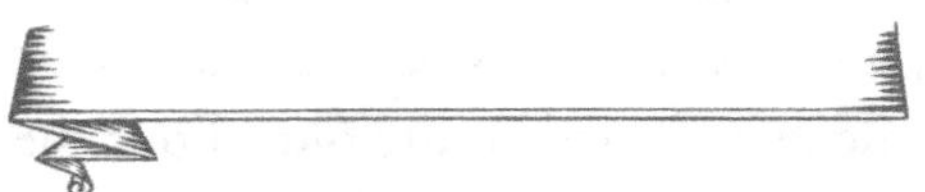

A few glorious weeks floated sweetly by, especially for Isobel, whose heart missed a beat whenever she set her eyes on Oswald. Each day buzzed along with an exciting rhythm, and the sun shone without a single menacing cloud frowning down from the face of the sky.

The three teenage outsiders had become inseparable, and each felt relief to be roaming free away from the constraints of adults with whom they were often at odds. Oswald introduced Issy to all his birds; they stole his father's booze and climbed and swung in the trees. On one occasion, the two boys deliberately started a fire in a field and then had fun whacking out the flames while Issy watched in awe.

Occasionally, Ozzy's sister Ariel joined them, and then it was possible to have piggyback fights late at night in the darkness of Isobel's front garden. As they tumbled to the ground after increasingly rough battles, they lay exhausted, their bodies shaking with uncontrollable laughter. The lonely town girl was no longer afraid of the dark and relished every moment she spent with her new friends. She wished the long summer holiday would never end.

Then came the day when Peter was nowhere to be found. Isobel nervously knocked on his front door, and Peter's kind father announced that he had to go to the hospital.

Feeling despondent, Isobel walked down to the stream that ran along the bottom of both gardens. There she sat with her head propped in her hands, staring into the clear amber waters.

'Come on fysh take a bitte. Whan the sun shineth make hay, is what I say.'

Isobel was startled as she thought she had been alone and kept her head bowed low, hoping whoever had spoken would disappear.

'Geten it!' the stranger yelped with delight. She couldn't help but look to her left, and there he was, as plain as day, a small man in a black hooded tunic, who looked quite old, about the same age as her Grandfather, with roughly cut short grey hair. The old man was pulling hard on a fishing rod when suddenly, he stood up and gave the stick one last yank and up came a small thrashing fish. 'Thanks be to God for geten me thy fysh, now I have mine supper,' he announced to himself.

Isobel sat up, staring, bemused and stunned by the man's peculiar speech.

'What be thou staring at lad, hasn't thou ever seen a man catch ye fysh afore? I have permission from our gentil Lorde to fysh in thee riverlet.'

'I was just thinking how clever you are to catch one; my father hardly ever gets anything.'

'You must have patience young sir.' He smiled at Isobel and then sat down on the bank. 'How should one address thee?'

'My friends call me Issy.'

'I be Richard, Richard Long. Thy name be amiss for a lad. I hasn't seen thou in these parts afore.'

'No, I am new.' She was about to correct him and explain that she was a girl but didn't want to have to enlighten him on why she chose to wear such boyish clothes. Also, it was clear that besides his foreign tongue, there was something very odd about the trespasser.

'I have seest another boy, methinks he be amiss, hey nay speaks just walks away. I pray thee that he not be one of thee King's spies. Things they be wrong, and I be sorely troubled as ruin has seized thy land.'

'What do you mean?'

'All I can say young sir is speaketh not when Lorde Raymond Langley is here abouts. He is a fellow of the King, and if thou sayeth mistaken words, in this mortal world, you will nay stayeth long.' He looked Issy full in the face, but she couldn't read the meaning in his eyes. 'I taketh my leave of you now as I have much to do. Go carefully, lad.' With that, he jumped up and began walking up the garden, muttering to himself as he went.

Meanwhile, Issy intensely watched every move he made, compelled by a desire to discover anything she could about the stranger. Then, to her complete astonishment, she saw him walk straight through the front garden hedge as though it wasn't there. She stood staring, caught between fear and curiosity. Issy then ran up the garden and crouched down behind a bush, peered around and watched as he crossed the road. There in the castle wall appeared a small door; the man opened it, and Issy heard the screech of its rusty hinges and saw him bend low to enter. Then both door and man melted away. On the return trip home, she decided not to tell anyone about her experience because she was unsure whether it was just a vision created by her mind or something real.

Chapter Six

Isobel was beginning to embrace all the new experiences that country life had to offer, so when Peter explained that he, Oz and his sister were going on a midnight walk to the old mill, she was desperate to be included.

'At bedtime, pretend to your mum that you are tired and make sure you are in your room by ten because I will text you at eleven,' Peter had instructed. Isobel was growing to understand that he liked everything; to be precise, he was a planner, unlike Ozzy, who was completely mad and unpredictable in character. 'Make sure you bring a torch and snacks.'

Isobel had been weary, fallen asleep, and not heard the bleep of Peter's text. Finally, her neighbour tapping on the glass startled her awake. Soon after this, in the dead of night, Issy found herself sauntering down a narrow lane deep in the countryside. It was the witching hour, and she was surprised to discover that the darkness was teaming with life. They saw two foxes, and for the first time, she saw glow worms in the long grass, large moths flying past, and the odd spider scuttling out of the undergrowth.

Then there it was—a towering white wooden water mill, illuminated by the full moon. All eyes were locked on the mesmerising structure when, to their surprise, the silence was shattered with a heart-stopping screeching as some large white birds swooped down from the roof. Everyone froze and stood pale-faced, trying to control the thumping in his or her chest—all that is, except Ozzy.

'You are all such chickens, it's only Barn Owls.' Oswald laughed.

'This sucks; I want to go back,' cried Ariel, who, at seventeen, was much more serious and anxious compared to her brother. 'Dad will be so mad if he finds out we are here.'

'Peter and I have done this load of times. The night is the same as the day, just darker. No harm has ever come to us, and besides, Dad will be drunk by now.'

'I want to go back. Who will come with me? Issy?'

'Don't be such a jackass, Sis.'

Isobel was a little scared but also found the whole adventure exhilarating. She wanted to continue, and she believed that even if they were caught, her grandparents would understand, as they had told her stories of their youthful explorations, which had sounded just as daring.

'This place is awesome, and nobody wants to go back, so you will have to come with us,' Oswald shouted.

'You are such a jerk.'

For a time, Ariel lingered behind, sulking, but Ozzy was playing the clown and soon had them all in fits of laughter.

'Come on, Issy, I'll give you a piggyback ride. Let's have a race. Ariel climb on Peter's back.' Ozzy's joy of life was so endearing that nobody who really knew him ever refused him for long, and so Ariel complied. They all made it to the velvety grass of the riverbank, where they collapsed. The air was suffocating, and they were all dripping with sweat. Peter took a drinking bottle full of cider from his backpack and shared it around.

'What do you want to do, Peter, when you leave school?' Issy inquired, genuinely curious.

'Don't listen to him, he is such a dork,' Oswald interjected.

'I want to be a scientist or an astronomer. I have my own telescope and a couple of times; I have seen things which I can't explain. One night, I was looking up at a clear starry heaven when I noticed seven stars shining with an intensity way beyond the others then they disappeared for quite a few seconds and then reappeared. They blinked on and off for many minutes before they finally vanished. I am still trying to find out what they could have been.'

'That sounds buzzing, man, UFOs. Could I have a look sometime?' Issy asked with enthusiasm.

'Well, if by UFOs you mean an alien spaceship, I have to tell you I don't believe in that mumbo jumbo because nothing organic could travel that far or fast. But you can have a look—it's fascinating.' He paused and then turned to face Ozzy. 'What are you going to do when you leave school, Oz?'

'Join the circus. I will be an acrobat. I am good at doing tricks. Watch this.' He stood up and gave them all a demonstration on how to do a perfect somersault, and then he astounded them all with a series of backflips, his tall, skinny body making a perfect arch.

Ariel, lying on her side with her head resting on her hand, was more cynical as she was used to her brother's antics.

'You know Dad wants you to take over as head falconer one day.'

'Sorry, Sis, but I am not staying with him. You know he hates me, and he thinks I am some kind of psycho killer.' Looking slightly dour, he collapsed back down onto the grass. There followed a moment's silence. Feeling weary and slightly intoxicated, they stared at the hypnotic flashing of the river that seemed to be flowing very fast.

'I know, let's cross the water and go up to the burial mound—we could show Issy the elephant tree,' Peter announced, aware that the mood needed lightning.

'Even I like the elephant tree,' Ariel stated with enthusiasm. 'It has a bough that is like a long curving trunk. We sit on it, and someone else grabs the end and bounces it up and down. Then you have to hold on tight.'

'Yeah, let's go.' Isobel tried to sound as enthusiastic as possible, but in truth, she was becoming increasingly sleepy.

'We would have to walk quite a long way downstream to cross the bridge,' Peter reminded them.

'Or we could cross by the fallen tree,' Ozzy said.

'Don't be a jerk, it's too dangerous,' Ariel squeaked, genuinely worried.

'You can go on your bums. I have done it lots of times,' he argued, his eager eyes beaming at them.

He was like a boy possessed; nothing was going to stop him, and he was defiant and sure of his abilities. Without hesitation, he approached the fallen trunk.

'Look at me, I am a tightrope walker. One day, I will do this over Niagara Falls,' he shouted out at them as all their horrified eyes turned towards him to watch. With his head facing forward and his arms outstretched, he proceeded to cross the uneven surface of the tree trunk. Beneath the cool water gurgled and spat up, making the wood slippery. Those standing on the riverbank had registered all the potential hazards and wordlessly stared, not daring to breathe. It was like watching someone recklessly skating on thin ice. However, he made it past the midway point.

They were all beginning to think that their misgivings might have been unnecessary when suddenly a blindingly bright bolt of lightning came from nowhere, cracked open the sky and struck the river. Startled, Ozzy slipped on the slimy surface and vanished into the electrified water. They all heard a hollow splash, the sound of which indicated to them that the river was very deep. There were loud intakes of breath, and all three screamed, 'Oz, Oz, swim Oz.' For a moment, he briefly appeared from beneath the crushing confusion of the surface. However, by the time Peter had found a stick and lay on the grass to save his friend, he had resurfaced much further away and had rapidly glided down the watery slide, out of sight and out of reach.

A fierce-looking black cloud rumbled over from the burial mound, and torrential rain shot its stinging bullets down onto the panicked group.

'Has anyone got a phone?' Peter screamed.

'I have,' Issy said.

'Then call the goddamn police! Call everyone, quick!'

With trembling hands, Issy pressed the numbers.

'Police! I need the police! I need everyone! Come quickly, our friend is drowning at the old mill.' The person on the other end of the line questioned Isobel further in disbelief that a group of teenagers would be playing near a river so late at night.

Ariel was sent back up the track to the road to wait for help while the remaining two friends searched along the riverbank, praying for any sight of the missing boy, longing and willing him to suddenly appear.

Everyone arrived at once: the emergency services and the teenager's parents. Isobel ran up to her grandfather, who had arrived with her mother Jean, flung her arms around him and burst into tears. 'I am so sorry, we should never have come.'

Peter was still searching the riverbank, his head bowed, watching the water, hardly able to see through the veil of tears and rain as his father, Bill, approached and gently placed his arm around his son's shoulder. The three adults understood that this was no time for reproach or punishment.

'Peter, come on, Son. It's time to let the police do their job.'

Ariel stood by herself watching the rescue workers, so Isobel's mother went to her side to offer some comfort.

A kindly policeman, Officer Cox, approached and cautiously asked the three teenagers what had happened.

'We were on a midnight walk, just exploring for a bit of fun. I promise we didn't mean to do any harm. We were just going to show the girls the mill and then return home,' Peter spoke up, trying to prevent any blame from coming his way.

'So, tell me, how did your friend come to fall into the river?' Mr Cox inquired, trying to be sympathetic but not really knowing the correct tone or words.

'It was Oswald's idea,' Isobel added. 'He wanted to cross the river by the fallen tree. We tried to stop him, but he was too quick. He was always too fast with everything he did, never thinking about what could happen.' Isobel was wondering if they could have prevented him from such a foolish act and was feeling guilty that they hadn't tried harder.

'We all tried to rescue him, but the river was flowing too fast,' Peter added.

'Don't blame yourselves. These tragic accidents happen, but it would be a bad decision for anyone to be out here at this time of night. The darkness hides many potential dangers. I hope from now on you will take your safety more seriously.'

He scribbled all the information in his notebook and then gave them all permission to leave, adding that he may need to speak to them further in the next few days. Then, just as they were wondering what to do with Ariel, as the adults were anxious to lead their children away from any potentially offending sight and the increasing danger of slippery mud, a stout, red-faced man came marching towards them.

'Come here, girl. I want an explanation. What's going on, where is your brother?'

They all watched as Ariel rushed up to him, her deathly pale face shining in a sudden burst of moonlight as she stared up into the angry, unkind eyes. Tears fell as the man cursed, grabbed her arm and dragged her down to the riverbank.

The other families looked on in astonished horror. The man was somehow enjoying the fact that he had the power to inflict all his pain on another human being. There was a terrible tension in the air as his evil tongue lashed out at anyone in close proximity.

'Where is my son? You are all wasting time.'

'Calm down, Sir, we are doing our best. Just allow us to do our job,' Mr Cox said.

Isobel's mother bravely approached the figure that was pacing up and down the bank.

'Excuse me, we would be happy to take Ariel home with us. She could stay the night, and you could collect her tomorrow?'

'The girl stays here with me,' he replied sharply.

At the rebuff, both families began to walk briskly back down the path towards their waiting cars. Isobel glanced over her shoulder at the sound of a splash and, out of the corner of her eyes, saw the madman plunge into the white water; words of hate roared from his mouth as he thrashed around, digging up the liquid and searching in the twisted shadows of the overhanging undergrowth for his lost son.

Later, Isobel was lying in bed listening to the distant rumble as the early morning storm drifted away. She felt numb; the night's events seemed to blend into one big, unfathomable blur. All the laughter had gone, and she just kept wishing that the following day, they would announce that they had found her friend safe and well.

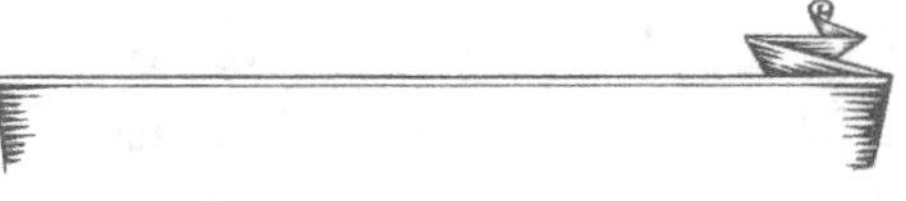

Chapter Seven

A couple of weeks passed. Both Peter and Isobel were set strict boundaries that kept them mostly confined to their homes. Not that either of them felt like going anywhere else, as they had learnt their lesson in the cruellest of ways.

The nightmare lingered in the air of the whole village. Mothers warned their children about the perils of the water and kept a closer eye on their wanderings. Strangely, Ozzy's body was never found, and soon, a rumour circulated that he had somehow survived and run off to the circus.

Finally, a memorial service was held at the church. They all stood in the tense, chilly atmosphere of the ancient building. Peter sat next to Isobel.

'This is fucking lame, I don't believe in this shit. When we passed Ariel walking into church, did you notice how she blanked me? I said hello, and she just ignored me,' Peter whispered as they all stood for the first song.

'Yes, I saw, but don't take it personally. Her brother has just died.'

'I don't think Ozzy's gone, I think he escaped but just didn't want to go home. I mean, would you look at Ozzy's jerk of a father? He looks evil, a right fudge. He hasn't got two brain cells to rub together. His suit doesn't fit, and I bet he has been drinking. I hate him—it's his fault that all this shit has happened. We should try and get Ariel away from him, and you can be sure he slaps her up.'

Isobel looked over at the madman who stood silently at the front, staring frozen with what looked like disbelief and pain with his distraught daughter silently weeping at his side with no mother to offer her any comfort.

'Peter, stop. The poor man is grieving, and they both look sad to me.'

They then all knelt in prayer. Peter and Isobel sniggered.

'Be quiet, you two,' Isobel's mother angrily hissed.

When the ceremony was over, the rest of the village quickly forgot the dreadful reminder of their mortality, and life seemed to return to normal. However, the tortured father could be heard screeching his car around the village in the early hours of the morning, and sometimes there could be heard a spine-chilling howling like that of a wild animal as he battled to come to terms with his grief and anger towards the world.

On the following Sunday morning, Isobel awoke to the chimes of the church bells, and from her bed, she could see through her window to the stream at the bottom of their gardens and saw Peter sitting cross-legged staring in the water as though he remembered his friend. The strange thing was that he was in her garden. Nobody would have minded this, as the hedge dividing the two bungalows seemed to deliberately fall short, leaving a wide gap so people could stroll as far as they wanted in either direction along the river.

Issy quickly got dressed, hurried out of the house and crept through the long, dew-soaked grass. Silently, she crouched down beside her friend.

'It was our fault, Issy. We should have stopped him.'

'We couldn't have, he was determined to give us a show. Besides, it all happened too quickly, and they haven't found him, so he might still be out there somewhere.' She paused, wondering if she was saying the right things, considering the depth of Peter's sorrow. 'Have you seen Ariel?'

'No, her drunk of a dad won't let her out, and I heard a terrible story that, in one of his tempers, he killed Sir Lancelot.'

'No, he couldn't have! That's sick.' Isobel was genuinely shocked and appalled by such a notion.

'It's true. I heard it from one of the gardeners, mad George had told him the bird had turned vicious since his son's death and that it attacked him, so he broke its neck.'

'Shit, that's gross.' Now, Isobel was feeling desperate to change the conversation. She couldn't bear any more bad news.

'Hey, do you believe in ghosts?' she asked, revealing what she had determined to keep hidden.

'No, not really; I think everything has a logical explanation,' the boy replied, peering at her curiously through the thick lenses of his glasses.

'Well, have you seen the man in black?'

'Have you seen him, then?'

'Yes, I've spoken with him.'

'Whoa, that's a relief. I thought it was just me. He fishes down here in our stream. I think he is a monk because that's how they dress,' Peter explained enthusiastically, his renewed appetite for a mystery tossing him from his dark pit back into the light. As they talked about the shadowy figure, they entered a magical place where their imaginations could run free from their cares and where they were brought closer together.

'He used to come and go randomly, but just lately, I have seen him far more frequently. Always on a Friday,' Peter added.

'Let's make sure we are down here on Friday.' Isobel smiled enthusiastically. They high-fived in agreement. 'I have got to help Granddad paint the hall, but I shall watch out for him and keep notes on what I see. You could do the same.'

'Yeah, my dad has given me lots of jobs to do. Let's finish them quickly. If we keep the folks happy, they might allow us our freedom back.' They smiled at each other, pleased with their smart plan. With renewed energy, they jumped up and made their way to their homes to complete their various tasks.

ON THE NEXT FRIDAY morning, Isobel woke up to a sunny dawn and a mist hovering over the lawn. Everyone in the house was still sleeping, so she pulled on her jeans and T-shirt and tiptoed down the hall and out of the back door.

Not long after, Peter appeared holding a picnic blanket.

'We could be waiting for some time, and we don't want to get wet.' He spread the soft, woolly material over the bouncy, rough grass and flopped down. Together, they lay on their backs, soaking up the growing heat and gazing at a buzzard circling overhead. As they watched, two crows appeared and began to mob the larger bird. It reminded Peter of his mother's story of how she believed nature was turning against people. Absent-minded, he made his hand into a gun and pretended to shoot them. Then, to the utter astonishment of the watchers, the two crows immediately tumbled downwards, spiralling as though they had been killed.

'Oh, my God, Peter, how did you do that?' Isobel shouted and sat up.

'I didn't do anything. I just made out I had a gun, and they fell from the sky. It must just be a coincidence.'

'Flipping heck, that is so weird. What were the chances of that happening?' She lay back, and they both stared at the blue in disbelief. After some time, Isobel recovered and felt able to speak.

'By the way, he seems to think that I am a boy. It would be too complicated to say any different.'

'Okay, I will keep your secret.'

They were on the edge of dozing off when a familiar muttering came floating towards them in the breeze. Immediately, the two friends pushed themselves up and twisted around to see the little man in the black tunic approaching them as though in a dream-like state.

He sat down stiffly, his bare legs stuck out in front of him. In his hand was a very straight stick with what looked like a violin string hanging down with a hook tied to the end. The teenagers watched as he squeezed some kind of a worm on the point, which he dropped into the stream. Absorbed in his task, he continued to mumble low to himself, excluding them from his one-sided conversation. 'Oh, river that floweth through time give me up some fysh this day.' Tirelessly, he sat waiting for the waters to yield their bounty, but nothing came. 'It's Herons they hath taken all ye fysh or some foe has poisoned thee waters,' he moaned into the air.

'He doesn't seem so friendly today and doesn't seem to know we are here,' Isobel whispered softly.

'Talk to him then,' Peter replied, feeling overawed by the situation.

'Hello again,' Isobel nervously spoke.

'Hush lad you will afrighten them away.'

'My friend Peter is here today.'

I bid thee welcome young sir, but this is my mark. My Lorde would rather chop thy hands off at a blow than see thou on his land.'

Not long after the conversation, Richard angrily threw his rod down.

'Are you going?' Peter asked Richard.

'I bid thee a sad farewell. Canest you not see, they fysh be dying.'

The teenagers sat up, gazed at the river, and saw splashing around on the surface—a writhing mass of dying fish gulping at the poisonous air.

'As thou findest things, so must thou leave them,' the old man muttered to either himself or the teenagers. The monk then collected his rod and began to walk back up to the garden.

'Quick, let's follow him,' Isobel urged, already stumbling to her feet.

She noticed Peter proceeding to roll up the blanket. 'Leave that. You're so bloody fussy, and we don't have much time. We must stick as close to him as possible.'

Without another word, Peter abandoned his task and followed his friend. When the Monk went through the hedge, they went around. They made no secret about travelling in the same direction; nevertheless, the man seemed unaware of their proximity. He moved slowly, dreamily, as if he was under some kind of spell. As they crossed the narrow road, a small wooden door appeared in the wall.

'Let's follow him, Peter. We need to hurry.'

'Okay, okay, stop panicking.'

They heard the squeak of the rusty hinges, and as the Monk bent down to enter, they were only a few paces behind. Without a second thought and full of curiosity, they, too, squeezed through the small opening.

Chapter Eight

They were so close to the scurrying little man that they didn't want to startle him, so they hung back a little. They were slightly disorientated and confused; outwardly, everything appeared to have changed. The fortified house had disappeared entirely, and the old keep had uncrumpled itself and stood proudly on the hill in a much more complete and magnificent state. It appeared lived in, no longer a derelict ruin. However, the surrounding landscape looked much rougher, and the trees and bushes grew less profusely. Also, Isobel noticed that no decorative fountains squirted into the afternoon sky.

'Where are we?' Isobel enquired, finding Peter as bemused as she was—he stood staring aghast with his mouth dropping open.

'I don't know. I honestly haven't a clue. I think we are in the castle grounds, but perhaps as it used to be.' Then he realised that they had hesitated too long and that the Monk was disappearing into the shadows. 'Come on, we must try to catch up.'

Richard was making his way along a track that ran between the castle wall and a thick tangle of bushes and trees, which concealed them all from the open lawn. The teenagers stalked their prey like two hunters. Isobel kept running her hand along the rough surface of the old stonewall for comfort and reassurance, as it was the only recognisably consistent feature. They saw it as a border between their world and the monk's alien territory.

They walked for a very long time; the wall stretched far into the distance, and the path gradually climbed, making their pursuit harder.

'Did you know there was once an Isobel who lived in the castle?' Isobel stated, partly to show off her knowledge and partly to entertain Peter.'

'What, the Lord's wife?'

'Yes, but it was a different family back then, and Gramps told me that her son was later executed for treason, can you imagine that? If our monk is from medieval times, he most probably had a shitty life. Peasant families had to work plots of the Lord's Manorial Estate, and they would have to hand over what they produced as a kind of rent. They also had to make themselves available to work for the Lord whenever he needed anyone, especially at harvest times.'

Isobel was so engrossed in her tale that she stumbled on a protruding rock but quickly gained her footing and continued to speak. 'The men would be required to serve him anytime he fancied a fight. If our monk or anyone was caught killing game birds, he would risk having his hand or arm cut off, as he would be stealing the Lord's property. If you killed anything else, like a deer, you would be hanged.'

'Gross. So, were all Lords like that?'

'Yes, I think so. They saw it as their 'God-given right'.

'I am glad I didn't live in those times,' Peter replied, genuinely appreciating that he was a child of the twenty-first century.

'Me neither. It seems that the people lived in constant fear.'

'Was there anything good about life back then?'

'No, I don't think so because they suffered the "Black Death" and many other plagues and then there was the peasant's revolt. I remember that from my cesspit of a school. I think to them it was the apocalypse.'

'I don't want to bore the shit out of you, but there is a scientific theory that says nothing exists unless it is observed, so how do we know that this place exists when we are not looking at it? I have also heard that there is a sub-atomic particle in the brain that is completely unpredictable and does its own thing, the intelligent gene.'

'Peter, I don't understand a word you are saying. You're such a geek, but I love your crazy ideas,' she smiled with deep warmth, and for a moment, Peter wished that he could freeze time and always have her at his side.

Finally, they came out of the dark tunnel into the blazing sunlight. Looking around them, they saw areas of open space awash with a sea of long, pale, golden grass that waved gently in the breeze. There were patches where very tall old trees grew, and amongst these could be seen more deer in one herd than either of them had ever seen.

The track then became less distinct and more treacherous with a mixture of protruding rocks and the gnarled, crooked fingers of tree roots. They were at the perimeter of the Lord's land and the beginning of the North Downs Way, the ridge of hills and woods that ran towards Canterbury. At last, they saw in the distance Monk Richard enter a stone house that was partly built into the end of the wall.

The teenagers stopped and quivered with excited anticipation. At a much slower pace, they walked with trepidation toward the building.

When they arrived, the wooden door was shut, and from the inside, they heard two voices. Signalling to each other, the two trespassers crept around the building, looking for a window. They found one open, but it was small, but beside it on the ground, a wooden barrel had been placed to collect water. Isobel deftly climbed onto the rim and, holding onto the window ledge, leaned forward and peered into a tiny room, overcrowded with all kinds of unusual objects.

She saw Richard busily gathering a variety of plants and vegetables, which he dropped into a large pot. While he was carrying out this task, he was also talking to someone sitting out of view in the shadows.

'I hardly dare speak, but I must tell thee, lad, the secret for which I have been entrusted as it lies heavy on my soul.'

'What be thy secret?' the stranger asked.

'Are you not my apprentice in all matters holy and in time thou anticipatest to be a Knight to thee Lorde? Then understand this, what

I tell ye pertains to thee alone and none other. Thoust must pledge to God thy silence for all time.'

'Dear Friar, you have my word of honour, and to God, I plight thee my troth.'

'Then I shalst speaketh my tale yet only what thou needest to know.'

'Soothly I say to you, the hill up by yonder mill, tis where Gods people were interned. They were worthy in the finest degree, although some called them barbarians. It is told that they knew the magic at the root of all living things and that they applied labour to the land and were bindeth thereof, desiring nay riches. Their wisdom sayeth that all born of thee land should wear the same crown and should bear honour and respect as though all were of one family. They sought to payeth back the earth for all they taketh. What be more they pay'd nay homage to feudal Lordes. Beasts and man alike were one family.'

'Alas, it runs against all reason, but there came a challenge to this harmony in the form of the Devil himself. Evil men did not oppose the Devil's reign and bowed low before his thrown. God shunned our earth, disappointed by the sins of man and saw fit to forge a new world. For the good, God's essence is buried in the heart of all things, waiting dormant.'

'What becometh of our Earth?' A small, quaking voice was heard from the dark corner.

'When thy God scattered his seeds of life, the Devil planted his own grains of destruction. He maketh a group of soul suckers that walk among us. They have false hearts, nay emotions, but on the outside, be like thou and thee. They be conquerors, destroyers and slave masters.'

'A long time ago, I was entrusted with a loathsome secret that the Bible be not the only book, there be another, called 'Diabolus Consilium', in common speech it be the 'Devil's Book'. Twas not like any other and was wrote down in a strange tongue. In days long gone, afore my birth, twas interned deep in the Holy Land. Twas in a lead-lined box but the soul suckers unearthed it, and that's when thee plagues came upon us.'

'Knights there came, full-worthy of the task who dug up the offending book, so others could not. Mayhap, a gentil Knight, 'William Delamore', the head of the Knights Templars took it under his protection. He be nay man's fool, but the fates turned against him and all his kind as they be burnt at the stake. Through wise, good fortune he had placed the murderous book in other hands afore the sad events.'

'Only a person with a pure heart and soul could carry such a thing without its evil devouring their lifeblood, and so to thray monks it was trusted.'

'Did they manage to be rid of the evil object?' the shadow voice enquired.

Isobel could barely see, but she was able to make out the silhouette of the monk brandishing a knife as he attacked what looked like a Swede. He wiped the sweat from his forehead with his sleeve and lowered his voice to a whisper as he continued his story.

'Tway of the Monks became corrupted, they let the devil in. They be quarrelsome and could nay come upon agreement on what to do with thy book. The tyrannous evil spoke in separate tongues to them, enticing them with the power hidden in its pages, telling them that each was its rightful owner. A murderous fight ensued; tway suffered mortal wounds and died. Out of fear of damnation, the surviving monk buried the devil's works, there and then, under a pile of lead.'

'Isobel, what's happening, let me look?' Peter whispered.

'Just wait a minute, this is important,' Isobel hissed back impatiently.

Back in the house, the shadow figure, now hungry for more of the story, sensed that the monk was about to fall into silence.

'So, we are all safe now?'

'The soul suckers, although everywhere, have little power without the book. They wander aimlessly like slaves without a master.'

'So, what concerns thee?'

'I take little comfort as all is not yet done. Alas, I fear the beast is rising. Thou art in wrong times, a breach hath there been in the boundaries of time, and everything is falling out of balance. Thou seest that the book has been released from its grave, and the devil once more will gain his advantage. Unless a noble army of saints ride forth to do battle, it will be the end of the world for all time.'

'I my son am old, I can do nay more to put back the world as twas. Tis for the young to seek out the evil and to bury it in the deepest crack of our Earth.' There followed a moment's silence while the two men considered the fate of humankind. 'Lorde Raymond favours you and has taken thou on to follow the path of a Knight and that be a great honour and privilege. One day it will be your duty to defend us all. If thee taketh this on lad, I warn thee, beware of those who promise thou impossible rewards for little return. Above all, listen to your heart because that's where God lies.'

Suddenly, Isobel felt a whoosh of air and a scrambling flapping sound just behind where she was precariously balancing.

'Issy, Issy, look,' Peter prompted.

Isobel turned, and in a split-second, she saw the golden shape of Sir Lancelot picking at some carrion hidden amongst the leaf mulch. She was so shocked by the sight that she lost her footing and slipped, falling with a loud splash into the barrel of water.

'Intruders! Intruders!' screeched Sir Lancelot.'

'Well, young Oswald, I think I smell witches. Let's take a look.' The old man whispered.

Isobel clambered out of the barrel and stood dripping wet. Then, the teenagers listened hard as they heard the monk and his follower approach from the other side of the house. They were unable to move and stood rooted to the ground with the huge bird pecking at their feet. It really hurt as they were only wearing trainers. They tried desperately to kick him away as Isobel muttered to Peter under her breath, 'Oh my God, did you hear that? The frigging bird talks.'

'Either that or we've both gone mad.'

The Monk stood before them, and to their utter amazement, so did Ozzy.

'Ozzy, Ozzy, you are okay!' Peter stepped forward to greet his friend, but the response he received was icy, so he quickly withdrew.

'Who art thou? You act as if thou knowest me yet I hast nay mind of your face.'

'I pray thee be gone faithful bird,' the Monk instructed. The bird stretched the long expanse of his wings and gently flew up and rested on the branch of a nearby tree.

'Thou mayest be a stranger to Oswald, but I knowest thee. 'Tis you sirs who hast put a hex on thee riverlet and poisoned thy fysh. Thee water runs barren and be bewitched. Thoust hast catched nay but weeds since the last full moon. Now here thee be outside thy abode, waiting in ambush like spies who wilt betray my words.'

'Methinks, lad, we should take these kill-cows up to the castle to be placed on trial as witches. Thy Lorde shalt determine thy fate.' There was a stern frown carved between his eyes and a mask of gloom fixed to his face, which told the teenagers that this man's intentions were serious, that if necessary, he would have them burnt to death. Isobel and Peter internally trembled as every cell in their bodies filled with dread. They had heard all the stories at school about how ruthlessly and quickly their ancestors despatched witches, and they really believed that their lives could be about to end.

'We are not witches. We just come from a different place,' Isobel pleaded.

'We are pilgrims,' Peter added.

'Thoust speaketh with the flattering tongue of the devil. I say again Lord Langley will judge thee.'

'Look, if you are worried about your secret, it is definitely safe with us. You can let us go, and we won't say a word, not even to Lord Langley.' Suddenly, the Monk's demeanour changed; his clasped hands began to shake, and a look of fear and panic flooded his eyes. Oswald began to pace up and down behind his master with his hand covering his face as though he was trying to hide from some terrible sight.

'Oswald, hasten away and fetch your sword. With good speed, let us end this treachery.' Ozzy scuttled off obediently. The two teenagers thought it would be a good time to run, but when they glanced up to the tree, they could see Lance watching their every move like a spring waiting to be sprung.

'We really don't mean you any harm. I know where that book is. I will bring it to you,' Isobel spluttered.

Oswald returned with a long sword in his hand, the monk gestured to him to come close and bend low, as the lad was taller than his master was, and then he whispered something in his ear.

Then, the Monk's apprentice roughly pushed the two intruders towards the track.

'With thee, thou must cometh. I shall cast thee out beyond the castle wall.'

The small group retraced the steps they had made earlier in deathly silence, each lost in their own private thoughts, with Lance scrutinising their every action like a dog watching over its owner.

Once they were back in the tunnel of trees and they felt a safe distance from the house, Peter thought it was time to speak up. 'Did he believe us?' he addressed Ozzy.

'Nay, my master trusts you not; he wants me to kill thee. It would be too dangerous for you to reveal thy secret. Besides, how wouldst thou know wherest the book be?'

Of course, Peter didn't know. He didn't even know what they were all talking about, and he had assumed Isobel had been bluffing to extricate them from the jaws of death. He decided that arguing was not the best way and instead began to plan a way of escaping.

'I swear I know where the book is. I can't explain, but if it is that important to you, at least give me a chance to return it to you both,' Isobel pleaded.

The apprentice remained unmoved and continued to keep his head firmly facing forward.

After some time, with all kinds of thoughts racing through his brain, Peter realised they were approaching the door in the wall. Without a second's thought, he grabbed Isobel's arm and screamed, 'Run, Issy, run.' They both sprang into action, sprinting down the track as fast as they could, with Ozzy following close behind.

'They escape,' Lance screeched as he flapped around Isobel, obscuring her view and causing her to stumble to the ground.

Peter was a step away from the gate when Ozzy caught up with him, grabbed his thin arm with an iron grip and flung him hard against the wall. Peter was winded, and he gasped for breath. However, he was forced not to react, as he was aware that the sharp point of the sword was poking into the soft skin under his chin. He stood frozen, his lips parted, and his eyes were wild with fear.

His attacker drew so close that Peter could feel him breathe, and his glasses began to mist up, so it was hard to see. They were face to face, and Ozzy was staring at him searchingly as though he was looking in a mirror for some offending mark.

'Your face is familiar. I can't remember where I know you from, but I do feel that we have met before.' With these words, he lowered the blade.

'Perhaps in another life,' Peter stuttered with relief.

'Your secret is safe with us. If we don't return with the book by this time next week, then you can do what you like with us,' Isobel uttered weakly.

'I shalt let thee go, but if thy don't return that book safely back to us, then stay away from these parts for all time, or I will have no choice other than to kill thee both.' With that, he turned and marched briskly away. The two youths stood watching until he vanished into the darkness of the trees while they recovered from the shock of the situation.

Then they pulled the stiff gate open, stepped back over the boundary of time and out into freedom. Once shut, the door melted away and was replaced by various forms of creepers that spread their tentacles throughout the wall.

Peter glanced at his watch. 'It seemed that we were there forever, but actually, at the most, we were only away for a couple of hours. You had better try and explain what you heard through the window, Issy.'

Isobel started from the beginning and relayed the story as best she could as they strolled across the road and back into her garden.

SOON AFTER THIS, WITH clothes still damp and stained with dirt, Isobel opened the back door and entered the kitchen, expecting to hear the happy flow of family banter. Straight away, she noticed that the atmosphere was subdued; her grandfather was at the sink washing plates thoughtfully. Her grandmother was at the Arga cooker stirring a sauce while her mother was seated at the wooden table, mindlessly cutting up vegetables.

'Ouch, damn! I have cut my finger,' her mother screamed as she quickly rose and rushed to the sink. John held it under the tap.

'That's quite a cut, Jeanie; perhaps we should get you to the doctor,' John advised.

'I wouldn't risk that right now. besides, a tight plaster usually does the trick.' Gran was already searching amongst the accumulated rubbish in the cupboard for the medical box.

'Why, what's wrong with the doctors? If it's bad, Mum, you should get a stitch.' Suddenly, they all turned and looked at Isobel as though they had not been aware of her presence.

'Oh, it's nothing to worry about, Issy,' her mother stated as the older lady wrapped a large plaster tightly around the dripping red finger.

'Jeanie, she is not a baby, she reads the paper almost every day and loves a good story.'

'What's happened?' Issy enquired as her mother wearily collapsed back onto her chair, and for the first time, she saw that her eyes were moist and that she had been crying. John decided to get his version of events out first.

'Well, it's all very strange. The papers are really only trickling out information, but your mother went into town to visit the hospital today and was turned away. However, there was a small group of busybodies outside who also had their appointments cancelled, and they informed your Gran that the hospital was only receiving emergency cases and the Museum and all public buildings would be closed for a while due to a virulent virus outbreak.'

'Yes, but that does happen sometimes. Our school was shut once because of the same thing.'

'Ah, but that's not all. A woman on the village bus said that her husband was a porter at the hospital, and the rumour going around is that it's a new form of the plague,' the old man added with a twinkle in his eyes, not really believing such an absurd story.

'No, really,' Isobel was genuinely concerned, especially after experiencing the strangest day of her life. Her brain immediately started to unravel the tangled threads of the monk's bizarre story.

'That's enough, Dad,' her mother shouted with exasperation. Her grandma Daisy, who was a woman of few words, had a flushed face and a mournful look in her eyes added to the sinister feel.

'It's a bad omen when a plague comes—even worst is usually to follow. The plague once wiped out fifty per cent of the population in these parts,' she said, dragging her hand across her whiskered top lip to remove the droplets of sweat.

'Mother, that was centuries ago, and they can cure it now.'

'All I am saying is that it's a bad sign.' The old woman hunched over and shuffled around the room, busily laying plates on the table and continuing with the preparations for their meal.

'Listen to you two; you can't seriously believe that gossip. Naturally, you are concerned about the baby, but it has got this far, and the way it kicks, I think it must be strong and healthy.'

'You don't really think there is an outbreak of plague, do you, Mum?'

'No, it's as Granddad says—just silly gossip.'

'Well, I believe it's possible they still have the disease in other countries,' Daisy mumbled.

Isobel slumped down at the kitchen table and, with her head resting in her hands, stared into the void and visualised the plague-like a black tsunami wave rushing towards the shore and washing away all life. Neither disease nor flood has any mercy, the forces of nature do not discriminate between old and young, rich or poor.

The teenager felt a lurking dread, she didn't want her dreams to be dashed against the rocks and her life ended by her succumbing to a hideous disease.

She glanced around at her family and wondered why they appeared not to be experiencing the same sense of urgency. Would they really just stand, stare, and wait to be engulfed by a fast-moving tide of destruction?

Chapter Nine

'Thanks for coming, especially at such great risk to your safety. You are indeed a good man,' Archbishop Sir Philip Wighard said as he opened the door of his private apartments to his friend Mathew, who was the Head of Antiquities at the Museum.

'It's good to see you, Archbishop, but I wouldn't come too close. I am already ill,' Mathew replied. Philip looked into his guest's glazed eyes and saw death grinning back, crouching in wait for the man's inevitable demise. His brow was covered in beads of sweat, and his chest was heaving with the effort of climbing the stairs. With considerable determination, he struggled to ease a heavy rucksack off his back, which he allowed to fall with a soft thud onto the thick carpet.

'Please, take a seat, Mathew. I will get you a glass of wine.' Calmly, the old man walked over to a sideboard and poured two drinks. 'This is a terrible situation. When the legend of the Diabolus Conilium was passed on to me, it was just that, a story—something I listened to with intrigue but quickly dismissed. Now, I have apparently been proved wrong.' He returned with the drinks and handed the glass over to his guest's outstretched, shaky hand.

'Thank you, I have a savage thirst. It all seems to be horribly true.' Mathew tragically sighed and swallowed the red liquid down in one gulp.

'Have you got it with you?' Archbishop enquired as he nervously perched on the edge of the chair opposite.

'Yes, indeed, in the bag, but I can't just hand it over to you. I need you to promise that it will only be given to the most carefully chosen people, that it will be buried so deep and in such a remote place that it may never be dug up again.' As he spoke these words, his crazed, fevered mind wanted nothing more than to abandon the evil object. He was beginning to long for death and just wanted to sneak away and hide like a sick dog.

'I know it isn't safe here, but it is not safe with you either. Look, it won't corrupt me, and I shall keep it locked away until the right people are found for the mission. I know only too well that if it falls into the wrong hands, the devil will be triumphant. You have my word that I will do my best, but other than that, we are all in God's hands.'

'I have no choice but to trust you, my dear friend, and if anyone is worthy of that trust, it has to be you,' Mathew uttered with despair as pain ripped through his body. He clasped his hand to his swollen neck, his face crumpled in agony as he pushed himself up into a standing position.

'I am truly sorry, but I must go. It's all in your hands now. I hope you don't mind, but could I take that bottle of wine with me.'

'Of course, my good man, I am only sorry that I could not have welcomed you under better circumstances. I shall be praying every minute of every day for our salvation.' Philip rose from his chair and took the man's arm in an attempt to help his guest to the door, but Mathew snatched it back.

'Stay away from me, Philip!' he screamed vehemently, frothing at the mouth. 'Can't you see I am a sick man? I will let myself out.'

Mathew left, leaving the door slightly ajar, as it was hard to pull over the thick carpet and disappeared as quickly as he could.

Archbishop Philip collapsed back down into his chair that swaddled him with the normality of everyday comfort; tears of sadness filled his eyes at the thought that Mathew and many other young, bright people would have their lives cut short by a disease that should only exist in the pages of history. Then, the mundane-looking bag caught his attention. He cursed what lay inside and wished that it had not been his role to intervene in the impending disaster. He just couldn't believe that he had in his possession the most corrupting artefact ever known to man.

Finally, he stood up and, with quaking legs and a beating heart, took a few paces towards the offensive item. Grabbing the two straps, he tried to lift the bag off the floor, but it was too heavy. Then, he made a second attempt, taking a deep breath and dredging up every ounce of energy. He heaved it up and just managed to throw it onto a sturdy wooden coffee table.

'What are you doing, Archbishop?' The Bishop of Dover, Francis, enquired.

'What are you doing here, Francis? I wasn't expecting you to arrive until tomorrow.'

'I had to come, it's absolute pandemonium. We have received news of a case of the sickness in Dover. People are starting to panic.'

'I know fifty people have died here so far, and they were all young adults and those with no underlying illness. They are talking about quarantining the city tomorrow. How did you get into the house? I sent my secretary and all my other officials as far away as possible.'

'Just as I was about to ring the bell, a very unhealthy-looking man stumbled out through your front door, so I thought rather than disturb you, I would come straight up.'

Philip was taken aback, he hadn't planned for the unpredictable and wasn't sure what to do next. He fell back into his chair, feeling exhausted and a little nauseous.

'Help yourself to a drink, Francis, if you don't mind. I am tired, and it's been a very long, distressing day.'

Francis poured a drink, which was unlike him as he usually refused anything that might cloud his ability to control others.

Philip felt uneasy. He had never liked the Bishop. His instincts told him that he was a man of no pity but a great deal of deceit, was too ambitious, and all he appeared to care about was his own self-advancement. The man was a performer—a game player who was only charitable when it fitted into his overall plans. How he had progressed so far in life was a mystery to Philip, but he was certainly not someone to be trusted. These thoughts left Philip with a dilemma; he needed to be rid of the interloper as soon as possible while appearing to be hospitable at the same time.

'I really appreciate you coming to help us manage our current crisis, but under the circumstances, I now think that it might be better if you returned to your town before they impose the quarantine. If we can contain this thing in one place, we may be able to overcome a countrywide disaster. Journey back tonight, save yourself and the rest of your community.'

Francis stood rigidly by the sideboard with a peculiar expression on his face as his brain explored the whole situation, trying to find the path that would personally benefit him the most. He was a young man for a Bishop, and dying of a horrible disease was not what he had ever expected from life. It was a relief to have been permitted to escape the horror.

'I think you might be right, Archbishop. I am reluctant to leave you with such a terrible burden, but I feel there is very little I could do to help. I would be of much more use and probably be more able to be proactive from my office.'

'That's agreed then. You will return tonight, and we will work closely together over the phone and the Internet.'

Philip followed his adversary's movements as he sat in the same chair that Mathew had occupied not long before and felt a rising dread as he saw the man's eyes lock onto the bag.

'I saw you struggling with that bag when I came in. What on earth is in it that has made it so heavy?'

'Oh, it's nothing really. It's just an artefact that the Head of Antiquities wanted me to take a look at. He often brings me various objects to examine as I have extensive knowledge of the ancient text. I probably won't bother with it now. I shall have it placed in a vault tomorrow and probably forget about it. The man's very sick, not quite there, and I only agreed to keep him happy.'

'I could look at it for you. I also have knowledge of such matters.'

'No, it's fine. I think we have more important things to worry about.' Philip saw the look of rejection and disappointment in his guest's eyes. *Perhaps he genuinely wanted to feel included, and besides, he would have to show him something, or he might grow even more curious,* Philip thought.

'As you pointed out, it does weigh a great deal. I think it's a lead-lined box. Perhaps you could help me carry it to the safe, and then I had better go to bed. I am feeling very weary and have much to do tomorrow.'

'Of course, I would only be too pleased to help, and then I will have to be on my way.'

Together, the two men struggled to extract the object from the bag. As the artefact was revealed, both men's jaws dropped with astonishment. All animosity was forgotten as they gazed at each other with incredulous expressions.

'I thought it was made of wood,' gasped Philip.

What lay before them was what reminded Philip of a small sarcophagus covered in a skin of gold, which had every part of its surface beautifully embossed with dragons, fighting men, demons and symbols. Both men examined every detail without uttering a word.

'Where's your safe? You are going to need to keep this a closely guarded secret,' Francis spoke up, breaking the silence.

'In the hall,' Philip answered in a daze.

United in their task, the men took either end of the box and, with great care, began to ease the object up and off the table. Slowly, they manoeuvred themselves towards the door and out into the hall, where they lay it gently down onto the soft carpet. Philip was dripping with sweat and gasping for breath, while Francis seemed strangely unaffected.

'You are much fitter than I.'

'Don't you feel it? The more you carry it, the lighter it becomes, or I am growing stronger.'

Philip wasn't listening, as he was already busy sliding the cabinet that concealed the safe further along the wall. Then he crouched down and began to turn the lock, desperately trying to remember the correct combination. He made several attempts, and eventually, the door satisfyingly sprung open.

'Look, I will show you. Stand back.'

Philip complied and stepped back as, with both hands, Francis easily lifted the box two feet off the floor and into the opening.

'Well, thank you for your help. That should be secure there until all this is over. Then we will be free to take a proper look.'

'It was no trouble. I must go now, as it's very late. I will speak to you in the morning, and I will pray for you all,' Francis stated without conviction.

With much relief, Philip showed Francis to the door of his apartment, feeling sure that he would not betray their secret.

The Bishop of Dover scurried off as quickly as he could towards his car. He was anxious to escape the grime and disease. However, once seated in the security of his metal cage, he began to feel a kind of discontent, and his mind slowly turned back to the enticing, lustrous golden flesh of the Archbishop's treasure. Since touching the object, he had felt a strange sensation of invincibility sweeping up through his soul, a glorious, triumphant power as though he had just run a hundred metres and won.

His car had been parked just beyond the arch that was the entrance to the Cathedral's grounds, and in the solitude of the night, he sat staring up at the illuminated golden tower and pondered his circumstances—should he stay or go? *There were always those who triumph during times of disaster,* he thought to himself. Curiosity was beginning to take control; he felt that the artefact must be very holy to have such a positive effect on a person with just one touch. He had a burning longing to set eyes on it one more time, to open the lid and feel the beat of its sacred heart.

For hours, he remained rigid, struggling with his dilemma, his conscience slowly freezing over as his hunger increased, and he felt compelled to respond to the calling of the book. His allegiance was to God, not man, and he convinced himself that such a precious object would be safer under his guardianship.

Not long before dawn, his greed and courage reached their zenith, and he felt it was time for him to take action.

Without any sense of guilt, Francis crept back into the house—this had always been his destiny, or he would have shut the door on leaving. Treading cautiously, he ascended the stairs, determined to carry out his plan without incident. Of course, he had noted the pattern of numbers as Philip had unlocked the safe, so the door released instantly. He moved quickly but efficiently so that before he could even think, his eyes were once again alighted on the sacred artefact.

Possessed by his base evil, and without hesitation, he lifted the golden lid. His eager eyes gazed down on the highly decorative pages with fanatical enthusiasm. Irresistibly, he ran his fingers over the text, and all its secrets were immediately disclosed to him. He was hooked like an addict and shuddered at the sweetness of the evil nectar that surged through his soul.

He had waited all his life for something significant to occur, to belong to something truly greater than himself, a tangible and physical belief. Now, he was close to the naked truth, and the meaning of everything was hammering into his brain. There could be no question of him leaving without such a miraculous find.

Believing that the old man was asleep and that nobody could hear him, he rushed back to the front room to retrieve the rucksack.

However, once in bed, Philip had not been able to sleep, the humid atmosphere and feelings of foreboding caused him to toss and turn. The burden of the day's events weighed on his conscience, and he was acutely aware that even the wisest of sages would not be able to solve the current pattern of disaster that he projected would grow in complexity daily. He wished that he could wake up and find out that everything had turned back to how they were when heaven was on Earth.

As the grey light of dawn began to grow outside his window and the first birds began to sing, he thought he heard the sound of movement coming from the hall. He lay alert, listening, tormented by images of a violent intruder. They had entered his front room.

'Who's there?'

'Don't concern yourself, it's Francis. I changed my mind. I shall just sleep on your sofa. Don't trouble yourself—we may talk tomorrow. Go back to sleep,' he quickly replied, sounding too demanding.

In his exhausted state, Philip was confused. There was something strange about the man's voice that prevented him from accurately reading what was happening. For some time, he listened and dwelled on what action to take; then, he decided to rise and confront the Bishop. When he entered the room, he saw Francis placing the box in the bag with the greatest of ease.

'What are you doing?'

'This is safer with me.'

'No, you are stealing.'

Francis paused for a moment and stood up to try to outwit the older man. They stared directly at each other. Philip saw defiant, fanatical eyes, and Francis saw fear and weakness.

'You don't know, but that object is evil personified. Having that in your possession will cause you nothing but pain. Your free soul will evaporate, and you will be chained to the altar of hell for all eternity.'

'What you don't understand, and I do, is that this is the chosen way, this is the right and only way. It's been there for all to see all the time. The signs are so clear for those who dare to look.'

'You are being duped; it's an illusion, and I can't allow you to take it.'

Francis ignored the old man's feeble arguments and proceeded to lift the bag that now held his treasure on his shoulders and made to leave.

Full of dread and horror as the man turned his back, Philip rushed at him and, picking up a marble statuette, struck the thief half-heartedly on the head. There followed a stunned silence, and everything proceeded forward in slow motion for Philip.

Francis remained standing and then turned to face his attacker. He glared out from a twisted, grotesque and demonic mask. Rage flooded through him and consumed the air in the room as flames exuded from every pore, licking viciously at everything nearby. Leaping forward, he grabbed the Archbishop around his throat, lifted him off the ground and pinned him up against the far wall.

'This is your judgement day,' he hissed, his viper's tongue smelling the stink of holiness.

Momentarily, Philip struggled, choking, and then his face lost all colour, and his lips turned a ghastly purple. His swollen tongue protruded out of his mouth. In seconds, his eyes froze, his body went limp, and when the Bishop loosened his grip, the soulless vessel fell to the floor.

Francis had not wanted that to happen, but when attacked, *a man had to defend himself,* he thought as he picked up the bag he had dropped and calmly placed it on the table. *It was a shame that the Archbishop had succumbed to the plague. He should have stayed in*

London, but it was good that he, Francis, was always there to fill the gap, he mused to himself.

Chapter Ten

In the early hours, Bishop Francis, under the shelter of the cloisters, stood gazing out at the machine-gun rain bouncing off the neat square of bright green grass. Every minute for the past week, the 'book' was constantly on his mind. When he wasn't running his fingers over the cool surface of its symbols and studying everything he could about the box and its contents, he was enjoying its life-enhancing powers. Day after day, he watched the Cathedral fill up with the worried well as he grew healthy and stronger. Sleep came to him less and less: at first, his dreams dwindled to nothing, and then, finally, he gave up rest altogether as it was no longer needed. He was reaching the point where he was unsure if all that was happening to him was real or part of a vast illusion while at the same time not caring. It was all too late, and he was enjoying the intoxicating rush of power.

He had dealt with the police perfectly, without conscience, guilt or any other type of emotion. Of course, they were very annoyed to discover that the Monks had felt it wise to immediately cremate the Archbishop's body and had strongly warned Francis that their investigations would continue and be very thorough. It had satisfied the Bishop to witness the detective visibly grimacing when he had locked onto him with his black ice eyes and gently touched him on the arm. It had been so easy. All he had to do was visualise plagued, diseased flesh in his head, and the sickness was transferred through him and into the body of the detective. Since then, the presence of the police had evaporated. They were all cringing like frightened animals in their dark holes.

Above the cloistered grounds, a black cloud burst open, and forked lightning cracked into the earth, causing the air to shudder with excitement. *I know it now; I'm the chosen one, and today, I will have to make a stand and tell the people what they need to hear. This was how it was always meant to be, and a hundred years from now, from the moment when I step into the pulpit, I will be remembered as one of the greatest men to ever exist.*

With a thrill of adrenaline keeping his stony heart beating and with the devil walking closely at his side, he entered a small side door that would take him to the main body of the Cathedral.

A cacophony of the self-righteous hammered into his head. He could hear all their thoughts as well as their verbal speech and those who cried secretly in dark corners. For a moment, he stood in the shadows by the place that marked Thomas Becket's assassination and held his ears against the unremitting blast. Millions of like-minded voices all scrambling around in fear, desperate to discover a way out, all realising that whatever style of life they lead, the great equaliser of death would not discriminate now they had entered his slaughterhouse.

The Bishop hurried to the pulpit and looked out over the crowds that filled the nave, the north aisles and south all crammed, waiting for a leader.

'Pray, may we please have silence,' his voice boomed out an anxious command. People mostly complied like a herd of cows, and the Bishop breathed a sigh of relief.

'As most of you know, I fill in for the Archbishop when his presence is required in London. Unfortunately, I am now standing in his place due to more devastating circumstances. You have all heard about the premature demise of our Archbishop, Sir Philip Wighard; God rest his soul. I am afraid this disease has no respect for the holiness of such a great man,' Francis paused to allow people to consider their fates.

He stared around at the gawping, witless humans that ate up his every word.

'Some of you might not like what you are about to hear, and in light of that fact, I would like to remind you that you are free to leave. I have, however, something to offer all of you who have pure souls a way of escaping this terrible situation and reaching salvation. I fear the truth is we have been living in a lunatic society for some time now. Lust, aggression, and greed have eroded our morality and ravished us as humans and the children of God. This might be an outdated view, but I believe our Lord and Master is sending us a message that it is time to defend ourselves against the 'hostiles'—the madmen that scurry through our streets in the shadows like rats. They are happy to oppress us, mug our elderly, and destroy our livelihoods and dreams. We need to remove this stain of evil from our community, to wipe out all the weak and feeble-minded.'

The crowd of innocent strangers stared up at Francis, aghast, not quite believing what they were hearing, and the vast building was blanketed in stunned silence.

'I would like you all to look at the table that I have placed in the crossing. Under that, the cloth is the holiest book of all time; it supersedes the Bible. We have kept it here at the Cathedral for centuries, and I was instructed that it was only to be revealed to the public in times of exceptional strife as it is of such great value to mankind. For those who feel able, I would ask you to come up to the makeshift altar, touch the book and repeat an oath to re-establish your relationship with our Lord. Leave your life of sin behind and save your souls.' Francis fell silent as he waited for a response, and many minutes passed by.

Then, a muffled voice called out from the shadows of the doorway. 'I will take your oath.' With his body drooping low, his face hidden by a hooded coat, a strange figure slowly limped down the south aisle. The audience watched with anticipation, not wanting to be the first to act but holding a debate with their inner selves that grew in urgency and ferocity.

Francis stood tall above the stranger who was crouching down at his feet.

'Why, my son, do you cover your face and hide from the eyes of God? Stand up,' the Bishop coldly spoke.

The man complied, and Francis bent forwards pulled the man's hood down and lifted his sunglasses away from his eyes.

'Help me, please,' the man begged.

'Turn around, my son, be brave and face the congregation,' his voice was tinged with a malicious brittleness.

In abject despair, the man revealed himself to the onlookers and was greeted by gasps of horror as the whole crowd drew back, retreating as far from the sickness as possible without trampling each other. The once-young man stood crying tears of blood, black pustule swellings burst out of his face, and he shook with fever.

'I am sorry this book won't help you, but I shall bless you to make your passing easier. Come here,' Francis said with fake compassion. Once again, Francis leaned forward, rested his hand gently on the man's head, and uttered a blessing. 'Go now. Be strong, and may God be with you, my son.' The wretched creature took back his dark glasses and hurried towards the door and out of the building. Francis looked around him and heard the united mumblings of the people meditating on their own agonised deaths, and he thanked the devil for helping to orchestrate a change in the mood of the crowd.

'Make your choice. Do you want the doors to close on your life, or do you want eternal freedom from pain?'

Suddenly, there was a thunderous roar of approval that almost shattered the stained-glass windows. People clapped, cheered and shouted, 'I will take the oath.' The sound grew louder and louder. The Bishop of Dover stood watching, allowing it to reach fever pitch. *Fear was a great thing,* Francis thought.

Finally, he felt it was time to calm the crowd. 'I will ask you to form yourself in orderly queues and approach the book in reverential silence,' he calmly ordered while glorying in the awful power of absolute control.

One by one, they filed before him, gently touching the human skin and repeating the oath while not understanding the strange language, all hungry for salvation, all desperate to survive the slaughter.

The Bishop watched as their eyes glazed over, and they transformed into hollow slaves, free of emotions and dreams, and unable to see the beauty in a flower, the rising sun or the human face. They were deaf to all forms of music, as they expressed no emotions except for the beat of war drums. No one wavered or hesitated—they all acted as one large mass, like a ball of ants.

Since the Archbishop's death, the army had placed an almost impenetrable cordon around the city, and all schools and public buildings were closed down. Only those with a specific purpose of national importance were allowed to pass through the checkpoints. Fifty per cent of the population had succumbed to the new form of plague, which was proving to be resistant to all antibiotic treatments. Any animal that was suspected of carrying the flea responsible for the disease was destroyed.

Soon, the rumour spread that those healthy people who daily worshipped at the Cathedral were miraculously immune from the illness and wandered freely throughout the city, preaching to those who were not yet sick to surrender to the sanctuary of the majestic building and take Bishop Francis's oath.

Bishop Francis conducted daily services where he instructed his followers about their purpose and role in the Architect's grand plan, sending them out to breach the boundaries and into the wider world to spread the word. Day after day, he waited and watched. Eventually, the cordon crumbled as soldiers became sick or chose to abandon their loyalties to the Queen and country and follow the thousands of modern pilgrims who, out of fear, felt compelled to travel to the hub of hope.

The disciples made the selection of who should live and who should die. They searched people's souls for any human frailties and wove a tale that was tailored to give solutions to their fears. However, there was no place in this new conquering society for those who could see through their words of deception—the questioners, intellectuals or those who possessed any qualities of emotional intelligence, these people were sentenced to death. Soon, all gentleness and love were gone from the heart of the population.

The new picture was that of a mighty machine made up of blank-eyed warriors destined to dominate without personality, driven to reach out towards a greater purpose. They were all tools in the devil's toolbox. Although the plague rapidly spread throughout the world, along with other disasters for those communities that needed further convincing, the disciples were eventually able to impose a type of order in the chaos.

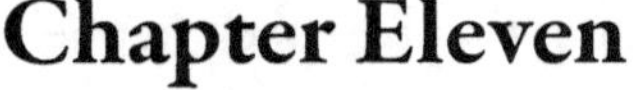

Chapter Eleven

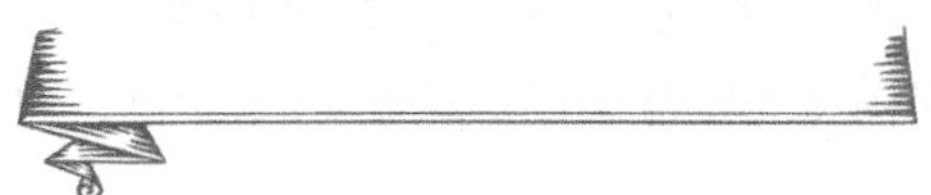

Isobel leapt out of her bed. She had been waiting for Peter to tap on the window to indicate that the coast was clear. Both their families had chosen a route of self-imposed captivity to batten down the hatches and hide. As the adults withdrew from the world, the teenagers felt more empowered and refused to become prisoners of fear. Full of defiance and energised by youthful exuberance, they decided to valiantly investigate the story of which Monk Richard had spoken.

As quietly as possible, Isobel climbed out her bedroom window and into an autumn night of wind and rain. From beneath the hood of his oversized coat, Peter greeted Issy with a warm, welcoming smile. Over time, they had grown to read each other perfectly, every gesture, facial expression or nuance of body language was immediately understood.

'It's a shitty night to go exploring,' Issy whispered.

'I know, but I feel that we are being called. Behind that Castle wall is the missing key to all this, and it is up to us to find it. As my father would say, a stone has been thrown into the pond, and the ripples are spreading out. We have little time, Isobel.'

As they climbed over the wall, the teenagers felt an inner flood of excitement and a keen desire for adventure. However, on the other side, everything seemed dead, only the wind in the trees was alive. During the day, they had noticed an absence of birdsong, the shells of butterflies, insects and dead things lying scattered everywhere. All the animal life seemed to have abandoned their posts and gone into hiding.

Even the wild boar failed to react to their presence, preferring instead to sink low into their muddy pools.

Their sole intention for that night was to explore the ruins of the monk's house for any clues that had been left behind with the passing of time. With their torches turned onto the strongest beam, they hurried along the slippery, rain-drenched path that was now becoming so familiar.

Isobel glanced around, noticed that some lights were ablaze in the fortified house and felt a shot of adrenaline at the thought that perhaps some malicious entity or mad George was observing their movements. The gossip exchanged in the village was that the Lord had gone on a pilgrimage to Canterbury and returned a changed man, dishing out orders to the locals and imposing a curfew. Anyone seen out during the hours of darkness was immediately arrested and held in a makeshift cell in the basement of the village police station.

By the time they reached Richard's house, they could barely stand; a wild wind like no other was circling all around and growing in ferocity. Trees were exploding, crashing down with a thunderous roar and shaking the ground. Peter and Isobel were terrified. No doors or windows were remaining in the ruin, but there were the remnants of a leaky roof. Together, they crouched in tight balls on the mud floor, their hands pushed hard against their ears in an attempt to block out the painfully loud noise.

'Peter, this is fucking scary, I am wetting myself here. God, I wish it would stop.' Isobel screamed her words as loudly as she could to be heard above the roaring wind.

'Shit! Shit!' Peter cursed as a branch torn from a tree shot like an arrow out of nowhere and into his cheek.

'Are you ok?'

'Yes, I'm fine,' he replied with an agitated tone as he held his hand over his face, trying to stem the flow. Isobel managed to pull a tissue out from her pocket and hand it to him.

'We are not safe here. We should have never come out.'

'It wasn't this bad when we left,' Isobel replied, her voice already hoarse and her throat sore.

In silence, they watched tree after tree sway, then bend, crack and crash to the ground.

It was impossible to stand up, so they both remained as still as stone, scarcely breathing. Then, a gust of wind charged through from one end of the single room to the other, scouring away everything in its path like a herd of stampeding horses, leaving perilously little of the building standing. Bravely, Peter opened his eyes and peered out. It was then that he spotted the hatch door in the middle of the floor.

Peter indicated his intentions to Isobel as his voice would not have been heard above the din, and she nodded her agreement. Together, they scrambled across the floor, lifted the rotten wooden door, and shone their torches into the deep, dark hole. They saw a thick rope hanging down, and without any hesitation, Peter grabbed it and slid into the darkness. Isobel had no choice but to follow. About a foot from the bottom, the rope gave way, and she fell with a hard thud next to Peter. They were then both engulfed by a cloud of falling dust.

'Are you ok?' Peter inquired as he watched Isobel struggle to blink the dirt from her eyes.

'Wait here a minute. I can't see.'

They were in no hurry, as they felt safer below ground than above, where the wind groaned and wailed its agonised anger out at the world.

'It's quieter down here, although hard to breathe. Do you think we are going to suffocate?'

'Well, we can't get back out the way we came, so we have no choice but to trace the path of this tunnel and see where it leads. Take my hand, Issy; we had better start walking.'

Inundated with trepidation, they cautiously stepped forward into the lonely darkness in silence, both understanding that if they were trapped nobody would hear their cries. After almost an hour of walking, they were wordlessly beginning to grow frantic as it dawned on them that their endeavours could be fruitless and that they might never find an exit. In addition to this, they were now paddling in the water, which seemed to be gradually rising.

'Come on, Issy, walk faster. We must find a way out of here.'

'Peter, I am scared, really scared. We have made a mistake. We shouldn't be in here.'

'I am sure it won't be much further, one step at a time, and besides, we weren't safe in that storm either.'

Sure enough, the passage took a sharp turn to the right and there, full of waist-deep water, was a large room. Isobel felt the hairs bristle on the back of her neck as their torchlights illuminated substantial rusty iron cages lining all the walls.

'What were they for?' Isobel wondered aloud.

'I don't know, but I don't think they were for anything good. Look, there are some steps over there. Let's get out of here.'

With a renewed resolve, they waded as fast as they could through the water towards the exit, longing to escape the merciless atmosphere of the dungeon.

The heavy wooden door was not locked, but it took their combined strength to open it far enough to squeeze through. They emerged into the grey light of dawn. To their relief, the storm had dispersed and was rumbling in the far distance.

They found themselves on a soggy bank, and rising high above them was the white wooden structure of the watermill. Far below cascaded the swollen river, and on the other side of this was the bright patch of short grass where a group of innocent teenagers had once rested after a long walk.

'We are on the far side of the mill,' Isobel said, stating the obvious. Her mood immediately lifted as she was free and once again able to breathe fresh air.

'Let's head up the hill to the mound and see what the damage is.' Peter equally felt the exhilaration that comes to those who have just conquered a fear.

They began to climb carefully, picking their way over an array of broken things that once grew, trees felled by some giant enemy, stones, and rocks scattered in the wrong places. As they approached the grassy summit, they were almost blinded by the brightest of light above, which was a strange formation of swirling copper clouds. Over the brow of the burial mound, they looked down into a large opening in the ground where a tree had been uprooted. There in the centre of a glowing golden ball, crouched an iridescent figure with flowing rust-coloured hair and with the most dazzling, magnificent, sun-yellow, feathered wings stretching out from between its shoulders.

Peter and Isobel were mesmerised by the extraordinary sight and stood staring in disbelief. Suddenly aware it was being observed, the angel-like being looked up at the watchers and smiled the sweetest of smiles, full of goodness and wisdom. In the next split second, the wings spread and gently flapped and as light as air, the figure rose into the brightness, followed by three wisps coiling up like smoke. The form disappeared into a crack in the sky.

The teenagers emerged from their trance-like state and looked upon a more familiar grey morning.

'I can't believe I just saw what I think I saw. Did you see it?'

'It was there, whatever it was, it was truly there. A mirage created by the strange atmosphere, perhaps,' Peter uttered, not convinced.

'Or an angel,' Isobel murmured.

As if to convince them further at that moment, three golden feathers floated gently down and settled softly on the ground where the figure had been bent over. Without a thought, the youths ran forward to collect the evidence.

'You take them, Issy. You will keep them safer than me, but I think it must be kept a secret for now.'

'You must at least take one in case we are ever parted.'

'What's that sticking out of the ground?'

Isobel scanned the soil and spotted what looked like an axe. However, before she could say a word, it was already lying in Peter's hands along with the feather. It was a flint axe with some kind of carved bone handle that appeared unaffected by time.

'I am keeping this. Wow, it's amazing!' Peter stated, and it was clear from his eyes that he was utterly entranced by the object, which, after a few moments, he slid under his belt.

'Well, in that case, I am keeping this,' Isobel replied, holding up a necklace of beautiful blue-green beads, which she immediately dropped over her head. Peter examined it closely, and as he twisted it around her neck, his eyes rested on a beautiful jewel.

'You should look at this.'

Isobel bowed her head. 'Wow! What is it?

'It looks like an eye with a turquoise iris and a jet pupil.'

Tired and in awe of what they had experienced, they fell silent. Together, they walked back up the hill engulfed in darkness as the rain began to fall once more down onto the torn skin of the earth. They crossed the bridge that had only just survived the onslaught of the ferocious river. Then, in dazed silence, they slowly walked along the track towards the main road that would take them towards the village. In the distance, they heard the ringing of church bells as though mourning the death of the many trees.

Finally, they separated to go to their own back doors, bracing themselves for whatever consequences for their inexplicable actions would be thrown at them on entering. Isobel skulked into the kitchen, fearing the wrath of her mother. No one was there, so she headed for the passage, hoping to sneak back to her bedroom before anyone noticed her absence.

As she entered the hallway, she was confronted by the image of her mother bent over, holding her swollen belly in both hands. Next to her was Daisy, her arm locked into the younger woman in a gesture of support.

'Mum! What's the matter?'

The woman seemed remote—her face was pale, and her trembling lips repeatedly repeated, 'My baby, my baby.'

The soothing voice of her grandmother offered reassurance. 'It's all going to be fine. We will go to the doctor's house. It is safe there and free of plague.'

'What's happening?' Isobel shouted with tears of tiredness and frustration brimming in her eyes.

'You had better get those dripping clothes off,' the old woman stated with a sharp voice and then immediately turned her attention back to her patient, ignoring the disobedient teenager.

Without another word, they disappeared into the kitchen and out of the back door. Then her grandfather came rushing towards her, frantically trying to get his arm in the sleeve of his raincoat while at the same time searching for his car keys.

'Granddad, where's Mum going?'

'Nothing for you to worry about. The baby is coming, dear.'

With that, he retrieved the keys from the windowsill by the phone and raced out of the house, leaving Isobel alone, listening to the roar of the engine and the crunching of the wheels over the gravel drive.

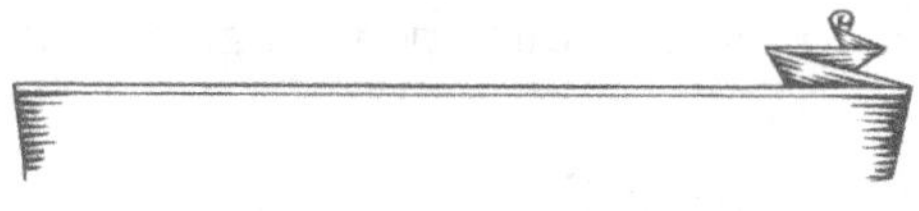

Chapter Twelve

Francis placed his inhuman hair-covered hand in that of the reporter's, conscious that he had to temper his sharpened strength so as not to crush the man's bones.

'Good morning, Bishop. My name is Mr Crane from the BBC. We spoke on the phone yesterday. I hope you don't mind us asking you a few questions?' A group of demented journalists from various areas of the media jostled for positions and held their microphones outstretched in eager anticipation.

'No, I would be happy to. But one thing I would ask is for one question at a time, please; I'm a little sensitive to sound and would wish to give each question my complete attention and consideration.' Francis focussed on a distant point to switch off the mind speak that he continued to hear in the silence.

'Bishop, is it true that the church has cut itself off from government and that you no longer want to discuss some of today's most important issues with the leaders of this country?'

'The church has never felt that it was their place to involve themselves in politics, and during this current national disaster, we find ourselves unable to agree with the government's views on how we progress forward. Too much time and money has been spent on propping up the weak sinners of our society. The world is awash with parasites. Our Lord has spoken. He has demonstrated his anger, and it is clear that he will only save the strong and righteous. We are just trying to restore form and structure to a way of being that has no shape.'

'Doesn't that go against Christian belief? Are we not supposed to help those less able in our society?'

'Your interpretation of the Lord's wishes is a man-made corruption. The words you have listened to for far too long are not from the heavens. They are Earth-bound.' Francis's control slipped, and he received the full blast of snarling contempt from the half-wits questioning brains. He adjusted his focus, stared up at a gargoyle on the roof of the Cathedral, and regained his composure. 'You are all welcome to attend a service here at the Cathedral where I hope I may extend your understanding on matters of faith. Now, another question, please, and I think it must be the last as the light is fading, and I fear another storm is brewing.'

'Is it true that all those within the City walls are safe from disease?'

'Not quite true. About fifty per cent of the population has died of the plague, and there are still a few who resist the Lord who has been struck down. However, for all those who have sought sanctuary within the Cathedral walls and who have embraced the oath and been blessed by myself or other members of the fellowship, they have indeed become the undying. I hope I have been able to answer all your questions, and you are all welcome to join us in praise to our Creator.' Without another word, he turned and rushed towards the building that roared up at the funereal sky like a giant black lion in the darkening skies. He wanted to escape the stench of humans and their verbal and non-verbal callings, silently begging to be saved while screaming.

'Bishop, just one picture for the cameras.'

Reluctantly, he stood in the doorway under the carved statues of saints as large drops of rain began to fall. The cameras flashed, and he felt his eyes blaze with a fiery rage. They should not have delayed him, as he could only keep his power contained for short periods. Above his head, the ancient stone began to crumble to the ground.

Annoyed by the man from the BBC who stood too close and was smiling inanely, he burnt into the reporter's pupils with his piercing eyes like the sun through a magnifying glass. The man crumpled to the ground. Then, with a machine-like grip, the uncontrollable force in his head reached out, grasped the heart of a random person in the crowd and shook it until he also collapsed. Finally working with the spirit of the building, he hurled stone nuggets at the bewildered audience, who stood for a moment in shock and then grabbed all their equipment and ran as the missiles headed their way.

Bishop Francis roared with laughter. Gregory, his head disciple investigating the commotion, opened the door into the porch and stood next to his master.

'What's wrong with them?'

'They are children of the enemy. They will only survive long enough to get our message out. Talking of children, we need to find a siren's call for them—ways of bringing even the youngest into the fold, or just destroy them all and start again.'

'Francis, we have a problem. There are just too many people coming to take the oath. They are even travelling from as far afield as America as the plague spreads. Is there a way we could take the words from the book, go to the people and set up churches in other countries?'

The Bishop bowed his head and stroked his chin with his bony fingers, deep in thought, as he wandered back into the building. Based at the Cathedral school, he had acquired an efficient machine of disciples who had taken turns around the clock to convert people. It was time to send his army out to conquer new territory, but would it be possible without people being able to touch the book? He needed to study it further; perhaps it was the words and symbols that hooked people into the alternate universe.

'Gregory, I want each member of the fellowship to copy down every word and symbol from the first few chapters of the book, the bits with the oath, to study it in-depth and understand even the most intricate details. Then, we will see who is ready to branch out. Anyone who can't or won't learn will have to be dispatched. Our crusaders must be invincible, the indisputable leaders of future generations throughout the world.'

'How are we going to solve the immediate problem of the crowds?'

'The moment they have been baptised, send them away. Tell them to wait until they are called upon. Once they are part of our faith, they will have nothing to fear, and their strength will only increase. Anyone you feel could be of special use, detain.'

FAR AWAY FROM THE CATHEDRAL that was heaving with life, the Houses of Parliament and all the Palaces of London stood empty, abandoned by the rich and influential. The golden tower of Big Ben pointed up into the blood-red gash that cut across the sky as the sun sunk over the city. Down below in the spreading shadows, people protested, holding up placards, shouting, chanting and banging on anything they could to attract the attention of their leaders, seemingly unaware that the corridors were deserted.

Elsewhere, full of despair and frustration, rioters stampede through the commercial areas of the city, systematically looting without fear of prosecution, as the police had become a dwindling, ineffective force with little power. The turbulent atmosphere whirled down every street where fires and funeral piers were left to blaze out of control, endangering homes and more lives. A poisonous cocktail of arson, murder and a variety of other crimes was rapidly corroding society's structure. London was sinking.

Prime Minister Duncan Galsworthy gazed out of the window of the remote castle like a prisoner longing for freedom. All the doors were locked and guarded. Behind him, his crisis team sat outwardly calm—internally, each praying that their country's crippling pain would soon be over so that peace could be restored.

Duncan was aware that he was intermittently clenching his jaws with annoyance. His stomach was permanently knotted so that he could barely eat, and he could feel his eyes twitching. He hoped that one of his men would be able to ease his bitter burden. Perhaps the head of the armed forces had a plan that could prevent doomsday from drawing any closer. He turned to face the grim-faced group.

'Thank you all for coming, and I won't waste any of our precious moments with the normal formalities. I believe the time has come for us to change course and take drastic action. Our city has become a festering wound that we must heal. What do you military men think?'

'Well, we need to enforce martial law properly, but with our reduced numbers, this will be difficult. I suggest we recall our forces, abandon other conflicts and focus our strength on the capital. We need to set an example for the rest of the country. Looters need to be shot, and a curfew put in place, and rigorously enforced,' the head of the armed forces said with conviction.

'Do we all agree with this proposal?' Duncan responded, hoping that his audience would follow the only possible way forward.

'No, I don't,' spoke up an adviser to the Department of Health.

'What's your opinion, Doctor?'

'We are near to a breakthrough with our combinations of antibiotic treatments. We have been working very closely with the Africans, who still have regular outbreaks of plague. Some of our patients are making progress. To go around shooting people on a whim will just make matters worse. You just can't go to war with your people.'

At this point, the flames of heated debate flared up, fuelled by the pent-up anger and feelings of helplessness that had lain dormant in each individual. It was like chasing the chaotic pattern of a pinball, and soon Duncan lost track of all the different ideas and opinions. He began to pace as if searching for a better signal.

'That's enough! We can't have anarchy in this room.' Everyone stopped squabbling as Duncan gained everyone's attention. He was determined to be heard. 'I have listened as much as I am able to your arguments, and I have come to a decision. I feel that our medical research is still lagging too far behind. There are few flea-carrying animals left, so I don't understand why we still hear of new cases of plague daily. That needs investigating. In the meantime, I am turning the Capital and other Cities over to the army.'

'But Prime Minister, the plague once in the human body is easily spread. It is a bacterial infection. It is more efficient infrastructure that we need,' the adviser for health persisted.

'Your point has been taken, Doctor. Now, to other matters, as you have all heard and seen on the news, we have another problem. With the untimely demise of the Archbishop of Canterbury, Sir Philip Wighard, it seems that the utterly corrupt and loathsome Bishop of Dover has undemocratically stepped into his shoes. He thinks himself above the law and is adding to the turmoil by claiming to be able to cure all ills.'

The silence in the room was palpable. Then came a growing, united mumbling of words of disdain for a man they all felt was corrupted and evil.

'This is a matter I would like to deal with personally,' Duncan added. There followed nods of agreement. 'I think that is enough for now. I would like to arrange another meeting tomorrow morning at nine.'

The group rose, turned their backs on the Prime Minister, and quietly talked amongst themselves as they left the room. Duncan then called back the heads of the army and the police.

'I need your help. I am sure you are in agreement that we need to rid our country of this vile interloper,' Duncan whispered. The men stood huddled together, their heads bowed as they secretly discussed the fate of the country's most-wanted villain. Finally, a plan was in place. 'All this must be kept top secret and only discussed amongst our chosen group of trusted friends. Have I got your word?'

'We will be onto it right away. This is one problem that should be easy to erase,' the head of the armed forces replied and smirked with a sense of victory.

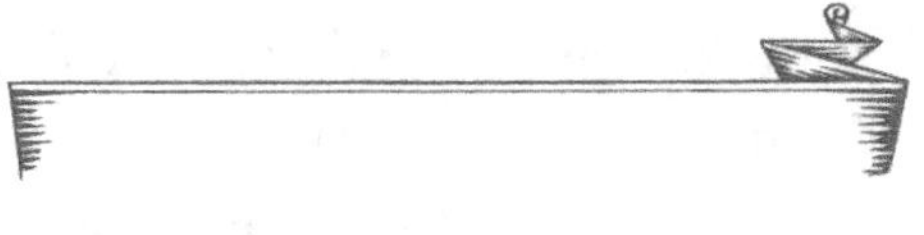

Chapter Thirteen

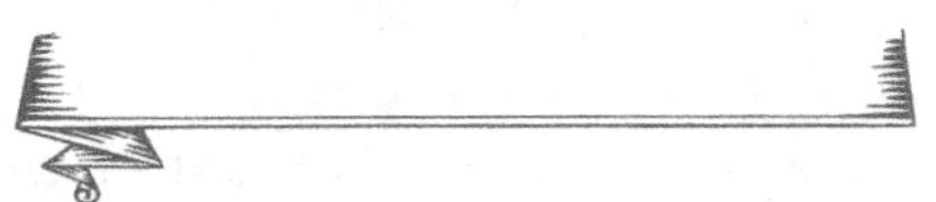

Leonard, the owner of the Black Horse, was so busy he barely had time to think. He was missing his wife, who, at the beginning of the crisis, had gone to Australia on a holiday of a lifetime to visit their oldest son. Then, due to the tragedy that had befallen the country, he had advised her not to come home until the situation had returned to normal.

Since the sickness struck, the small room of the pub had been inundated with customers. They were all men, and at that age, they were too old to care about their mortality but suffered from fears for the young.

As each person creaked open the door, he saw their eyes dart around the room, searching for anything that looked suspicious. Some would sit alone, not saying a word, their mood dour, and others would gossip furiously in animated groups. They were all doing more than just quenching their thirst; they were drinking excessively to forget. By closing time, neighbours who had been friends for years would take their frustration out on each other in a violent dispute. Feelings of dread amplified everyone's emotions, and nobody bothered to excuse their bad behaviour.

Still, it was lunchtime, and the atmosphere was muted compared to what it was bound to be later into the night when the village would transform once more into the Wild West as few obeyed the curfew.

Leonard's hearing was divided between a group of farmers discussing the devastation wreaked by the hurricane and another that was talking about how to claim the village back from the influx of pilgrims who had decided to walk to Canterbury rather than take their cars. Apparently, they had felt that travelling in large groups was safer and staying away from the roads meant they could avoid the army.

The door banged shut as John entered the room. For a moment, all eyes shot in his direction and then relaxed as people returned to their far more pressing conversations. Leonard watched as his friend shuffled towards the bar, where he pulled out a stool and sat staring pensively. The man he had known as a deep thinker and a kind, gentle soul appeared transformed. His face was creased with lines of pain and worry. Leonard approached with concern.

'What can I get you, John?'

'A shot of whiskey and a beer, please.'

'That's not like you. Has the baby been keeping you up?' As he spoke, he turned from the tortured face and grabbed a bottle of whiskey in the expectation that his customer would need more than just one shot.

'What a terrible time to be born,' the old man stated to himself.

'Yes, but the baby is strong and healthy, isn't he?'

'He is—but for how long? Even taking Jeanie to the doctor was a drama. We had to abandon the car and walk because of all the fallen trees. Now, none of us can sleep; my daughter checks the baby all the time for signs of illness. I had to come up here just to escape the arguments between the women and all the tension.'

'How's Isobel? Does she like having a baby brother?'

'I think Isobel is the only one with any sense, she spends all her time out with Peter roaming the countryside, staying out of the way. She has never liked being indoors anyway.' John paused and looked sad. 'Her mother is so obsessed with keeping the baby safe that our Issy is almost neglected. It's a good deal she has a friend like Peter,' the old man whispered, not wanting the whole pub to hear his business.

Leonard poured his friend another whiskey. 'That ones on the house,' he said. Then he gestured to John to come closer, and the two men leaned in, their heads almost touching.

'I meant to ask you. Do you remember some time ago you told me of a strange ghost-like person who you had seen sitting in my pub?' John nodded his acknowledgement.

'Yes, yes, I have seen him quite frequently lately. I don't mention it because I don't want to frighten the girls, and besides, they all think I am going senile.'

'Well, I have seen him too. He usually visits in the early hours after the rabble has gone.'

'Where do you see him?'

'Well, that's the peculiar thing—he lurks around in the kitchen, often bent over like he is examining the floor. It's as though he has lost something, or he is searching for something.'

'Can he see you?'

'I am not sure, I tend to hide in the doorway so that I can watch him and discover what he is up to.'

'Do you think he is the ghost of one of those skeletons you found? Perhaps he is looking for that box.' John's head was swimming; he no longer felt crippled with anxiety and could feel the deep furrows on his forehead soften. He loved a mystery.

'Why don't you stay over one night, and we can do a ghost hunt?'

'Yes, I would like that. I will phone you up when I am off duty on the home front.'

'We'll have a few drinks and become detectives for the night.'

'That sounds great. I will look forward to the visit.' Leonard was then called upon to attend to another customer, so John sat drinking in silent thought. When his glasses were empty, he shouted over to his friend, who was talking to the farmers. 'I am going to leave you now, my good friend. I plan to go home and have a nice siesta. See you soon.'

John smiled and, with a more elevated mood, pushed the stool out from under him and wavered towards the door.

'See you, John. Take care of that family of yours,' Leonard shouted after the old man.

THE NARROW ROAD WAS like a river of people. Peter and Isobel stood by the garden gate, watching the lost souls flow by as they wondered how they would enter the Castle grounds without drawing too much attention. Isobel glanced up the road, looking for a gap, and recognised her grandfather's familiar gait. He approached with a self-satisfied smile on his face.

'Hello Issy, Peter. What are you two up to?'

'Oh, just hanging about.'

'I hope you have checked with your mother to see if she needs any help.'

'I have been doing chores all morning. Mum and Ben are asleep now, and Gran's reading a book.'

'Fair enough, but be careful. These are perilous times. I think I might get some rest myself. See you later.' With that, John walked with almost sprightly steps towards the bungalow.

Out of the corner of his eye, Peter caught sight of someone in the crowd that he recognised. He nudged Isobel.

'Isn't that George?' Isobel turned and followed Peter's gaze.

'Yes, and that's Ariel he's dragging along.' The teenagers regarded each other with expressions of mingled surprise and horror. Then Isobel rushed forward and grabbed her friend by the arm. Ariel turned and glared at the girl, shot her a look of indignation, and pushed her away.

'Go away, Issy,' she commanded with alarm.

'Where are you going?'

'None of your business.' The stern reply came from the dishevelled figure of her father, who towered over them both menacingly. Peter, who had been standing close by, pulled his friend out of the crowd to the other side of the road.

'Leave them; it's not our problem if they are idiots.'

'But I wanted to tell her about Ozzy.'

Unbeknown to the teenagers, the artefacts they carried, the axe and the dragon tear necklace, meant that the divide between past and present no longer existed. For them, time had merged into one, and they were free to wander back and forth through the gate. When they turned to face the wall and saw the small door, they were so desperate to escape the commotion of the pilgrims that they opened it and stepped back into the medieval peace without question.

Instantly, Isobel crashed with a hard thud to the ground, where some angry beast trampled her. Instinctively, she covered her head. Then she felt her clothes being tugged at, and she was dragged up into a standing position.

When she opened her eyes, she saw Ozzy was holding her against the wall. She turned and saw Peter trembling beside her, his face white with shock and alarm. The person whom he had previously considered to be his friend was now his tormentor.

'Does thou cometh with thee book? Would thou be so foolish as to return empty-handed? I shalt have no mercy upon thee and wouldst slay thee like any foe,' his voice was cold, and his fingers trembled on the hilt of his sword.

'Slow down, you are racing ahead of yourself. We have come with an important message for your master,' Peter bravely spoke with the flats of his hands pressing down on the air in a calming gesture.

'Kill them, kill them,' Lance screeched from the top of a tree.

'Fear not Oswald me lad; we will listen to thy tale. Besides, thee book be weighted with evil and may only be moved by the strong,' Richard stated as he stepped out from the thick shadows of the pines. 'So, what say thee?'

Battered and shaking from her encounter with the wild boar, Isobel was left speechless, and she was more frightened of the shadowy shapes that she could see mining the soft earth beneath the trees.

'Your silence ire's thee. Speak thee out?' the monk was growing impatient.

'I don't know what year it is for you —I suppose about 1380? Well, we come from the twenty-first century. We are from the future.'

Richard looked up at Peter through eyes that were glazed over and perplexed.

'I knew thoust be witches —or worse, demons.'

'No, no,' Isobel interjected. 'Look, your trees are still standing and where we come from, they have all fallen. We speak differently to you, and please, we need your help.' Isobel rambled on, knowing that she was floundering...

'Speak on, lad,' the monk instructed Isobel.

'In our time, the book you spoke of was dug up, and since then, our world has experienced one disaster after another: plagues, hurricanes and storms. We are living in hell.'

'Indeed, afore the 'Devil's' book was buried, we also fought through times when the furnaces of hell ravished our souls, each day we spent on thy knees begging for mercy. There be much drinking, riots and debauchery, us wretches thinketh that each sunrise to be our last. There be hard times, but as long as we keep our lips fastened, God be kind to thee. Why then wouldst we turn thine ears to witches? We be not cod's-head, we wilt nay step into thou snare of evil.'

'You are worried, too. Your river has been poisoned, so you can't fish. You don't want to step back into hell, but it is leaking from our time back into your present.' Isobel was stunned by her own words and speaking them made all the horror more real. 'Babies are dying—my brother could die.'

Richard fell silent and looked at them for a long time as he ruminated over what to do next. A shaft of sunlight shot through a gap in the canopy and illuminated the group. It was then, for the first time, that he saw Isobel's necklace. A gentle smile of recognition spread across Richard's face, and he visibly relaxed. Then, as his eyes scanned over the sickly-looking boy, he spotted an axe protruding out from his belt.

'I beg thou forgiveness, kind sirs; thou art both welcome on thy land.'

The teenagers stared at the monk, bewildered by the swift transition of mood from sombre to friendly.

'Come lad, set thee eyes upon these gifts,' he beckoned to Oswald. 'See here, our young sir wears the 'dragon tear necklace', and the other lad carries the 'angel axe', he explained excitedly. Ozzy cautiously approached and scrutinised the treasures.

'What are you talking about? These are just grave goods that we found after the hurricane.' Peter glared at them cynically. He was feeling irritated by all the supernatural qualities and interpretations people were so willing to attribute to the most mundane objects.

'Thou doest carry the memories of our ancestors, the elements of eternal goodness. Thou art the chosen ones, touched by thee angle and we be obliged to assist thee by all possible means. Follow me, he uttered, coaxing them forward. 'I have something to show thee.'

'I would like to just say I am not a boy; I am a girl, 'Isobel,' Isobel stated.

Ozzy took a close look at the sparkling light of her eyes, and his heart quivered as he felt he recognised the deep spirit that danced in their rich dark beauty. With renewed buoyancy, he smiled at her shyly and stepped politely back.

'It's lovely to meet you, my lady,' he coyly spoke.

Overwhelmed with feelings of relief, Isobel followed the small man and his companion, who both raced along the path with great agility and speed. The wild boar disappeared from view, and so she relaxed. At times, they almost ran, then walked. Finally, the pace dwindled as they broke out of the trees and into the sun. Sir Lancelot rose high, floating on currents of warm air. Deer, alarmed by the intruders, took flight and vanished. Peter stood for a moment, panting, trying to catch his breath.

'Are you ok?' Isobel enquired.

'I'll be fine—just asthma.' He took a blue inhaler out of his pocket and sucked hard on it.

'Issy, what do you make of this? One minute, they want to kill us, and the next, we are being treated like their best buddies. I don't trust them,' Peter hurriedly whispered.

'I don't know, but they are nice, so let's go along with it for now.'

Oswald had been dancing along next to the monk, but they both stopped and looked around.

'What's that?' Ozzy shouted back.

'It's something that helps Peter breathe. He will be alright in a minute. We just need to walk slower.'

As they strolled along, they began to see groups of chickens pecking at the soil, and their number increased as they approached the monk's house.

Richard went straight to the water butt, took a metal cup that was dangling from a piece of string and scooped up some water.

'Here takes a drink, Master Peter, and if you need medicines I have herbs that will cure all ailments,' Richard explained. 'When thee be well, I shalt take thee both underground. What you see there, you must swear to keep a secret, and I beg of thee, show nay fear. Oswald, I will ask thou to stayest here and keep guard.' The boy nodded his agreement and called for his bird, which immediately swooped down onto his outstretched arm.

'Do I have your guarantee, lad, and you, my lady?'

'You do, we promise that we won't tell a soul,' they replied enthusiastically, not wanting to tell Richard that they had already explored the extending passages.

The monk took a stick with what looked like dried grass tied to one end and thrust it into the embers of his fire. Flames flared up and then died back, creating a dull glow. Richard opened the trap door. Isobel looked down the dark hole and was relieved to see that the rope was still there and that it seemed new. This time, the teenagers were able to descend without incident.

The first thing that struck them was the noxious fumes. The stench was unbearable, and Peter began to cough. Isobel held a tissue over her nose, but Richard proceeded as though he was completely unaware of any odours. The smell of rot and decay increased with every step, making the long walk into a loathsome trial.

After what seemed to be forever, Richard stopped and turned to face the teenagers.

'What thee are about to lay witness to, hast little reason in the world of men. It hast been bestowed upon thee to have guardianship of what survives of thy 'monster race'. I keepeth Oswald from cometh down here, as he loves all beasts and with nay, thoughts would set them free. If that be and Lorde Langley finds thy precious collection gone, he would summon the 'derrick' for thee as I be thee lad's master.'

'Take heed of my warning thee monsters be unpredictable and mostly uncontrollable. They be hostile, as thou would be, held captive behind bars. Please be brave, showest nay fear and stayest back.'

'Where do they come from?' Isobel enquired to delay them meeting the mysterious beasts.

'They used to live on the perimeter of our world and were barely ever seen. When God saw man as a destructive creature rather than a creative one, he deserted our world. Then the first plague came, and other disasters took place, so the monster race began to travel further into man's territory. Folks were fearful, it be their belief that they were the reason for all that be wrong and set about hunting them down until there were but a few left. Most returned from whence they came and hid back in the shadows. Our Lord of the manor loves to collect things, and these poor creatures are part of his collection.'

As they took the sharp bend to the right, Isobel noticed that the floor was at least dry as opposed to their last visit during the storm. Then, they found themselves once again in a room with a high vaulted ceiling. It was hard to make out the creatures in the weak light, but it was clear that they were all standing and alert, awakened by the sound of approaching voices.

Richard went closer to the first cage and held his torch up at the monster. There, standing over eight feet, was a man-like creature covered in silver-grey hair, his body as skinny as the branches of a willow tree. The stickman began to pace up and down, followed by a cloud of flies appearing like an amplified misty shadow. His small, black, beady eyes were sunk deep into his head and stared out starkly at the unexpected visitors.

'Why has he got that thick chain around his ankle?' Isobel asked.

'He might not look it, but he be very strong and hast broken the bars many times afore. He be named Virtus. Methinks he mayest be mad by now,' uttered the monk as he moved on to the next cage.

There was a magnificent beast, a black-fur wolf-like creature. It stood taller than any wolf Issy or Peter had ever seen, and its powerful front legs were longer than the back legs, causing her spine to slope down. It was altogether heftier than its modern-day counterparts were and had sabre teeth, which were as long as a pencil. It prowled around the cage, in her endless routine of waiting a minute after a long minute to breathe fresh air again and feel the warm sun and the cool of the moonlight. Eventually, her curiosity waned, and she slowly crawled into the darkest corner of the cage and lay down while watching the intruders' every move like a rat from its hole.

'I call her Umbra, as she is all blackness except for the red eyes.'

As Umbra had lost interest, Richard moved on to the last cage and held the light up high.

Isobel first noticed sharp black talons wrapped around the bars of the cage, they were clinging tightly while trying to shake the iron poles. Startled, they all jumped back. Isobel's instincts told her to run straight home, as out of the darkness, a huge head thrust forward. Its mouth was a cavernous black, full of yellow teeth and two sets of fangs. Its roar shook the building. Thick, gooey green saliva dropped onto the dirt floor, and its venomous, noxious breath oozed into the watchers' lungs.

The monk had stood back but had re-composed himself while the children stood rooted to the spot and, unable to control their fear, trembled.

'Be not alarmed, he canst escape,' Richard tried to reassure the teenagers.

The beast roared again, and this time, Umbra bounded towards the bars and began to howl mournfully. Then Virtus joined in, shaking the shackles of his captivity.

'We had best take thy leave. We nay want the whole world to hear their cries. When the Lord captured Morse, the dragon, he was in a cave surrounded by a large booty. He loves to steal things a bit like a magpie,' Richard added as an aside as he turned away from Morse.

As Richard went ahead towards the door that led to the mill, he chattered on, trying to distract the young people from their secret terror. Once they began to leave, the animals calmed themselves and dragged themselves back into their pitiful sitting positions. Isobel took one glance back, shuddered, and cringed at the sight of such poignant desolation.

As they climbed their way back up into the light, Peter asked with an annoyed tone, 'Why did you bring us here... to show us such an inhumane sight?'

'It be the Lordes cruel way, young Oswald be correct, they can't stay locked away, but we can't just open the doors and let them flee. They need to be returned safely to the perimeter world. I thought you, with your powers, might be able to help.'

'We are not magicians or witches,' Peter replied.

'It just be me hopes. I need to return to the lad now. Do thou cometh?'

'No, I think we will cut across the fields at the bottom of the mound and go through the poplar wood. We need some time to think.' Peter spoke for them, both understanding that neither he nor Issy was ready to descend back into that hell.

Aware that Richard was watching them, the two teenagers scrambled up the bank, grappling with a confusion of emotions when they heard him call out.

'By the way, do you know where the book has gone?'

Peter stopped, turned and shouted back. 'Yes, we do, but we don't know how to get it.'

'I have searched where I thought it was but can't find anything. Everything has changed. Come back soon. We must acquire it before it's too late.'

'We will come back,' Issy called while still climbing, trying to escape the cages and create a distance between past and present. Once they were safely over the brow of the hill, Issy turned to Peter and idly asked, 'What's the time?'

The teenager glanced down at his watch. 'It's stopped at about the time we walked through the door.'

'I hope that doesn't mean that we are stuck in the past,' Issy replied anxiously.

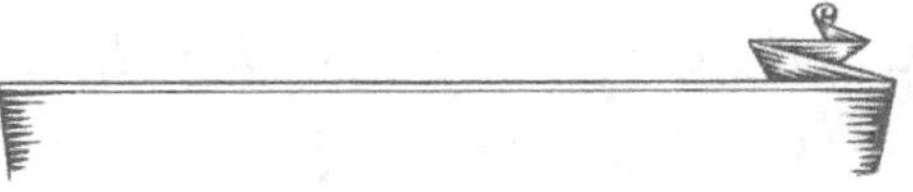

Chapter Fourteen

It was the early hours of the morning; the noisy crowds had gone, and the city was asleep. Others dreaded the darkness of night pressing around them, but Bishop Francis was drawn into its rich emptiness and the peace it provided him away from the commotion of humans.

He stooped over the black document, hungrily running his fingers over the pages of the book. He now was able to move with the greatest of ease, as his iron-strong muscles made everything feel weightless. His mind was still bound by the spell of the most fantastically thrilling living dream of his life. It was no mortal dream but something truly beyond everything else in how it felt.

In this living dream, he had been standing at the lectern preaching from the book when there came a loud hammering on the main entrance door. Then, a strong wind punched it open, and in flew a cloud of crows that flapped madly around the heads of his congregation of hooded monks. Then the door slammed shut, the building shuddered, and the demonic creatures took up positions, perching like guards on every available surface.

Standing before him in the aisle was the strangest figure he had ever seen. A creature of considerable height, neither, man nor woman, a vision of shimmering blue-green. It had no other recognisable features. Around where its feet would have been fluttered, blue flames and it appeared to hover above the ground. Although constantly moving and fading in and out, it was still a substantial awe-inspiring presence.

Francis stared at the entity long and hard, and as he did so, he felt as though his soul had been plunged into a furnace leaving him cleansed and able to understand everything with profound clarity.

'You have summoned Diabolus Angelus. You have brought about the collision of our universes,' the visitor's voice boomed and echoed around the whole Cathedral. 'I am Diabolus Angelus evermore, the prophet from the shadow Universe, the perpetual storm. It's our immortals that overthrew your God and hung Jesus from the cross. We are the hunters, the rope around the wretch on the scaffold, the bullet, and the knife.' His voice thundered into everyone's brains. All the monks of the fellowship had listened and were mesmerised. 'This is man's exit time. We are come to take what is ours. There will be no opposition to our celestial Monarchy. Your meagre souls are a stain, a cancer in the system, and humans are no more than our fodder.'

'You, Bishop have declared your ambition to join our number, to be counted, to be saved. You are anointed as warriors of our kingdom.'

With these final words, a tempest of cold flame swept like a swollen ocean, consuming everything in its path. The Bishop had felt pure ecstasy as the fires licked over every part of his body, and on awakening, he knew that he was somehow transformed.

The changes to his body had been rapid of late. At some point, his weak and feeble human flesh had decomposed and atom by atom, the form of what some would call a demon, had taken its place. The thick hair that now covered everything except his face and the unexpected appearance of wings were hard to conceal. At first, he had noticed two buds on his back, which day after day began to swell. Finally, one night, he found himself curled up on the well-trodden stone floor, wracked in almost unendurable pain as his skin slowly split open, and for the first time, he was able to unfold his awe-inspiring wings. When he confronted his image in a mirror, he was amazed by what he saw. A tall, powerfully muscled, hairy beast met his eyes, and when he spread out the dusky purple, leathery skin, the black fire in his heart roared up in ecstasy. Since then, he had grown accustomed to wearing long flowing robes to hide his monstrous characteristics.

That night, the vast space of the Cathedral felt alive; every crack and shadow was buzzing with movement and magic. Beneath the ground of the Cathedral, he could hear the dead shudder awake. At the entrances to the building, his elite guards muttered curses about the frailties of the inferior race.

Francis felt as though he was standing on the edge of a precipice, a giant looking down at the approaching minions, waiting for the call to arms. He knew they were coming, the Prime Minister's pilgrims, as he could hear their whispered conversations.

A subtle, light breeze blew around the space, brushing his face as the massive doors opened at the front of the building. *What fools to enter in such an obvious way,* he thought as he turned his dark head to watch the soldiers move into the candlelit gloom.

The soldiers, not wanting to attract any attention by making too much noise, moved cautiously forward and with their guns fitted with silencers, they were ready to shatter the Disciples' vital organs. This antagonised the demon disciples and ignited the fire in their muscles so that they sprung high into the air, avoiding the spray of bullets. As they spread their wings, the air rippled out, so the men struggled to remain standing. The flying beasts wove in and out of the terrified group just out of their reach. One by one, the soldiers were picked off so quickly that some of them never knew what had killed them, something driving through their flesh or incinerating their hearts. One man had his eyes gouged out by retractable talons and ran around sightless, crying in pain. Francis couldn't stand the noise, so he reached out with his mind and crushed his throat.

The sheer strength and power of him and his followers caused the Bishop's whole being to throb with excitement. Then he realised that some lunatics had managed to enter the building the back way, as he saw a whispery blue light coil around one of the pillars, which meant that one of the fellowship had been struck down. A group of the Prime Minister's warriors approached him warily with their guns trembling in their hands. He watched without any emotions as the serpentine spirit curled its way up the nearest soldier's body unnoticed until he reached a small space of bare neck between the man's helmet and body armour. Two fangs appeared and jabbed into his skin like syringes as the almost invisible vampire drank the life out of the helpless creature that collapsed to the floor and vaporised into another blue snake-like form. The Bishop was surprised as the vampires rarely attacked adults, preferring the souls of children, as they were purer. He wondered if perhaps the soldier had been an uncorrupted recruit. *The Prime Minister's son was in the army,* he mused.

Francis threw off his cloak, stretched out his wings and raised higher and higher, riding the air and circling as far below in a state of uncontrollable fear as the humans shot their bullets up at the moving target. After playing with them for a while, he swooped over to where his guards were no longer fighting and scooped a sword off the ground. Then, in a flash of lightning speed, he accurately ran the blade through the soldiers' necks like a farmer swiftly scything down the hay. All were dead except one creature who, almost immobilised by the quaking of his limbs, stumbled into the shadows and towards the back entrance of the Cathedral.

When all the commotion had ceased, Francis landed by the bodies, folded his wings and crouched down so that he could drink the blood of the dead and quench his thirst. His disciples were unmoved and didn't even flinch at such a hideous sight. When he had sated all his cravings, he stood up and looked around.

Gregory came up to him and fearlessly looked into the demon's blood-red eyeballs that seemed to be popping out of his head.

'What do you want us to do with all this mess?'

The Bishop lifted his head back and, from his cavernous mouth, fired super-heated air onto the group of corpses until all that remained was glowing embers.

'Just sweep it all up,' he said in a matter-of-fact tone. 'I have decided that the time is right for me to travel to London and address the rest of our congregation. I am going to take the book with me, so I need you here to continue as best as you can with the conversions and immediately direct the rest of our fellowship into the other continents to spread the word. To draw less attention, I shall travel by car, so I should be there by midday. Probably dispatch a few soldiers on the way,' he laughed, and the sound echoed throughout the Cathedral. 'I will leave you in charge of publicity. I want people to know that my arrival is imminent.'

'You know, Master Bishop, my loyalties lie with you, above and beyond anything else in this universe. I will carry out everything you command of me.'

'Good, we need to make haste. This country and the world will soon be under our rule. Humankind is obsolete, but we are destined to progress forward and have evolution rocket us into a future where a new species shall reign.'

AFTER A SMOOTH JOURNEY along almost empty roads, Francis decided to delay entering London as he wanted to be sure that everything was in place and properly stage-managed. However, he needn't have been concerned. There were crowds upon crowds of supporters lining the streets. Mostly, they were his clones, the duplications of his disciples. They reacted the moment his 4-by-4 entered the outskirts of the City. Those who had taken the oath were easily identified, as they stood rigid tall, with expressionless faces stilled by the silent beating of their ice hearts. Drunk on their elevated status, they coolly saluted their leader. For the Bishop's ground troops, self-loathing and depression were things of the past; all their ambitions were now sharply focused on Francis and the new world order.

As the Bishop scanned the crowds, he realised that what had elevated him to the zenith of his political power were the ecstatic cries of the emotionally oppressed. The plagues, riots, and the inability of the government to act in times of crisis had sent the population of uninitiated, searching for something different, an antidote to the futility of their lives.

Francis observed people from every walk of life, even trim youths holding up placards and chanting for change. In addition to them was the cheering, waving arms of those who had lost their livelihoods or who had not received medical attention because of the collapse of the health service. Then there were the twisted faces of the hobbling, hopeless, hungry and frightened, all desperate to escape their tragic melodramas.

There would be no place for love and emotions in the Bishop's new civilisation, everyone would be an equal anesthetised by the state.

Surprisingly, Francis met with no resistance when his car was escorted up to the Prime Minister's residence. He opened the car door to deafening applause, and outside, he paused to address the crowd and the reporters.

'I come here as the ambassador of our Lord and Master to unveil a new way of being, to free every one of you from the constraints of poverty and lack of civilised rule. We are the righteous, the everyday people who have toiled our whole lives for little reward. There is no problem that anyone of you may have that can't be solved. However, beware all those among us who are terrorists, criminals and all those who possess a murderous hatred towards civilised people, as their punishments will be severe.' The Bishop paused and looked around, trying to gauge the reaction of his audience, and was greeted with expressions of approval.

'If you are still unsure how the seeds of faith may bloom into the flowers of hope in your life, I would like to remind you that the only defence against our enemies of the plague and the other terrors that have engulfed our nation has been to seek salvation through our Creator.'

'Also, if our current government is able to find the courage to return to our Capital, the fellowship and I would be only too happy to work alongside them in improving the future for all citizens,' Francis said, taking a deep breath and sighed with relief, *the audience is still with me.* 'I would further like to thank you for all the support you have given our ministry today, but now I must go and begin to restore order to the chaos.'

Francis noted that Gregory had organised everything perfectly. Just as he finished his speech, a servant opened the door to the Prime Minister's residence. However, as he approached the building, he noticed a foul smell cough out of the open door. *Children, the Prime Minister has children,* he thought and tried to prevent himself from retching in disgust. He hated the spawn of humans, and although they were long gone, he recoiled from the stench and the ugly image of family life. Francis strolled back to his car as though he had forgotten something. Then he turned to face the horde one last time.

'If anyone needs to consult with me, I shall be residing at the Houses of Parliament,' with that, he climbed into his car and slowly fought his way back through his adoring masses.

THE NEXT DAY, THE CAPITAL awoke to brilliant sunshine. However, the rest of the island was encased in leaden, funereal clouds, and a storm raged with a ferocity that was beyond anyone's living memory. The resulting deluge flooded vast swathes of the countryside, forming an almost impenetrable barrier around the perimeter of the

City as rivers burst their banks, bridges collapsed, and wave upon wave washed over sea defences and into the streets.

Prime Minister Galsworthy found himself once again staring out of the window in disbelief. He swallowed down the pills that he was beginning to rely on to keep him awake and functioning. Every cell in his brain was swollen with the humiliation of defeat; none of his plans had worked, and he was acutely aware that he had failed at every turn.

He swung around to face his crisis team and perched on the low windowsill. 'He thinks he is the Messiah, but he is just a madman, totally insane,' he shouted, gesticulating wildly to emphasise his agitation while frothing at the mouth.

'We handed him the metropolis on a plate, sir. We shouldn't have left,' the head of the Bank of England whined.

'If we had stayed, we would have most probably died of the plague. How would that have helped? This whole situation is absurd. We need to return power to the decent, sensible people and rid our country of this fanatic. It's outrageous how he has gotten away with fooling so much of the population. He must be stopped at all costs unless you also wish to be overpowered by the misrule of an evil totalitarian leader,' Duncan raged.

Duncan rambled on for some time, trying to stir his dysfunctional committee into action, but they remained silent, listening, despondent, and unable to act. 'What it comes down to is courage. We need to take an ultimate stand, throw everything we have got at this tyrant and the rest of his cult and hit them all in the gut. My orders are for our army to head for London and to destroy anyone who stands in their way or shows signs that their allegiances lie with this maniac. Is that clear?'

The subdued group nodded their agreement, resigned to the fact that none of them had any kind of alternative plan. The whole situation had erupted with such little warning; they had petrified as though caught in the blast of a pyroclastic flow.

For the next few days, the army went on the attack, forging their way through the flooded land. These were valiant men determined to do their best to save their country. The maniacal machine of the prophet's demons managed to dodge out of reach of the tanks, bombs, and guns.

Far away from the action, the Prime Minister watched the pictures beamed to his room through his television screen of the heroic dead lying unburied in the streets. The crippled, blind and those suffering mental trauma that looked out at the world with perpetual tears in their eyes began to search for a way back home.

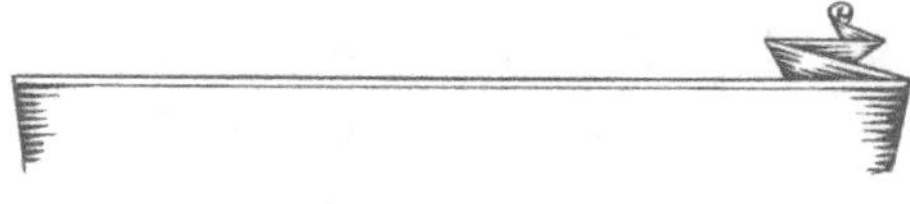

Chapter Fifteen

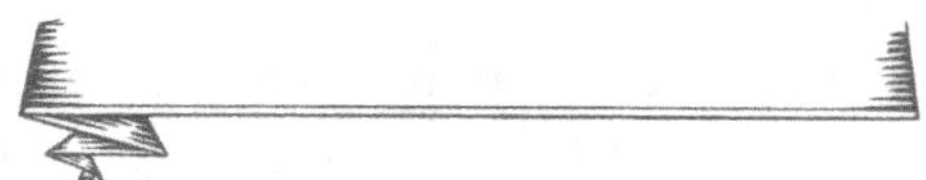

John and Leonard had decided that it was late enough to start their vigil for the ghost. As John stepped out of his house, the wild storm closed around him. The road had turned into a river, and it vaguely crossed his mind that water could engulf his home, but he dismissed this idea, as such an advent had never occurred in his living memory. Carefully, he manoeuvred over fallen branches and other wind-swept debris until he finally climbed the hill and no longer had to wade through water as here the tarmac was the more normal mirrored black.

He tapped gently on the door of the Black Horse not wishing to draw attention to himself as the curfew was now supposed to be strictly enforced. When he was greeted by Leonard's smiling face, he felt a sense of relief and the thrill, which comes from taking a risk.

'I am so glad you made it. Come, take your coat off and have a drink.' Leonard helped John off with his coat and then took away the old man's wet clothes and placed them by the open fire. Then, both men sauntered towards the bar and sat down side by side. Leonard already had a warming bottle of whisky nearby.

'John, I have found something out about our friend from some old records that the vicar discovered hidden away in the church. Of course, the account was written a long time after the event, so it might just be a story.'

'What have you learned, Leonard? Tell me?' John gently probed. His glass trembled in his stiff fingers with the sudden surge of adrenaline.

'Have you ever seen the grave upon the downs, placed on a crossroads of ancient tracks?'

'Yes, of course, I have walked that way for years.'

'Well, have you ever wondered who was buried there?'

'I knew it was a suicide as they were always buried at a crossroads so that their spirits couldn't find their way back home. Sometimes, they would also thrust a stake through their heart. Nobody, I asked, could ever give me an explanation as to whom it was, though.'

'I know who it is,' the younger man paused and realised how silent it was within the thick walls of the pub.

'Who, who is it then?'

'It's our monk. He started his adult life at the abbey, where he looked after the fish and other livestock. The Lord of the Manor took an interest in him because of his skills with animals; apparently, he was able to cure any creature of its ills. While working as the feudal Lord's favourite, he became involved with members of the community who secretly worshipped the old religion. Gradually, these experiences changed him; his internal cosmos transformed, and he was seen conversing with the animals in his care. People were shocked and grew suspicious—remember, the fear of witchcraft was rife in those times.'

'What happened to him?' John enquired, realising that he was now on his third whisky and feeling comfortably warm. Leonard continued.

'This is the tragic part. Under pressure from certain unknown people, the Lord felt obliged to act and warned the monk that he would have to go on trial. However, in recognition of all his good works, the Lord gave him a night to die with a little more dignity. The next day, he was found hanging from a tree in the castle grounds. Now, his blighted soul haunts the village.'

John sat in amazement, lost for a moment in deep thought.

'That is terrible, poor sod.'

'That's not all, there is worse to come. I think the damage was done the moment he left the abbey.'

'Hang on a minute. You are losing me here. I am a spent force these days. I can't keep up with you younger ones. Please, one step at a time.'

'One of the guards from the museum is staying on the farm across the main road. He overheard the old curator telling some official that when that book was found with the skeletons, he believed they belonged to two monks and that there had been a third with them who hadn't died. There are records to show that three monks left Canterbury at the same time on a mission. Something or someone derailed their plans.' Leonard waited for a response.

John was struggling. He was shaking, cold and aware of a creeping feeling of dread. A chill draft stroked the back of his neck, causing him to shudder. The pub seemed to have turned from a hospitable environment to a hostile one.

'What's the matter, John? You have gone deathly white?'

'Oh, it's nothing. I am probably coming down with a cold or something. All this rain makes you ill. So, what you are saying is that we need to look to the past to solve our current crisis.'

'Yes, that's exactly what I am saying. I think that whatever happened back then has got something to do with our problems now.' John then thought he heard a faint knocking but decided not to mention it to his friend. Then, there was an ear-splitting crash as though something weighty had smashed to the floor.

John gasped, and then the two men turned to face each other and stared in shocked horror.

'What was that?' Leonard whispered.

'It must be him. It came from your kitchen.'

Leonard covered his mouth with his hand to muffle his words. 'We had better take a look.'

As though they were glued together with a half-bent gait, they crept uneasily around the bar and out the back towards the source of the commotion. They hid behind the door, poking their heads into the room to see what was causing the racket. They were mesmerised by the turbulence as objects catapulted themselves off shelves, and saucepans and utensils hanging from a ceiling rack crashed onto the stone floor. The clamorous flight of mundane objects was disturbing, and at the centre of this storm was the small bowed figure of the monk. His agitated hands were throwing into the air; anything he felt was an obstacle in his hunt for some precious commodity.

In one swift motion, he spun around and looked towards them. 'I know you are there, hiding like cowards. Where is it? Just tell me, and then I will leave. What have you stupid people done with it?' he sneered.

'I don't know what you mean?' Leonard bravely replied.

'The book, you fool, the book. It was buried in this room.'

John watched as his friend stepped from the shadows to confront the restless spirit.

'The book has gone. It was dug up and sent to the museum.'

Leonard saw the awful truth dawn on the little man's weary-looking face.

'I am sorry,' Leonard added.

'So, thee young master tell thee a truth. Thay sayd the book be gone but I thinketh how could that be. May God give protection to Lady Isobel, and Sir Peter for thine burden be heavy. There be nay more in this world for a poor monk such as thee.'

A profound silence and a feeling of futility engulfed the room. John walked out to stand by Leonard, and together they observed the figure fade as he was sucked back into an alternate dimension.

'My God, that was the craziest encounter I have ever experienced. Why did he mention Isobel and Peter unless he was talking about people from his time?' John stated in disbelief. For a moment, they stood frozen, absorbing their feelings of disquiet, taking deep breaths to calm their heavily beating hearts.

'It's a shame we didn't have a camera,' Leonard finally uttered. 'If we tell anyone, they will blame the whisky.'

'Leonard, I am sorry to break the visit short, but I need to return home in case the floodwaters have risen. I suddenly feel really disturbed, like something terrible is about to occur.'

'Me, too, and I don't feel easy about sleeping here tonight.'

'Come home with me then.'

Together, the two men journeyed back to the bungalow with the fear of more harm and pain to come.

IN THE DEAD OF NIGHT, Isobel's sleeping mind slowly began to creep towards wakefulness. She was conscious of her legs itching infuriatingly from mosquito bites. Finally, dripping with sweat, feeling nauseous and not sure which century she would wake into, as in her dreams they all merged into one time, she woke and gasped in the chill, moist air. A peculiar feeling was rising from her gut, informing her that something was wrong. She lay for a moment with her eyes shut, trying to suppress the gnawing anxiety, and then abruptly sat up to face her fear. Looking down from her bed, she saw a sheet of reflective water covering her bedroom floor.

Without further hesitation, she threw her legs over the side of her bed, lowered her bare feet into murky liquid, and, for the first time, noticed an acrid smell. She hitched up her nightdress, and with slothful movements, she crossed her room to the light switch. Initially, it blinked on, but then all further attempts failed.

Isobel's immediate thought was for the well-being of baby Ben, who slept in a cot in the next room. On entering the environment of the infant with its sweet smells and the modulating sounds of deep sleeping, everything seemed normal. As she leaned over the cot, she mused over the perfection of new life and then remembered that she was there to carry her brother to safety. Carefully she placed her hands beneath the bundle, and as he stirred, he made an innocent, happy gurgle. Fear gripped her stomach and squeezed.

They weren't alone. Tormented, she lowered Ben back into his cot and glanced around. The water was moving, rippling, and she focussed on a snake-like form that glowed with an inner blue light. As pure terror grew inside Isobel, the creature began to rise up, first like a wisp of smoke and then its shape enlarged and swelled into a malignant monster. Eventually, it loomed over them, a giant serpent. Its mouth opened, revealing a multitude of pin-sharp teeth and fangs. Isobel leaned back against the cot in a vain attempt to protect her brother.

In her panic, Isobel clung to the dragon tear necklace that hung around her neck to satisfy her need to touch something tangible for reassurance against what she was sure must be a nightmare. She was unaware of the iridescent light that was being emitted from the eye in the necklace and shining through her fingers. Isobel stared up at the loathsome creature, her eyes feeling hot and writhing uncontrollably in their sockets as her heart beat with intense hatred. Something in her had changed, and she raised an arm, pointed and a laser-like beam shot from her index finger.

The demonic vampire gave a demented wail as light seared through its evil soul, causing it to wither, shrink and melt into a bubbling acid pool that floated on the surface of the water.

Isobel grabbed up the baby and rushed into the hall, where she was met by the panicked expressions of her mother and grandmother.

'We need to leave immediately. The water is rising!' she shouted, handing Ben over to her mother. 'He is fine.'

'What was that terrible noise?' Daisy enquired

'That was me. I awoke from a bad dream to find the house flooded. I called, but none of you heard. I just panicked, sorry,' Isobel lied, not wanting to add to their anxieties.

'Don't worry, dear. We have all been through a very stressful time lately. I often feel like screaming,' Daisy said, trying to reassure Isobel, conscious that she, as the older woman, needed to take control. 'We will head up the hill to the school and stay there for the rest of the night.'

'Where's Granddad?'

'Oh, don't worry about him. The old fool went to visit Leonard at the Black Horse—fancy deserting us now of all times.'

Jean soothed her baby with gentle words as she placed it in its sling and then wrapped them both in her husband's oversized raincoat. Once they were all dressed against the elements, they abandoned their home. Daisy took Isobel's hand in hers, and together they cautiously walked side by side behind Jean, who speeded ahead through the deluge, occasionally crying for help.

'If only your father were here. I haven't had any contact for weeks.' These words brought an ugly image into Isobel's mind of the man she so loved and admired in hand-to-hand conflict with a demonic army. *Would he be more cunning than they would, wrestle them and drive them into their graves, or would he be the one to be slain?* At this thought, ferocious tears welled up in her eyes, and she cried silently as they struggled up the hill.

Halfway up, they saw two familiar shapes approaching—one slightly stooped, the other agiler.

'Gramps, you are safe. I am so glad to see you,' Isobel stated as she ran forward and wrapped her arms around him like she had not done since she was a child. He reciprocated by gently stroking the wet hair from her face.

'We will all be safe now. They have opened the school. Peter is already inside.'

Chapter Sixteen

It was as dark as night—only Major Jacob Miller guessed that it was probably about five in the afternoon, as his watch had broken about a week earlier. When all had fallen silent, he scrambled out of the rain-flooded pit. The last few days had been a true battle as their unit had been surrounded by beasts that never came close enough to be killed, except by chance, when they were caught by surprise, biting into the flesh of the dead. A pattern had formed—furious fighting, then an eerie silence as the enemy would regroup. And then they would be there again, the dreaded black wings emerging out of the sheets of rain.

Jacob took his last cigarette out of its packet and tried to light it under the shelter of his coat. Finally, it was lit, and he began to walk along aimlessly, not knowing where to go. *Head for high ground,* he thought. The swollen rivers, flooded roads and fields were treacherous. Somewhere inside, he understood that there were no men left for him to lead.

His mind was broken and confused; he wasn't even sure how he had survived. There was a high-pitched ringing in his ears. He could still hear gunfire, the coughing up of blood and the choking. He remembered waking in the soupy hole amongst severed heads, twisted limbs, the grinning faces of old and new corpses and the clawed fingers of those dying who tried to scramble out of the slippery mire.

He was not the same man who had been sent off by his smiling family, who would have never believed that he was going away to engage in the most brutal killing and butchery. As their faces entered his mind, he quickly pushed them away to avoid further pain. He felt lonely and small, all his courage and confidence shrivelled away to nothing. Even walking was hard as he was bruised and ached all over and knew that there was something wrong with his right knee. It kept giving out, and a pulsating pain radiated up and around his thigh.

Jacob was barely conscious of the fact, but he had been automatically staggering up a gradual slope to a small farmhouse that was partially concealed by the edge of a wood. The enemy, assuming everyone was dead, had moved on, and now the survivor felt a little less afraid.

He eventually arrived at the old property and stood outside the door for a while, shivering in the rain, breathless, with his heart thumping in his chest while he picked up the courage to knock. He tapped gently, and a middle-aged woman partially opened the door, which was on a chain.

'Who are you?' she inquired aggressively.

'I am sorry to disturb you,' he faltered, momentarily lost for words. 'All my friends are dead. I need to sleep.'

The woman reluctantly slid off the chain and allowed him to enter. He could see a mingling of fear and pity in her eyes. Then he noticed food laid out on the table, reminding him of how ravenous he was, as he couldn't remember when he had last eaten.

'Come on in. You are welcome here. I am sorry about the noise, but the boys are waiting for their tea, and the weather has meant that they haven't been out much.'

For a soldier who had been sleeping under canvas, in ditches and any soft place to lay his head was welcome. The country kitchen, with its large wooden table and two armchairs, pulled up by an open fire, was heaven.

'Sit by the fire and dry yourself off. Those clothes on the horse should be dry by now,' she said as she took his coat and then busied herself folding up various garments and placing them on the arm of the opposite chair.

To Jacob, everything was so miraculously ordinary, as though the place was untouched by the outside world. 'This is like stepping into the past,' he murmured as he eased himself carefully into the chair.

Two small boys of about seven and nine rushed into the room. 'Who's that mummy?' the eldest enquired.

'It's okay, boys. He is a soldier, our guest, and I would like you both to play a bit more quietly tonight. How about you get your Legos out?' She suggested, knowing that this was one toy that they were able to play with together without it ending in a fight.

'Oh, we have had our share of trouble, too,' she said, addressing the soldier. 'My husband —he just disappeared. He was often late coming to bed because he would do the books after seeing to the animals. I fell asleep and didn't notice he was gone until the next morning.'

The woman's voice was soft and motherly. Jacob thought that he would love to be able to go up to her, hug her and weep endlessly into her breasts as though he were a small boy again. However, as he rested in the chair by the fire, waves of sleep seized him, and at first, he dreamed happily. Then he saw the hopeless, fear-stricken faces, the staring eyes and heard the whimpering of young men in the night. He woke with a start, not knowing where he was. A woman was kneeling beside his chair, holding his hand.

'It's ok. You are safe. You fell asleep. Here, drink this coffee,' she handed him a mug from the table. Eventually, she saw the look of recognition in his eyes and smiled sweetly.

After he had finished his drink and his senses had returned, she announced that dinner was ready and called to her sons. They all sat up at the table, the boys staring at the weather-beaten, dishevelled soldier—at all his exposed frailties, his trembling hands, gaunt face and heavy, lidded eyes. In awe of a man who had fought demons and survived, they were hoping for permission to ask him questions about war, guns, and the honour of competing for a worthy cause and the demons, which, as yet, they had only seen from a distance.

Jacob, on the other hand, was basking in the warm normality of his surroundings, as though he was experiencing everything for the first time: a moth fluttering around the light that hung over the table, wood spitting out from the fire and finally, the lingering smell of a rich, meaty stew mingled with fresh crusty bread. He ate slowly, relishing every morsel that passed his lips. As he recovered, his mood lightened, and he found himself drawn to his host's shiny chestnut-brown hair, dimpled rosy cheeks and delicate busy fingers.

'What's your name?' he asked, smiling with a twinkle in his eyes.

'Ruth,' she replied, blushing red in a flirtatious manner.

The boys saw this as their opportunity to speak, and it was Josh, the eldest, who felt brave enough to ask the first question. 'Did you kill any of them monsters, Mr?'

'Yes, hundreds, but boys, never be in too much of a rush to go to war, however good the cause. The real heroes are those who battle each day in the fields, producing food so that we all may live. When a man fights, it's the devil and death that have the upper hand,' Jacob spoke, ignoring their age, deliberately wanting to squash their youthful idealism of a soldier's life.

The boy looked disappointed and fell silent.

'You have both done a brilliant job here guarding your mother and the farm. When your father returns, I am sure he will be so proud of you both,' Jacob added, wanting to ingratiate himself with the boys as he was desperate to be allowed to stay and was pleased when he saw them grow a little in response to his words.

Ruth changed the subject to talk about the Lego models they had brought to the table. Jacob felt a real joy listening to the family banter, and for a while, all the horrors of the previous days melted away.

That night, after a refreshing bath, to Jacob's surprise, he was invited to share Ruth's bed. There was a mutual need for human affection, softness, and warmth, and neither of them felt any of the reproach or shame that would typically have restrained their actions. Jacob had forgotten how seductively silky a woman's skin was, and soon, passion consumed all his afflictions and sorrows. Their intertwined bodies connected in ecstasy that they were both grateful they could still experience. United, they moaned with pleasure, shared the loveliness of lying wrapped together and then falling into a deep, dreamless slumber.

Jacob cherished every moment of his good fortune, and he felt that the week he spent in such wholesome company was a reward for all the pain he had suffered. Under the kindness of a doting woman and nourishing food, he thrived. Soon, his impoverished soul felt vibrant and renewed.

As the days went by, his contentment began to fracture as he felt a desire to return to the fight, to eliminate the destroyers of love, so that one day he may go back to his wife and children and dwell in peace.

Then, during a night of troubled sleep, Jacob jumped awake with fright. Before he was able to open his eyes, he heard a rustling and whispering of voices. Then, he listened to a tremendous air-cracking bang, which he recognised. His immediate reaction was to roll off the bed and onto the floor. As he lay quivering with his arms over his head, he heard more words.

'Run, James, run. We must hide.'

Jacob recognised the name James as being that of Ruth's youngest son. *The boys were in trouble,* he thought, and still only half-awake, he struggled to his feet. He turned to rouse Ruth, and his eyes were met with a sight of absolute carnage—she had been shot, and the right side of her head was a grotesque distortion, no longer a person but an organic soup of liquid and brains. Repulsed, Jacob turned away, bent over and vomited onto the floor. Then, being sure to keep his eyes averted from the damaging image, he grabbed the towel from the end of the bed and laid it as best he could over her without looking at her head.

Uncertain as to what had occurred, he grabbed the bloody gun that he found dropped on the carpet and went looking for Josh and James, still believing they were in some kind of peril. On entering their bedroom, he saw the luminous blue glow of a soul-sucking snake and shot at it. However, it was too quick and squeezed itself through a hole in the floorboards. It crossed his mind that the children had succumbed to the fangs of the vampire, but he shoved this thought aside as being too terrible to consider. After much searching, he abandoned the task, believing that the boys had concealed themselves well to recover from witnessing such horror.

Jacob took his waterproof poncho off the stand and a spade from the hall and went out into the chill, wild dawn. He dug a deep hole in the small garden by the cottage. Then, with all his emotions shut down, he walked back to the house and into the room, where he carried out the dismal task of wrapping the body of the once tender and loving woman. When his onerous work was completed, he carefully lifted her, laid her body over his shoulder, and, in a trance-like state, walked down the hall and out into the gloom.

For the next half an hour, he lifted spades full of soil and sprinkled it over her corpse until the hole was full. Exhausted and weighed down with grief, he collapsed to his knees in the mud. All his pent-up emotions were suddenly released, and as the rain poured down on him, he cried and howled like a wild beast, lamenting the possible loss of his own family.

Jacob was so absorbed in his melancholy that he was unaware that the missing children had crept out of their hiding place and were moving closer. A quick hand plucked the gun up from where it lay on the ground next to the weeping man. Disturbed by the movement, Jacob sprung to his feet, ready and alert, only to be confronted by Ruth's two boys. Josh stood just a few feet in front of him with the gun held firmly in both hands and pointing directly at the soldier.

In an instant, Jacob realised that they were the undying, with their unnaturally frozen expressions and menacing, stony stares. Then, in the swirling misty downpour, something caught his eyes not far away. A large coal-black animal was stealthily stalking the children. Jacob saw its eyes lock onto Josh as it burst into the air and hurtled down onto the child's back, sending him crashing into the mud. The soldier bent down, picked up his gun, and, dragging his injured leg behind, bolted off into the woods.

In a frantic panic, he stumbled over branches and through deep puddles until he felt safe enough to stop. Shivering and shaking to the depths of his soul, he turned and saw the wolf standing some distance away, regarding him calmly. The creature was nothing like anything he had ever seen before. It was large with a huge rib cage. When standing, its back sloped down. It was sabre-toothed and had frightening red eyes. Jacob sat down on a fallen tree trunk, and the animal echoing his movements relaxed down onto the ground.

Too weak to protest, he slowly accepted the animal's presence and went about trying to build a fire. Luckily, his experiences in the army meant that he always kept an emergency kit in the inside pocket of his coat. Despite this, it took some time to ignite the damp materials that he had at hand. All that time, the beautiful wild creature sat watching, its ears and nose always alert to any potential dangers.

Eventually, he was able to pull a log up to the meagre fire and attempt to ingest some warmth into his cold, numb body. He felt crushed under the burden of the curse that had been placed on the country he had once loved so deeply, and a part of him was ready to lie down and die. *Even if I were able to return home, what good would a broken man be to his family? I can feel the cracks in my compassion and the fire in my heart burning with an icy flame,* Jacob reasoned to himself as he acknowledged the cost to his soul from spending so much time in the company of evil. *In any case, it was most likely that his family and friends were already dead—or worse. The old Jacob, the father and husband, was lost when the world ended a long time ago,* he grieved.

Sitting upright with his head resting on his hands, Jacob began to slip in and out of restless sleep. He awoke sometime later to find two dead rabbits lying next to the fire. When he looked up, he saw the wolf lying in the same position, staring directly at him as though she hadn't moved. Somehow, the small act of kindness momentarily restored the man's will to live. 'Thanks, friend,' he called out to his wild companion. The wolf shook the rain out of his thick coat and yawned as if in response.

He took a sharp blade from his emergency kit, prepared the dead animals, and realised that basics, like food, still lifted his mood. When he had finished cooking the meal, he took some for himself and threw the rest on the ground in front of his new friend, who softly moved forward and accepted the offerings.

While he ate, he began to understand that it was the lack of control in his life that was killing him and that just cooking had helped him to feel a little more human. He decided that if he could hang onto a tiny element of this capacity, then he would survive, like the wolf and other animals. *People had asked for too much out of life, they had been blinded by the comforts of technology and lost sight of what mattered. From now I will forget the endless wanting of my previous life and focus on the nuggets of freedom, food, shelter, and sleep. In that way, I will be able to continue.*

Jacob sipped the water he had collected in a plastic bag, allowed his head to drop into his hands and was lost in a healing, untroubled sleep. It was a dull thud that awoke him sometime later, like something heavy had hit the ground. He opened his eyes and lifted his head. There, in front of him, he saw that the beast had something or someone pinned to the ground. Jacob heard the low rumbling growl and a woman's voice pleading.

'Please, stop, stop, I mean no harm.'

Calmly, the soldier walked over to his guard and looked down at the writhing creature, and he saw wide, wet eyes and a very human expression of fear.

'Let her go, my friend. She is no threat to us.'

Understanding the command, the wolf slouched away and resumed his sitting position while watching the stranger's every action.

The woman was about the same height as Jacob, who was not a tall man, and he could see that under the oversized camouflage coat that her body was equally thin and wiry.

'Come and sit by the fire.'

'Well, I am in a hurry,' she nervously spoke, glancing fearfully at the wolf.

'I don't think she intends to hurt us, and I am just an old soldier who has lost his way. I am quite harmless, too,' Jacob explained to the woman.

The pair huddled side by side on the log, hooded bent figures, their arms clasped around their middles as they tried to protect themselves from the endless downpour.

'Do you think this rain will ever stop?' her voice trembled from her chattering lips.

'I suppose it must, eventually. Where are you headed?'

'I am going southwest to join the resistance. How about you?'

'I am just trying to find a way out of these woods. I don't know.' Jacob then gave her a brief description of the previous week's events. She listened intently, occasionally sympathising, and by the time he had finished, he felt elevated from his pit of desolation and was touched by a twinge of hope. Then he worried about how long she would stay with a person who was obviously so adrift.

'I am sorry, what's your name?' she asked.

'Oh, Jacob.'

'I am Lilith. I am afraid I can't sit here any longer. I am too cold. I must keep moving, and you will die of exposure if you stay much longer. We must find shelter. I was a doctor, so I know about these things,' she spoke between violent bouts of shaking.

Jacob abruptly stood and shook off the rain and his feelings of despondent gloom. He held out his hand to the girl and, with renewed energy, said, 'Come on, let's get moving. I now know where I need to be, with the resistance.'

She took his hand and rose, smiling. He took out a tiny compass from his pocket, and together, they began to walk south.

'Come on, wolf, we are leaving. It's now or never.'

When he turned around, he saw that the beast had gone and vanished back into the shadows.

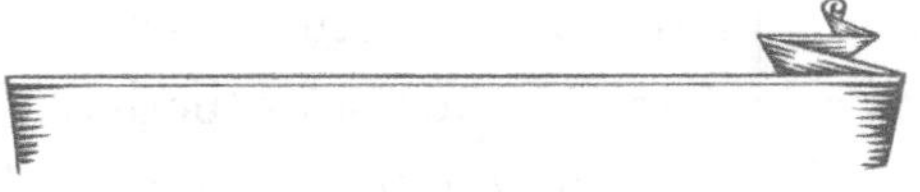

Chapter Seventeen

A few days later, Isobel awoke shivering to a golden light lancing through the school windows. Everyone else appeared to be sleeping, so she grabbed her coat, carefully stepped over the still dreaming, and ventured out into the playground that looked over the castle wall.

There seemed to have been a shift in the seasons. The sweet-smelling autumnal air had a sharp chill, and something within Isobel had also changed; emotionally, she had moved on. She felt older. All of creation had been holding its breath, waiting. Now, it was giving out a huge sigh of relief as the cogwheels began to move once more.

Isobel stood alone in the enormous silence, watching the sun creep higher up in the sky and the glittering beads of dew trembling on the leaves. She sucked in the fragrant air and meditated on the lyrical moment of nature's glory. The dark days had gone. The floodwaters had subsided, sunlight glinted from within all things, and hope abounded.

What Isobel couldn't have realised in her bubble of tranquillity was that far away, the puppet master was still pulling strings. The marble hearts now sat firmly in the seat of power, planning a new type of offensive. The umbilical cord of the previous government had been severed, and now in a position of dependence, they were easy to control like tamed pets. A mock truce had been agreed, with the promise of negotiations. Useless contracts were signed, and the punishments temporarily stopped. This was the eye of the storm, a chance to hide the massacres of the army and the innocent, to put on a new mask to lure the humans into a false sense of security. Furthermore, there was only one television channel and radio station, both run by the state. The switch on all other forms of modern technology had been flipped off, disabling communications and shrinking people's lives.

It was announced that Britain was free of the plague, but they failed to mention that because the immunity of the population had been weakened by so much upheaval, other viruses had seized the opportunity to strike, and illness still abounded. They also stated that within a week, the school would be re-opened and that children would be taught a new and improved curriculum. However, travel overseas had been stopped, and aeroplanes were grounded due to the outbreak of disease and a series of natural disasters that were ravaging the continents of the world.

Isobel heard footsteps approaching. She turned to look and saw her grandfather strutting towards her with a renewed spring in his step, and all the anguish melted from his face. He caught Isobel's gaze and smiled warmly.

'Look, a heron,' he said with a flourish of his arm, pointing at the cloudless blue. Side by side, they stood admiring the magnificent creature. 'What a glorious day,' John softly spoke.

'Yes, it is. Everything seems clean and new,' Isobel replied.

'I came to ask you if you had seen your mother. She has gone somewhere and taken the baby. I have to say, Issy, I have been quite worried about her lately. She has been under so much stress with your father's disappearance and caring for your baby brother.'

'I know, me too, but there has been so much happening. I have tried to help, but I just end up annoying her.'

'It's okay. It has been the same for all of us, but despite everything, I can reassure you that she does love you deeply. It's just that things have been so difficult.'

'I understand,' Isobel lied. She couldn't comprehend why her mother had excluded her and pushed her away at every opportunity.

The permanently sad-eyed woman had built up a thickening wall against them all, behind which she was silently crumbling.

'I expect she has left a note. She wouldn't just vanish,' Isobel added, feeling the surge of her new maturity.

'I will go and look,' John replied

'And I will get properly dressed and help.'

Isobel rushed off in the direction of the classroom where she had so comfortably slept. She let her coat fall to the floor, took off her nightdress and rapidly pulled on her jeans and a t-shirt. Her now long hair was a mess, and she hadn't brought a comb with her, so she smoothed it back as best as she could and pulled on a woollen hat. Just as she was easing, her arms into the sleeves of her thick fleece, Peter entered the sunlit room. His face looked sleepy, and his hair, which had grown too long, looked dishevelled. His eyes gleamed happily through the thick lenses of his glasses.

'Peter, Granddad, can't find mum,' Isobel said with exasperation.

'I know. I have just been speaking with him. He has found a note which says she is going to the Cathedral to have your brother blessed.'

'Peter, we need to find her before it is too late.'

'Your granddad doesn't seem worried.'

'Yes, but you know evil things are happening in that building. I thought you liked adventures, and we promised Richard we would locate the book.' She hadn't told him about her strange encounter on the night they had abandoned their homes, as she didn't want anything to deter him from assisting her efforts to find her mother. Isobel touched the cool, brightly coloured beads around her neck and felt reassured at the reminder that she had some protection against any onslaughts.

'Don't panic, Issy. I am sure she won't have covered much distance. We probably won't even need to go as far as the Cathedral.'

As he spoke, Isobel was already agilely moving through the groups of stirring, homeless villagers. Peter reluctantly followed a few paces behind. He had wanted to spend the day helping his father clean up their house but knew it would be fruitless to protest to his friend. Besides, it would not be chivalrous to allow her to go on her own.

'Where are you going?' John called out after them.

'To find Mum,' Isobel replied without faltering.

Once out of the school grounds, Isobel ran down the hill. At the bottom, she stopped as she saw an almost impenetrable barrier of people traipsing along through the black mud in various states of wretchedness. The well, the afflicted, the lost, and the deprived all mingled together like a turbulent, noisy river. A cloud of flies hovered over the group as though they were farmyard animals.

Peter had stopped to grab two bottles of water that were standing in crates outside the school and then followed at a slower pace. He finally caught up with his friend and bent double, panting and desperately trying to catch his breath.

'We will never find them,' Isobel cried out, full of anguish. As Peter recovered and stood up, he saw that her eyes were filled with tears.

'Issy, we will. It will be alright.'

In silence, they joined the trail of pilgrims heading for the city of mistakenly perceived hope.

Progress was painfully slow. They passed their two bungalows and their gardens, once so beautiful but were now swamp black, the bushes decorated with an unfamiliar array of debris. Then, it occurred to Isobel that it was probably all the litter dropped by the pilgrims. The teenagers looked at each other, acknowledging their shock and horror at the amount of damage and the extent of the work that would need to be carried out to restore their homes to their original glory.

Further along, as the trail widened and twisted through the dark, dense woods people spread out, and there seemed to be more room. They began to see clusters of the impoverished smeared with mud and grime begging and the weak resting or doubled up in pain. As they passed, Isobel clung tightly to Peter's arm, anxious that they would be challenged for money. Peter, enjoying his new role as her protector, urged her to keep her head bowed to avoid the pleading eyes and to ignore their entreating cries.

However, at some point, the density of the crowd increased, and Isobel lost her grip on Peter. She was dragged along by the human tide and lost all sight of her friend.

It took far too long to get to the city, and by the time they arrived, the bright blue was fading. Under the arch that leads into the Cathedral grounds, Isobel paused, waiting for Peter to catch her up. She looked towards the vast, imposing proportions of the building; its stone, once golden in the sunlight, now looked cool and grey in the afternoon shadows. People knocked into her as they pushed by, and as her eyes cast downwards, she noticed a very bright, luminous light emitting from her necklace. Not wanting to draw attention to herself, she lifted it over her head and, clasping it tightly in her hand, tried to conceal it in the pocket of her fleece.

At that moment, she thought she saw her mother entering the Cathedral, but she could barely make her out. Adrenaline shot through her heart, and she stormed forward, her eyes hooked on the wooden door. With each step that she took, feelings of foreboding shivered up and down her spine as she perceived the presence of malicious entities.

Inside the vast space, crowds of people milled around, looking confused until they were greeted by the black shapes of men or women in long flowing gowns, which Isobel presumed were monks of some kind. Inundated with fear, Isobel wanted nothing more than to leave before she was confronted. She took a couple of deep breaths and then studied her surroundings. There was no sign of her mother, Peter, or the book. The place was so altered from the uplifting environment she had known previously. It had a dark, frosty feel, and there was a strange, rancid stench. As she peered up at the stained-glass windows, she saw that their beautiful jewel-like quality was gone, replaced by a haunting melancholy.

Isobel decided that to stay would be too dangerous and that she should leave. Hopefully, she'd find Peter on her way out. As she hastily made her way towards the exit, she was mocked by a multitude of whispering voices and felt she was being suffocated by an avalanche of panic. In the doorway, she felt an icy touch on her shoulder. Startled, her heart leapt into her throat, and she whirled around to see who was trying to prevent her from fleeing.

It was Ariel. Isobel sighed with relief, glad to see a familiar face, and immediately reached out her arms to embrace her friend. For the briefest of times, their arms enfolded stiffly around each other, and then they drew back and regarded one another. Ariel's face grimly held Isobel's attention. It was strangely seductive —far more beautiful than she remembered. Her skin was pearl white, her expression mournful, and her eyes were still, very dark and hypnotic. Her clothes were even more bizarre, as she was wearing the same black cloak as the monks.

Isobel noticed that the monstrously evil whispering from before had faded, replaced by waves of the most sublime distant singing, which she somehow knew belonged to the lost soul of her friend. In her mind's eye, she saw the fleeting image of the teenager she had once known and realised that she bore little resemblance to the joyless, emotionless creature that was preventing her from leaving.

'Is it really you, Ariel?' She enquired with uncertainty in her voice.

'Yes, it's me. I am glad you are here, Isobel,' she replied with a robotic tone.

'I am not staying. I have to go, Peter's looking for me.'

'Peter's already here. I saw him heading towards the crypt. I think he is looking for you.'

'Oh Ariel, come with me, this place is bad. Come home. We have found your brother, and he is waiting for you to return and is desperate to see you,' Isobel pleaded, hoping to see an ember of feeling.

'I can't. I belong here, in the Cathedral. I am a privileged representative of the fellowship,' she replied coldly.

Isobel's eyes strayed one last time around the devil's lair, and feeling that it was futile to try to save the stranger turned and pulled the door open a fraction.

'I have seen your mother, too. She was with Peter,' Ariel murmured.

Isobel faltered, feeling repulsed by what she understood to be a deception. She was hooked in by the thought of her mother and knew that she couldn't just abandon her family to their fate.

With trepidation and taut nerves, Isobel reluctantly turned back into the darkness. Ariel had vanished into the crowds, so Isobel made her way towards the crypt. A no-entry sign barred her access to the steps that descended into the thick gloom. Then she heard the most serene, enchanting singing. Out of pure curiosity pushed the barrier to one side and crept down into the darkness.

In the crypt, the magical notes expired. She called out Peter's name in a loud whisper and put her hand in her pocket to feel the sense of security that her beads provided. She felt panic-stricken as she realised that she had been duped, her shield and only protection had gone, most likely stolen by Ariel.

In that moment of clarity, Ariel, who had been lying in wait, suddenly lunged forward out of the blackness and pounced on Isobel's back. Isobel fell forwards; her spine was crushed into the stone floor as she was thrown over onto her back, and bright torchlight shone into her eyes. She peered up through eyes blurred with tears and saw that Ariel's thin veneer of loveliness had cracked and peeled away to be replaced by the crazed visage of an old hag that snarled and spat like a rabid dog. Next, her bony fingers were gripping vice-like around Isobel's neck. In defence, Isobel scratched her face, clawed at her eyes and, struggling to breathe, tried to wriggle free. The monster's strength weakened for a second, and Isobel heard a shrill scream echo around the room and realised that it was her own agonised voice. Utilising every ounce of her inner forces, she managed in one movement to wriggle free and spring onto her feet, only to feel, in the next moment, the sharp, cool edge of metal on her cheek.

Too frightened to resist, she allowed her assailant to force her hands around to her back, where she felt her wrists being tightly bound. Ariel then sadistically kicked and shoved her toward a small door embedded in the wall, which she quickly opened.

Isobel was pushed into the coffin-like space that only had enough room for standing. In front of her face was a square cut out of the wood with iron bars through which the teenager screamed in desperation as she heard the key being turned in the lock.

'Let me out, you bitch!'

Once again, the torch flashed into her eyes, momentarily blinding her. Then Ariel came back into focus, and Isobel saw that she was holding her iridescent beads.

'Nobody can hear your cries. Enjoy your time in the hermit's hole. I am to save you for the Lord's return. He has something special planned for our enemies,' she chuckled and moved away, extinguishing the light as she went.

Darkness closed over Isobel. She was bruised and aching and wanted nothing more than to be able to collapse to the floor. The confines of the cell were claustrophobic and hot, and the pain of the bindings cutting into her wrists made her feel wretched. The absolute darkness and the need to escape the bleak cruelty caused her to swim through waves of drowsiness where she experienced brief but vivid dreams. It was in this state that she found herself looking up at Sir Lancelot circling in an eggshell blue sky. Then, in a moment of waking, she thought she heard a soft flapping motion in the air. She listened hard to the pleasant swishing and felt the atmosphere move as something in flight, flew down and landed gently close by.

'Who's there?' she whispered.

'It's me, Lance,' the eagle stated and then stopped to preen his wings. 'I saw you pass by the castle wall, and my master told me to follow you.'

'Please, can you deliver a message? I need help to escape this dreadful hole. Come near the door. I want to feel you close for a moment.'

As Sir Lancelot hung on with his strong talons to the edge of the wood, he could just make out the girl's eyes brimming with tears and could hear the lament in her voice.

'I will make haste and bring you help.'

Isobel basked for a second in the warmth of the bird's breath and imagined his beautiful curved beak gaping open and the small, quick pink tongue.

'Peter might need help, too.'

'Don't sorrow. You will soon be free of these vultures.'

In the darkness, Isobel heard the faint scraping release of the talons and the sweeping of wings, and then she knew he was gone. That one touch of breath filled the girl with a calming hope.

OUTSIDE, PETER FELT dwarfed by the towering walls. He was flustered and bent over, coughing. *Where was Isobel?* He had lost his friend in the crowd near the gate and was lagging about half an hour behind, although he wasn't sure, as even the clock on the cathedral had stopped. Now, he felt unwell and clammy. The light shining off the wet path hurt his eyes, and the bickering, berating, and prattle of the crowd caused his head to spin. At the same time, he was desperate to gain his composure before entering the building to continue his search.

As he forced himself to slowly rise, his eyes caught sight of a familiar figure. Isobel's mother was sitting on a bench opposite, nursing the baby. Gradually, he crossed the sodden grass to where the woman sat. He cleared his throat, and she looked up.

'Peter! I am so glad to see you. Is Isobel with you?'

'No, we have temporarily lost each other, but I am sure I will catch up with her soon.'

Ben stopped suckling, and Jean pulled her coat closed and rested the small form over her shoulder.

'I went into the cathedral and was shocked,' Jean said. 'It appeared so changed to how I have always known it, and once inside, I felt nauseous, quite sick. I could barely stand and had no choice but to leave. I came out here and sat down. Then a woman came up to me, and we talked, and she said I had wasted my time as they would not bless children. Isn't that strange?'

Peter listened thoughtfully. It was clear that Jean needed to describe her peculiar experience to someone, and it gave him a little more recovery time.

'That is strange. The closer I got to the building, the worse I felt until I was almost crippled with sickness. It's as though the building was rejecting me,' Peter explained.

'Yes, I felt like we must have tasted bad and were being spat out.'

Peter paused and at last, feeling stronger, lifted his face to the sky and deeply breathed in the sweet air. Circling overhead in the dusky firmament, he saw what he thought was the gleam of golden plumage. He wondered, *could it be Sir Lancelot?* Golden eagles were unheard of in England, except in captivity.

'What are you looking at?' Jean inquired.

'I thought I saw an eagle, but I suppose it can't be,' Peter replied vaguely as he lowered his head for a moment's rest.

'I can't see anything, and I am long-sighted,' Jean replied.

Drawn back to the sight, he looked back up and once again, his eyes rested on the shape of lustrous golden beauty.

'Lance,' he called up. The bird focused on his friend and plummeted towards the ground, landing gently at his feet. 'How come you are here?'

'I was told to follow. Beware of danger and betrayal. Leave now. We must seek help. There is no time.' Leaving Peter to ponder over his enigmatic words, he flapped his wings and soared back up high into the sky.

The boy called after, 'I will, Lance. I will leave and get help.'

'Peter, whatever is the matter with you talking to people who aren't there.'

'Didn't you see it, the eagle?'

'No, I didn't. I think it's time we leave. We will probably find Isobel has already made her way home. If not, her grandfather will have to take the risk and drive back to find her.'

Together, they retraced their steps and trudged along the muddy track towards the village. The baby slept peacefully in its sling. His mother seemed happy to have abandoned her quest for salvation and, for the first time in months, spoke cheerfully to Peter. However, Peter was anxious and frustrated by the idle pace as all he could think of was getting home and seeking help. Every slow step he took seemed like a betrayal that he was adding to the minutes that his friend could be suffering. His sense of urgency was so desperate and consuming that he felt obliged to make his excuses and rush ahead.

'I am sorry, Jean, but I think we should find out where Isobel is. I am going to go ahead. I need to know if she is at home. Sorry.'

'It's ok, I know we are slow. You know what you need to do,' Jean replied.

Peter sucked a couple of times on his inhaler and dashed off, weaving in and out of people as quickly as he could.

Chapter Eighteen

Peter emerged from the dull tunnel of trees to the recognisable refuge of his home, nestled in a slight dip someway from the narrow road. However, he saw straight away that the bungalows had transformed again from the image he held in his mind. His eyes strained to peer through the darkness, and he saw that the windows had been boarded up and words painted on the wood that read, 'Keep out! Looters will be prosecuted.'

A tall, stooped figure was toiling nearby, scraping mud off the path with a shovel.

'John, what has happened?' Peter called out.

The old man stiffly tried to straighten up. 'Looters, we have had looters, son. Isobel and Jean will be so upset when they get back.'

'Is Issy not here?'

'I thought she was with you.'

Peter had John's attention. He picked up his light and slowly, with jerky movements, made his way up the garden path to where the boy stood. When he finally stopped, he leaned on the gate to catch his breath. Then, once recovered, he straightened up to face his young neighbour.

Peter felt a pang of sadness as he looked into the man's eyes, which were fixed, staring with fatigue, his usual bright optimism withered. The boy also noticed that as John reached out to pat him on the shoulder, his hand trembled.

'Where is my beautiful granddaughter, son?' he asked with an anxious pleading in his voice.

'I am sorry, John. I was hoping she was here with you. Don't worry. I shall retrace my tracks and find her. You can be sure she will be absolutely fine—we just got lost in the crowds.' Peter could feel the old man's weight press down onto his body as he supported himself by continuing to cling to his shoulder.

'And Jean and Ben, are they safe?'

'Yes, they were not far behind me.'

'Good, good,' he smiled bravely. 'Peter, at my age, I have to let some things pass. I have learned not to worry and allow time to do its work. Your father and I have done our best to secure our homes. I don't know what's going on. I think these are very fret-worthy times. However, while I am the only man in the family, I think it's important to keep everyone calm and gently ease them through the stormy waters. The old have to retreat and make way for the young to be heroes. Only the young dare to bring about significant change. Do you understand?'

'Sort of.' Peter didn't want to offend John, but the man was rambling.

'Peter, I am tired, but I am no fool, and I know that things are happening beyond most people's comprehension. I am saying to you that under the circumstances, your father and I consider you a man and give you the permission to do whatever the young need to do to assuage our land of its troubles.' His grip tightened on the boy's shoulder. 'What I want to say is, please find my Isobel and bring her safely back home.' Peter was alarmed as he looked into the old man's entreating eyes and saw a multitude of fears writhing and knotting like a ball of worms.

'Of course, I will. I promise.' Peter felt the easing of pressure as John released his grip; John patted him twice and placed his hand back on the Iron Gate.

Peter, looking over John's shoulder, saw a dark shape lingering behind the side of the house.

'Is that my dad?'

'Yes, he is finishing some sweeping up.'

'Why hasn't he come over?'

'He is not feeling quite himself and doesn't want to pass his bug onto you young people.'

'Dad, come here,' Peter shouted out before he could be stopped.

The much smaller man briefly looked up, waved and then returned to his task.

'Dad, I need to speak with you,' his son implored.

Peter watched as his father Bill's resistance crumbled, and he sluggishly walked towards them, a drooping, weary shadow, using his broom as a crutch.

The youth was staggered by the sight of his father as he joined them at the gate and now stood in the splash of light. He had always been a small man but had been fit and energetic, enjoying cycling, canoeing, and running. Now, he appeared diminished and shrivelled. His eyes were blood red, and his shivering skin was grey with fever. His father grinned weakly to reassure his son, and Peter saw his broken teeth. The poor state of his father's mouth had always been a poignant reminder to Peter of how much he was loved because Bill had always intended to pay to have the dentist fix them but instead had chosen to spend any spare money on holidays and other things for his family.

'Dad, you are not well.'

'Son, it's just a bit of a cold. I will be fine after a good night's rest. I just don't want to expose anyone else to my germs. I agree with John your main concern now should be to find Isobel.'

'Is mum ok?'

'She is feeling a little low with this bug, too, but the doctor's wife has been kind enough to put her up in their house. She is taking antibiotics and will be fine. We just don't want you to get sick because of your asthma.'

Peter, devoured by despair, felt torn, stuck between the need to help a friend or his parents. At that moment, it was clear that being the only child, he should stay and help his father and mother.

'I am not going anywhere. Isobel will be fine. I know someone else who can go and find her.'

Then Bill coughed uncontrollably. Peter saw blood frothing from his mouth and turned his gaze from his father's face. The man quickly wiped his lips and gained his composure.

'I am not going anywhere,' Peter forcefully stated.

'You are not needed here, and we don't want you. My friend here is looking after me,' he grimly glanced up at John.

Peter was stung by his father's uncharacteristically harsh words. He turned to John, who gave him a wretched smile.

'Peter, your dad will be fine with Daisy and me. Go quickly now. It's getting late. We are going straight to the doctor's house, and we will make sure there is some supper left out for your return. Oh, look, there's Jeanie.' He smiled, happy to be able to change the subject.

Peter followed his gaze as he looked towards the leafy tunnel.

'Take my light, Peter. I will share Jean's torch.'

Peter thanked John, took the lamp and turned his back as father and daughter embraced. For a moment, he was focused on listening to the group talking and wiping away the troubles they had all encountered that day.

Then, the young man crossed the road and approached the figure that he knew so well, who had been waiting for him in the darkness. Death had taken Oswald's body but not his soul, and it saddened Peter to realise that his friend was unaware that he only existed because of some error in time and space. The mirage was so real; the same exuberance shone from Ozzy's eyes, and the noble bird perched on his arm completed the bold and heroic persona Peter had once so admired.

His wayward friend was such a contrast to his reserved, studious character and still could energise him and encourage him to become involved with a more adventurous approach to life.

'Lance has told me that Isobel is in danger. We must go at once and save her before it's too late,' he said, dancing around excitedly.

'How are we going to rescue her? She is probably being guarded.'

'I have my sword, and you have your axe. I have no time to stand around thinking whether or not this is right or wrong. If the Lord catches me gone and he wants me for some labour, there would be trouble.'

'What about the 'Monster Race'? You could release them, they would scare anyone away.'

Oswald was already bouncing down the street, forcing Peter to chase after him like a boy trying to catch a butterfly. Peter's mood was already lighter, brighter, and guiltily, he felt relieved to be set free from the oppressive presence of illness. As he passed John, his father and Jean still chatting, by the gate, he waved and felt reassured that at least they had each other and that his father was in safe hands. Peter caught up with his friend and just managed to catch his reply.

'They have already gone. I let them out a while ago. I sneaked down when Richard was asleep. It was easy. He was angry, but I think it is what he wanted, although he has been quiet since. My head will be on the block when the Lord finds out.'

'What! That's terrible,' Peter exclaimed.

'Don't let it concern you. The first sign of trouble and I will be off. I will join the travelling circus.'

'Where have they gone?'

'Home, they said they were going to return home.'

In the hollow of the trees, the road was now deserted. They could hear the odd whispering and rustling noises of people hiding and bedding down in the darkness, but there seemed to be no one around interested in a mad boy chasing an imaginary friend.

On the downs, they proceeded with more caution. Peter was tired and hungry and wondered if he really could travel much further. Then they both froze with alarm as something disturbed the cool night air.

'Did you hear that?' Peter whispered with alarm.

Oswald nodded. They calmed their breathing, listened hard, and then they heard it again.

'It sounds like a wolf howling at the moon,' Oswald whispered. Peter shone his torch into the darkest shadows but saw nothing unusual. They continued moving at a much faster pace.

Startled, they both jumped back as the black shape of some beast sprung out onto the path ahead of them and stood with its head down, growling and snarling.

'It's Umbra,' Oswald whispered as he gradually made his way towards the seemingly hostile creature. 'Umbra, it's me, Ozzy, and this is my friend Peter. Lance, tell her that we mean no harm.' Lance was perched on an overhanging branch above the beast's head to avoid its jaws.

Peter was scared. He stood back and saw that the animal's hair still bristled down its back, and its white fangs looked eager to attack. Every vein in his body was filling with blood, ready for action—to run as fast as he could or to attack with his axe.

'I thought they were going home. I wonder what's wrong?' Oswald said gently and bent down to stroke Umbra in greeting. Lance, not much liking the wolf, flew nervously from tree to tree. The sabre-toothed wolf settled and allowed the human to touch her back.

'Morse is trapped,' Lance screeched out. 'And she also told me to be wary of humans as they never delay in trying to destroy the creatures of the earth.' The wolf stared accusingly up at the stranger.

'Show me where he is,' Oswald commanded, directing his instructions at Umbra.

Peter reluctantly followed the pair into the woods. He could scarcely breathe and was conscious of every sound, from the cracking branches to the whispering leaves in the breeze. He was also keenly aware of a growing, stagnant, sickly odour. He would have much preferred to be elsewhere at that moment.

Then, there was a monstrous green-black shape coiled up in a clearing with the stickman Virtus whimpering, crouching beside him like a silver birch broken in half. The dragon's massive body heaved a tragic sigh and moaned in pain. As they approached, he turned his large head and breathed out scorching, hot, stinking air at them.

Under the light of a full moon and the lamp, Peter used his scientific curiosity to examine every detail. The beast's body was about the size of a huge horse, but its tail was equal in length and thrashed around like an anaconda held by its head. Its skin was like a Sting Ray's with a sandpaper texture, and running down its spine were spikes that jutted out in all directions. However, it was the head that disturbed the boy. Its eyes were large, almost human, but its jaws were strong, long and crowded with razor-edged teeth. Its nostrils flared on top of its snout like crocodiles, and sticking out from the thick bones of its forehead were two horns.

'Morse, it's Oswald. We have come to help.'

They all stood around the felled beast, who was the essence of defeated misery, and saw that his back-left leg had been caught in a snare, swollen and bleeding profusely. It was clear that they wouldn't be able to cut the wire from around his limb, but they could release him from the tree it was tied onto.

'Poor wretch. Did any of you try to free him?'

Virtus regarded them blankly, and Umbra snarled as though she understood Oswald's words and found them contemptuous.

'Peter, cut the wire with your axe.'

'Can't you?' Peter replied, feeling that freeing the venomous beast was probably not such a good idea.

'The power in that weapon only works for its owner.'

Without wasting any more time, Peter summoned up all his courage, placed the lamp on the ground, took the axe from his belt and, holding it in both hands, raised it high above his head. As the blade struck the binding, it emitted an intensely bright light that looked like the edge of lightning. Then Oswald crouched down and busily worked at loosening the cord of torture from the dragon's putrid wound.

At last, Morse was free. Wavering a little, he managed to stagger into a standing position.

'Stand back,' Lance squawked with alarm from high above them as he could see clearly that the dragon was about to move.

Everyone stepped back a distance and watched as Morse unfolded, shook his great wings and spread them out to their full length. They all stared at the magnificent beauty of the wild beast. Then he concertinaed the leather skin back again and, with great power, shot high into the air like a rocket. High above them, he performed for them in front of the backdrop of a jewelled sky, diving down, swooping up, tumbling, corkscrewing, and coughing out long plumes of orange flame.

'He is wonderful, that's his way of thanking us for freeing him,' Oswald explained to Peter. Lance swished down off the tree, landed on his master's head, and began pulling at his hair for attention. Oswald reached up, pulled the bird down, and cajoled him back onto his arm, just as Morse landed with an awkward three-legged thud back in the clearing. The dragon had always been the leader of the group, so Oswald wasted no more time.

'Lance, tell him that we urgently need their help tonight—this very minute! A lady has been taken captive in the City where our enemy has their base. We must set her free. Ask him if he would oblige us by joining us in our quest. It would only delay their journey by a day.'

Morse turned to Umbra and Virtus. Lance could hear the beast's thoughts and heard him say, 'What do you think, one last chance to destroy the spawn of man before we leave?'

Umbra's hunched, dark shape restlessly moved back and forth as she pondered whether she wanted to go into battle. Peter watched as the wolf glared at Morse, who was always ready for a fight. The dragon remained steadfast as he looked into the stern red eyes; he knew she was anxious to get back to her territory. Umbra growled with impatience. The dragon raised his head at Virtus and shook the woods with booming untranslatable words. The tree man quaked in the blast and then bent down, scooped up a nearby boulder and hurled it at the dragon, which missed its target. In an instant, Morse reacted by breathing out a tongue of orange flame, which licked the giant's silver fur, singeing it and sending him yelping and stomping off into the trees. With his back turned Peter noticed for the first time the long Mohican-style mane that ran from the top of Virtus's head down his back.

Umbra bared her teeth and growled. Morse put his head down to face her, and for a moment, their eyes were locked together in a silent challenge. After what seemed like many tense minutes, Umbra conceded, sloped off into the shadows and disappeared.

Oswald looked around and found that Peter was also gone. He was alone with the dragon.

'I don't know what disagreements you have, but I have saved you twice, why can't you help us in return?' The boy pleaded. Morse looked him up and down with an expression of disgust, puffed smoke from his flaring nostrils, spread the vast canopy of his wings and launched himself into the sparkling darkness. He flew around in ever-increasing circles as if saying farewell and then vanished.

'Lance, they have all gone, you can come down from that branch.' The bird swooped back down onto the boy's gloved arm. 'It looks like it's just you and me.'

Oswald found Peter on the track, shuffling along with his head bowed down. The boy felt the spirit approaching. Then the ghost touched his shoulder, and Peter flinched. Oswald saw that the boy had been crying and that his eyes were nervously darting all around.

'Don't worry. It's all going to be all right. They don't always get on, but they rarely do any real damage,' he said, trying to comfort his friend.

'It's grotesque. I can't stand to be near him, and he hates us. I don't want to be involved anymore. I am sorry, but I am going back.'

'Peter, if you do that, you will regret it.'

'I am hungry, and it's such a long way.'

Oswald's mood switched as his compassion dropped away. He had no time for cowards. *If something had to be done, then you had to keep going until the project was completed,* he thought as he and Lance stormed off, leaving the boy to stew in his own dilemma.

Virtus stepped from the edge of the dark woods with what looked like a whole cooked chicken in one hand and went directly up to Peter. He stared down at the quaking mess with a strange look in his eyes as though he was studying something in the boy's face. Then he tore a leg off the bird, handed it to Peter, and before the boy could protest, he pulled him high up into the air, sat him on his shoulders and sped off into the night.

Far behind, Oswald and Lance followed, aware of the occasionally glimpsed black shape swiftly moving through the woods to their left.

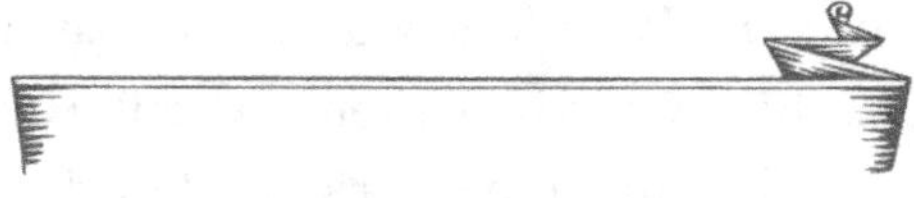

Chapter Nineteen

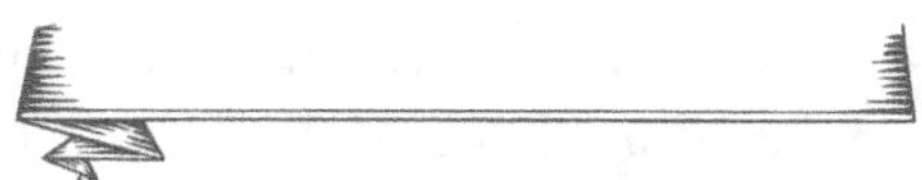

The rhythmic motion of the giant's body had sent Peter into periods of sleep. He awoke refreshed and feeling more secure in the warm mane of the giant's back. They came to an abrupt halt in front of the Cathedral. The boy rubbed the sleep from his eyes and marvelled at the illuminated, magnificent building that stretched endlessly into the night sky. Peter's super-human companion began to explore the smooth stone with his fingers as if fascinated by the detail in the ornamentation of the carving. Minute by minute went by as they waited and listened curiously to a melancholy murmuring coming from inside the thick walls. Eventually, Oswald and Lance appeared hastily crossing the open stretch of lawn. When Virtus turned and saw the familiar face of the falconer and his eagle, he gently lowered Peter to the ground.

'Has anything happened?' Oswald whispered, deciding to place any lingering feelings of annoyance to one side.

'There have been some strange noises coming from inside.'

'Let's try the door.'

Just as they realised that the door was locked, a monk on sentry duty came around the corner.

'The cathedral is shut to the public at night,' he sternly spoke.

'We have come a long way to take the oath,' Oswald replied. Peter was surprised as he realised the hostile monk had no problems seeing his friend.

'It is clear to me that you have come for trouble. Is that not a creature from the monster race? Our book states that their evil tribe of outsiders are nothing but destructive to man.'

There was a gust of cold air as the door burst open. Lance swooped over to the boundary wall while a circle of swirling black coats instantly surrounded the three companions. Last to walk out was Gregory, who was obviously enjoying his role as substitute leader.

'Well, brothers and sisters, what do you think our Bishop would do with these intruders?'

'Suck out their souls, crush their frail human hearts, dissolve their brains, pick the flesh off the bones!' The demons shrieked in unison. Soon, they were all screeching and hissing out diabolical words, methods of torture and various ways to kill.

'Well, let me know when you have finished. I will be in my chambers,' and with that, he flicked his coat and departed back into the dark mouth of the building.

Peter's stomach tightened. He knew he was about to die and dreaded the thought of pain tearing through his flesh. Cloaks were flung to the floor. There was a sudden upsurge of air as wings spread and the demons hovered above the group. Their claws were ready, and their eyes glowed red. They hung imminently, savouring the moment. Peter's heartbeat was so fast that his brain was clouded with confusion of thoughts. All he understood was that he was wavering on the brink, staring up at hell. He felt his windpipe being compressed by invisible hands. He struggled, unable to breathe. Desperately, he panicked; his eyes felt as though they would pop out of their sockets, and he was about to collapse.

'Use your axe, Peter!' Oswald cried out above the howling battle cries of their mighty opponents.

Virtus reached up and pulled the flapping creature nearest to Peter apart as if it was one of his chickens. From the broken body, pieces on the floor slithered out a worm-like blue light which tried to coil around the giant's leg.

A claw cut across Peter's forehead. Blood filled his eyes, and his vision was blurred. His axe was now in his hand, taking on a life of its own. The boy blindly struck out with laser-like precision at everything that came near, spinning around, hacking at the space above his head. Never had he moved so fast or accurately, a wild dance and burst of energy. As the lightning sparked out from his blade, he too became like a constant striking bolt of electricity. All around him, he heard the whoosh of bodies plummeting to the ground with bone-cracking thuds.

When silence reigned, he collapsed onto his knees, exhausted, and immediately spewed up the meal he had consumed earlier. Finally, he recovered. Wiping the blood from his eyes with the sleeve of his coat, he peered up at the others and saw them anxiously trying to free themselves from the blue snakes that seemed to be swelling in size by the second. He glanced down and saw that he was crouched in a pool of blood, limbs and seething organisms.

Above, the air shuddered as lead guttering and flakes of dirt fell from the roof. Peter noticed a sour stench, looked up, and saw Morse bursting out from behind the top of the building, rushing towards them and turning the whole sky red as he breathed out his flamethrower breath.

The dragon landed close by, folded his wings and hobbled painfully over to the group that was now thrashing around, trying to free themselves from the tightening, growing knots. He lowered his large head, dribbled some venom carefully onto one of his front talons, and very deftly began to cut their shackles. In the instant of their release, Oswald and Virtus leapt out of the reach of the soul suckers. Peter rose with his axe, crackling with electricity. He looked all around, his senses sharpened by fear and like all soldiers, forced to kill, was denied any further years of youth. He now stood like a man.

Once they were out of harm's way, Morse blasted the wriggling enemy with a flame of breath so that they shrivelled up or slithered into the cracks of darkness at the base of the building. Ravished by the pain of his increasingly swollen leg, the dragon flapped his wings vigorously, shot into the air and settled back on the roof to recover some strength and attend to his wound.

Oswald signalled to Lance, who silently swooped low over the grass, under the arch of the doorway and into the dark throat of the Cathedral. Without any trepidation, Peter followed the bird. Crouching low, Virtus entered soon after.

However, Oswald was delayed as he glimpsed something move out of the corner of his eye. He heard a soft, melancholy voice whisper in his ear. 'Hallo, brother.' He turned and found himself face to face with a young woman of exquisite beauty.

'Who are you?' he asked, puzzled but aware that something was tugging at his heart.

'Don't you recognise me? I am your sister, Ariel.'

'I am sorry, my lady, but I don't have a sister. I am an apprentice to the Monk Richard Long, and I am afraid I must go. I am in a hurry.' Anxiously, he stepped back.

'Please don't go. Remember, you used to make me laugh. We played together by the river and in the woods.'

The coaxing, sad lilt in her voice caused him to draw near. He studied her large dark eyes and felt a stirring inside, something close to memory.

'I might know you, but I can't think,' he struggled uneasily, trying to recall a long-forgotten family.

'Do you remember the river and the mill?'

At these words, Oswald felt as though a bomb had exploded within him, filling his soul with all the pain of purgatory and images of fierce, frothing water filled his head. He felt that he had stepped from the light and was falling into a deep, dark chasm.

'Oh no, God help me!' he screamed, pressing the palms of his hands over his eyes in an attempt to block out the truth.

'Oswald, you are dead—a phantom. You died that night at the river.'

A light shone all around the boy. He saw an autumnal misty morning of intense beauty, a glorious sunset, every intricate detail and colour of the earth and the serene loveliness of Sir Lancelot's outstretched wings as he swooped low over a bright green lawn. Somewhere inside himself, he knew his substance was flickering and fading. Then he felt a touch on his shoulder, and he was jolted back, standing once again by the Cathedral, walls gazing at his sister.

'Brother, I can save you. Give you your life back so that you live forever.' She stroked his arm gently, keeping him attached to the present. 'It is a gift I am able to give you as your sister. Follow me. You will be happy, and you won't regret it. Your lovely Isobel can't love a ghost.' Ariel took the boy's hand, and he meekly allowed himself to be led around the back of the main building towards the cloisters.

PETER AND VIRTUS VENTURED deeper into the murky gloom, which was poorly illuminated by candles, while Lance waited for them in the rafters. Peter cursed the scared boy he once was for leaving his lamp in the woods and, at the same time, plucked a candle up from its stand. The whole place seemed empty, as though a temporary truce had been called. The incurable malice and brutality of the demons filled him with bitterness and hatred. This time, there was no thought in any part of his being of leaving without Isobel. Even if he lost his soul, the man in him would fight forever to protect that goodness at the heart of all those like Isobel, her grandfather and his father and mother. They were the rays of sunshine that shone through the dark of the woods. 'We will beat them,' he muttered aloud to reinforce his sense of conviction.

Lance swooped down and perched on the plinth of a statue that stood close to the crypt entrance. Peter caught sight of the bird as he then glided under the arch and vanished into the black beyond.

Stealthily, Peter crept down into the hole. Vertus trailed behind, and when he caught up, he had to bend into a ball to be able to squeeze through the small gap. He stumbled down the smooth, worn steps and landed hard at the bottom. Stooping under the low ceiling, he shuffled cautiously towards the candlelight, where he found Lance standing on a tomb and the human holding a light-up against a door.

It was hard for Peter to see the precious captive as her head had fallen limp onto her chest, and she appeared unconscious.

'Isobel, wake up, it's Peter. You are not alone anymore.' There was no response from the cell. 'Lance, tell Virtus to force the bars apart.' The bird complied, and soon, the giant, with the greatest of ease, had pulled the metal out like a dentist extracting rotten teeth.

Peter gently lifted the girl's head and brushed the tangled hair from her face. 'Wake up, Issy,' he coaxed. Slowly, Isobel opened her eyes and fixed them upon her friend.

'Peter, I am so thirsty.'

'How are we going to get this door open? Oswald any ideas?' His request was met with silence, and as he turned around to his consternation, he realised that Oswald was no longer with them. 'Where has he gone?' he addressed Lance.

'He is not with us, master. I will go and find him.'

'No, stay until Isobel is safe.'

The giant stepped forward again and, placing his large hands on either side of the opening, pulled with all his might. There was a loud splitting and creaking, and the door fell forward enough for Virtus to be able to tug and lift the girl up and out of her pit. He cocooned her tenderly in his arms like a mother holding a baby. She had fallen silent again, a withered flower that had been seeded in poor soil.

'We must leave straight away,' Peter whispered directly at Virtus, realising that he understood his words.

Furtively, the group made their way toward the steps. Abruptly, a looming, sinister shape emerged from the entrance. It locked his hypnotic black eyes onto Peter's and leered down, revealing his pointed, serrated teeth. He floated down the steps slowly moved forwards and addressed Peter.

'You pitiful humans. You are of no use anymore. You are no longer at the top of the food chain, no longer Masters. You only exist to satisfy our hunger.' Gregory contemptuously sneered, threw his head back, released an ear-splitting demented shriek, then held his arms forth and pushed the air as though against some unseen force. In the same instance, Virtus's neck was squeezed in a vice-like grip. Blackness descended, and he and Isobel fell to the floor. The girl lay helpless, groaning.

Peter then saw a shape darker than the deepest shadow spring out of nowhere and land on the demon's back. There was no time for the fiend to resist as the wolf had pinned him to the floor and had already ripped out the back of his neck. While Umbra devoured her kill, Peter went over to Virtus. He lifted his arm, but it was limp, his bulging eyes stared to the heavens, and his breathing was still. Then he went over to Isobel and held her in a sitting position.

'Lance, could you come and cut her bindings?'

The bird compliantly flew down and pecked away at the knotted rope. Once freed, Peter helped Isobel into a standing position. 'We must go. We are not safe yet,' he whispered.

'What about Virtus?'

'Don't worry about him. He will follow us as soon as he feels better. He is waiting for Umbra.' Peter quickly navigated them around the slippery pool of blood that spread over a large area of the floor and went up the steps.

Peter and Isobel limped out into a cooling breeze and the pale light of dawn. Morse flew down to greet them. His whole demeanour was one of mourning; his head hung low, and his tail was still. The lizard's human-like eyes were full of grief, and his normally heaving chest barely moved as though his soul had fallen silent and his heart fossilised with the demise of another member of the monster race. Lance then appeared in the doorway, followed by Umbra, who was dragging the dead body of Virtus, which he dropped at the feet of Morse, who gently touched the felled giant with his hooked fingers. Then he opened his gigantic jaws, jiggled the middle of the corpse into his mouth, and without a sound, except for the flapping of his great wings, took to the sky.

'Where is he taking him, Lance?'

'Home, back to the graves of his ancestors. We don't forget those who went before us.'

Umbra stared for many moments at Peter with a stern contempt that sent a shudder down his spine, and he felt like a child who was a disappointment to his teacher because he failed to learn. Then the wolf turned and soundlessly sidled off towards the shadows of the buildings on the boundary of the holy grounds.

Oswald then walked around the corner of the building, and straight away, it was obvious that his sparkle had gone—he seemed diminished, dulled. He stepped towards Isobel, reached forward, eased the dragon tear necklace over her head, and softly kissed her cheek. The girl flushed, and a few tears trickled down her face.

'Thank you, Ozzy, where did you find it?'

'You don't want to know.'

He looked at her with a pensive and peculiarly troubled expression, causing Isobel to feel lonely, and at the same time, her heart ached, desperate for the love that was receding.

'Goodbye, my friends,' he dismally uttered and slowly walked back around the corner of the building with Lance, who had flown down onto his arm. Isobel rushed after him but was too late—he had vanished into the ether.

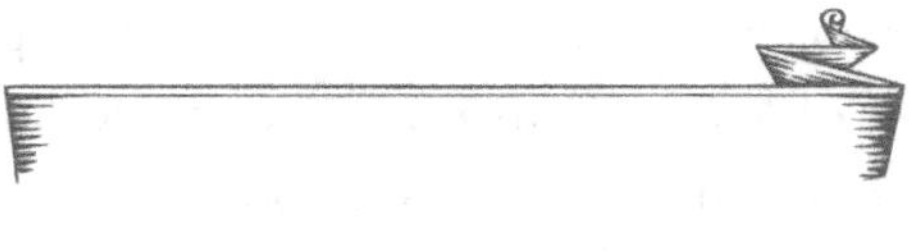

Chapter Twenty

In time, people can adapt to any new situation, and superficially, life in Britain returned to a form of normality. The plague had reduced the population significantly. Everyone was employed, mostly in mining or factory work, which was the preference of the new government. Scientists, or anyone who possessed specialised skills useful for the advancement of the fellowship, were imprisoned and coerced into working on the latest space project or cloning. Those who had taken the oath and joined the new religion were cogs in an endless production line, a hideous flow of ant-like humans. Supermarkets were reopened and, under a very efficient workforce, were well stocked and maintained with local produce, which created employment for anyone who was able to manufacture goods.

For the shrinking section of the population who had so far managed to avoid being sucked into the black swamp of the Bishop's inhuman desires, life on a daily basis was bleak and hard to negotiate. It was almost impossible to discern if trusted friends had become one of the 'un-touching', as they were secretly known, or were still empathetic mortals, as everyone pretended that their allegiance was to their new leaders. For their protection, the humans would hide behind expressionless masks, responding with disgust at the mere mention of music, poetry or any form of creative expression. Displaying visionary attributes or discussing dreams and desires could also alert the enemy. These free citizens had to be permanently hyper-vigilant to even the subtlest of their human responses. However, the biggest danger came from any overt displays of affection or emotion in public—a tear, a laugh, or the look of love in someone's eyes could lead to immediate arrest and incarceration by the fellowship police.

Others, mostly the elderly who felt that resistance was futile and who were worn down by all the disruption, were hiding in the remotest parts of the Islands, placidly waiting for change or to catch a fresh wave of ideology that would ride them into a different future. They were just thankful that, for now, the arguing and fighting had stopped and were happy to turn their backs on any sign of trouble.

Amongst the uncontrolled, the shadows of acute danger followed each moment, forcing them to step softly, cautiously waiting for the darkness of oblivion to descend. No one ever mentioned those who had disappeared or the loved ones who failed to make it home or put their heads above the parapet in any way—it was all too risky.

Isobel and Peter were also conscious of their every move as they visited his sick parents in the still-overcrowded hospital. Isobel reluctantly sat on a chair in the corridor, staring at the door opposite and twirling her thumbs, which would have revealed to any onlookers her state of internal anxiety. A disquieting awareness of her subtle movements caused her to abruptly stand and head for the nearest toilet, where she locked the door and was able to sit in quiet contemplation.

For comfort and reassurance, she took her beads from her pocket, where she kept them concealed. She gazed into the beautiful iridescent eye, and as a magical bubble of bliss enveloped her, she saw images of Oswald as he had been: his bright eyes and his richness of life, doing summersaults on the riverbank. Desperately, she wished that she had been able to tell him how much she had loved him, *had he not felt the same way, too?* She wondered. Isobel remembered how his touch had been frequent but quick as though he was too scared to linger and how he found it hard to look her in the eyes, but when he did, he couldn't then drag his gaze away.

Then, as she looked into the depths of the eye's pupil, she saw the hovering vision of a face. *Is it a reflection of my face?* Her meditations were interrupted by whoever was speaking directly inside her head.

'I don't know who you are, but I can see you. I can really see you. I will be quick because I don't know how long this will last or even if it will ever happen again. My name is Selene. I am seventeen. Who are you?'

Isobel answered in her head. 'Isobel, my name is Isobel.' The image in the eye faded and died.

Isobel quivered, and although it was cold outside, she dripped with sweat. Then a howling, screaming exploded in her head, and she realised that it was Peter releasing an outpouring of grief. *Oh no, Peter! I must stop him*, she thought. Internally, she rushed, while externally, she calmly walked to the room where her friend's parents lay. With a queasy dread, she eased open the door.

Gently, she briefly laid her hand on the shoulder of the boy who was perching on the edge of a chair and weeping over his mother's lifeless body. 'Peter, keep it inside until we are safe.'

'I can't. I loved them so much,'

'They will always be with you, but they wouldn't want us to be caught.'

Peter lifted his grim, pale face up to Isobel, who tenderly took his glasses from his eyes and wiped the tears away on a tissue and then off his cheeks. Isobel carefully replaced the thick lenses and then, taking his hand coaxed him into a standing position.

'Right now, look at me and do as I tell you. First, don't speak, don't think and lock down all those pent-up emotions for both our sakes. Just follow me.'

Not far away, they could hear someone approaching. Two nurses entered the room and went directly to the beds of the dead.

'They are dead. You can go back to school now. We are directed to take any bodies directly to the crematorium,' one of the nurses coldly spoke.

The shield of Peter's existence crumbled; he felt lifeless, drained, and empty. With a stony face, he nodded at the nurses, and he and Isobel left.

That night, as Peter, grief-stricken, hidden away in a dark corner of the school, Isobel sought out the comfort of her grandfather. She finally located him in the yard behind the building, only to discover that Leonard was already demanding his attention. For some reason, she decided not to go forth but to remain concealed in the shadows of the wall and listen to their conversation.

'Hey, my good old friend, what keeps you up so late on such a cold night?' Leonard said cheerily.

'Leonard, I never bargained for any of this. My heart is breaking. There is a young lad in there cut down by terrible grief that he isn't even permitted to express. They won't even allow him to bury the bodies of his parents.' John placed his hands on his knees, bent double and wept onto the tarmac, choked, and retched. 'I feel so sick I want to throw up all the anger and hatred that I am obliged to hide.' Then, the old man retched again and was sick.

'John, nothing lasts. This whole thing will all be over soon—we just need to ride the storm.' Leonard laid his hand on his friend's back, hoping the touch would console him.

'I can't bury our good friends, Emily and Bill, my neighbours for years, as under the new rotten regime, they are sent straight to the crematorium. Tell me where the justice in that is. Peter was a kind, studious boy. Now, his life has been cruelly changed. I hardly recognise him. His heart is bleeding, and he is stricken down with hatred.' John straightened his body and turned around to face his friend.

Leonard looked up into his blood-drained, tear-stained face and, grasping his arms in his firm grip, held him with his eyes.

'John, these are terrible, dark and barren days, but we must keep strong for the young and help them through. To stay free, we must continue to look for signs of the good in all things and marvel over those sweet, unforgettable days of our past. Come on, my friend, we need to hang on.' John nodded his agreement and seemed calmer, so Leonard allowed his arms to fall and instead crossed them against his body for warmth.

'I am sorry. I am fine now.'

'I promise you that it will all come right eventually. Remember, the mass evil of the Second World War was mostly over in five years.'

Transfixed, Isobel continued to watch and listen. She had never seen her grandfather so defeated. Usually, he was such a light, jolly man, but living in such an emotionally cold society, where people had so quickly learnt how to emulate the living dead, had impacted him terribly. Leonard continued the passionate discussion to distract John away from the agonising burden he was forced to bear.

'Hey, yesterday I re-encountered our friend, the monk on Hollow End Street. He was bent over, searching for something in the hedgerow. I asked him what he was looking for, and do you know what he said?' Leonard asked John, who shook his head. 'Toads, he said he was looking for toads to bring him luck.'

'You don't get toads this time of year.'

'Well, I didn't want to tell him it was winter. Then he went on muttering to himself, saying, my life is over; unless *a miracle happens, I will be dead by the morning.* So, I asked him why? He explained that the villagers had been told that he was a witch because he talked to animals, but he knew that the Lord of the Manor wanted him dead as he lost his temper when he wouldn't reveal where the book was hidden. Then, apparently, he discovered that his collection of animals had escaped. John, he seemed so real, and his sadness was palpable.'

'Leonard, I think we need to remember that he is a ghost, and if you mention this to anyone, they will think you are mad. And really, you were right, we should be spending our time convincing the villagers not to take that flaming oath and persuade them that if the police come to the village they need to hide.'

'I know, John, but I still feel that the answer lies with that poor spirit. The last thing he said to me was that his apprentice had run away and that there would be nobody to give him a proper burial, and he feared hell if he was interned at a crossroads.'

'Okay, Leonard, what point are you trying to make?'

'I think we should dig him up and give him a proper burial. That way, all this trouble may end. I think we need to say farewell to someone in the proper way and say some words for Emily and Bill, too.'

'You have gone insane, Leonard! This is no time to be dabbling around like that, and besides, where would we place him?'

'He wants to be laid to rest with his ancestors at the ancient mound. It wouldn't take long. I have got enough diesel left for one trip in the old Land Rover.'

'Leonard, I think that you need to lay off the whiskey for a while,' John smiled sympathetically at his friend.

'We could do it tomorrow night. There is little else to do here other than drink.'

'Okay, friend. We will do this one last thing, then it will be over, and we will be free to concentrate on helping the few families left.'

'Agreed.'

The two men smiled and heartily shook hands. They then strolled off together towards the back entrance of the school while Isobel hurried off to find Peter and distract him with the news about Richard.

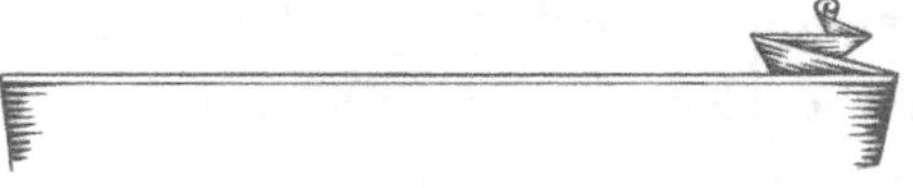

Chapter Twenty-one

After midnight on the following night, Leonard's Land Rover shuddered to a stop outside the school. John was waiting in the doorway with Daisy, who had a kind but exasperated expression on her face in response to what she believed to be a dangerous and foolish adventure. John raised the collar of his coat against the cold and rushed towards the vehicle.

'Have you got the spades?' he asked as he clambered into the passenger seat.

'I have got everything—a torch, tarpaulin, even an old wooden door in case his coffin has rotted away.'

The four-wheel-drive spluttered down the hill along Hollow End Street and choked up onto the stony track of the downs. When the vehicle finally stopped by the grave, John began to doubt the actual possibility of them being able to accomplish their task with such a decrepit machine.

The two men jumped out and went around the back to grab the spades.

'Take a good look, John, because we must leave everything as we find it.'

They removed the moss and grass-covered topsoil very carefully and found it surprisingly soft for such a cold night.

'Good job, there isn't a frost,' John said nervously, feeling guilty like a grave robber for disturbing the resting place of the dead.

After spending some time digging and diligently making a mound of the soft earth, the edge of their spades struck what appeared to be large, round, grey rocks. The men fell to their knees to scrutinise their find more closely.

Gooseflesh rippled over John's body. 'No wonder he couldn't rest. They didn't even bother to place him in a coffin.'

Warily, they began to lift the heavy stones, both caught up in the spell of curiosity while vigilantly glancing over their shoulders for fear of being caught. Eventually, the brittle white bones were revealed. The skull had been crushed, and they noticed the neck was broken.

'I am surprised they didn't stick a stake through his heart as well,' Leonard said with annoyance.

'They used to do terrible things to the bodies of suicides. They were terrified that if they left the body whole, it might rise from its grave and return to haunt the village. What a senseless waste,' John uttered as he examined the remains of the forgotten.

'Yeh, life is so unpredictable. One minute, you are going along quite happily, and the next, your fortunes change. How about a shot of whiskey, my friend, to calm the nerves?' Leonard added as he took a drinking flask from his inside pocket and handed it to John.

'Here's to you, brother,' he said, saluting the skeleton and holding the rim to his lips. 'We have come to put things right so that you may finally sleep forever.'

The two men sat for a while on the damp ground, taking long, hard swigs at the whiskey. Finally, when their mood became less sombre and they felt more relaxed, they set about carefully removing the bones and placing them on the door. Richard was covered in the tarpaulin, and taking either end, the men began to lift his remains into the Land Rover. Then, unexpectedly, something fell out from beneath the sheet and landed on the ground near John's feet.

'Hey Leonard, we have dropped something.'

'Let's lower him in the truck first, and then we can take a look.'

Richard was laid gently down, and the door was secured with bungee ties. John went back to examine the find.

'It's a small leather purse. You would've thought that would have been taken when they buried him.'

'They were probably too scared to touch anything in case it was cursed. What's inside?'

John shuddered and cringed as he picked up what might have been the suicide's possession, wondering if it had been added to the grave at a later date or had been with Richard for hundreds of years.

'It's a ring of some kind.'

Put it in your pocket, and we will drop it into his new resting place.'

Then the two men returned to their labour, this time working backwards, replacing the rocks and the soil and then patching together the blanket of green until they felt satisfied that everything had been restored, as close to its original state as possible.

Soon after, Leonard was shaking his vehicle along the rutted ground towards the mound. He switched off the engine, listened to the deep hush, and saw that, just in that spot, the clouds had blown away. He turned to John and smiled.

'We had better get to it.'

John nodded, yawned and opened the door. Together, they lifted Richard out of the truck and, like coffin bearers, carried him down the slight incline to the place where the skin of the mound had split open in the storm. They looped ropes under the door, suspended it over the hole and gently lowered it down to join the archive of his ancestor's souls.

John grabbed a handful of soil and sprinkled it into the crack.

'Rest in peace, Richard Long, and rest in peace, my dear friends Emily and Bill, the parents of Peter,' John softly spoke.

As the two men lowered their heads and wistfully contemplated the happy times they had all spent together, they felt warmth spread through them as though they were standing in a pool of sunlight. John sighed, looked up at the cluster of bright stars and breathed in the precious joy of such a sacred place. Lastly, the men worked tirelessly to fill the gap with as much earth as they could.

Satisfied that they had fulfilled an important ceremony, they wearily decided that it was time to go home. As the Land Rover rumbled down the abandoned field and into a valley, they felt that they had completed something and were free to fight with renewed vigour any obstacles that lay ahead.

At the bottom of the hill, the engine began to die. They managed to coax it on and off for a while so that they were halfway up the next hill when it came to a complete halt. Reluctantly, they climbed out of the vehicle and abandoned it to travel the rest of the way on foot.

John and Leonard trod softly and slowly through the field that gradually sloped up towards the raven-black woods. An inky dark sheet of cloud blanketed this part of the sky, so there were no stars or moon to add any extra light to their torch. Out of breath with the climb, the two men stopped and gasped in the damp rancid smelling air. The mood had changed; they could both feel the presence of something lurking and knew it was out there, somewhere, stalking them through the night.

'Leonard, we are not alone. There is something wrong,' John whispered.

'I know. I can feel it and smell its foul stink.'

'What shall we do? I am too old for confrontations.'

'It's probably someone camping in the woods, and the smell could be foxes. Take my knife if you are worried, and keep watching your back. But the only thing we can do is keep heading for your house so we can camp out there.' Leonard handed the old man the small sharp blade and then strode ahead into the misty gloom.

As they proceeded forward, every few paces, John stopped and swung around to check that nothing was creeping up behind them, ready to strike. Every ebony shape that moved in the shadows was analysed, and their ears tuned into even the most imperceptible sounds so that when an owl began to screech, they both nearly jumped out of their skins and then momentarily froze with fear.

On the edge of the cold woods, the noxious smell grew stronger. As they walked forward, they ran into a veil of sticky spider webs that hung down from the trees. Leonard dropped the torch as they thrashed their arms about, trying to break down the silky fibres, but with each step they took, the tangle of webs became thicker until they found themselves entwined and trapped in a tightening net. They tried to pull free of the bindings and flee, but their feet were fastened to the ground. Out of burrows in the wood, and the earth, thousands of tiny spiders emerged that scurried towards them, running up their bodies, entering their mouths and ears. They clogged their throats so that they choked and coughed and crawled over the surface of their eyes, blurring their vision.

The two captives struggled and shook, but the more they moved, the more trapped they became. They internally shuddered with mute fear as somewhere in front of them, they just perceived a looming shape in a black cloak, its face partially hidden by a hood. A strange phosphorescent glow surrounded it.

A flock of ravens flew up from the watching trees, and the spiders scurried back into their holes as the unspeakably terrifying figure crept closer to his victims. John was aware that while struggling with blindness, he had dropped the knife onto the soil, and he glanced down, just managed to make out the black shape, and then looked up at Leonard, who acknowledged his thoughts.

'Good evening, gentlemen. It's very late to be about, and I thought there was a curfew that had to be obeyed?' The stranger greeted them and lowered his hood to reveal his frightful face. He had jet-black eyes and gaunt skull-like features, as well as long shark-like teeth that were exposed as he grimaced.

'Yes, it is late, sir, and we are in a rush to get home. We never intended to be this late. We are returning from the Cathedral where we took the oath.'

'Ah, the oath, wise choice,' Bishop Francis flung his cloak over his shoulder, revealing a long, sheathed sword and a bag hanging down from his shoulder that contained a large object. 'In this bag,' he tapped it with his right hand, 'is a box that contains the most precious object in the whole of space and time. It is our Lord's own words, and anyone who is able to decipher its codes is freed from the ravages of all human frailties. If man follows these laws, he will possess the riches of many universes and will never have to toil again. Don't you think it would be wrong to prevent that kind of inevitable progress?' He paused and looked long and hard at the two men.

Both John and Leonard desperately tried to quell their fear and control the icy shudders that trembled in waves down their spines. Leonard was rendered speechless, so John summoned up all his courage and tried to ease their way out of their predicament.

'Yes, sir, it is wrong to prevent progress, but we are both tired and need to be on our way, but we have somehow got caught in this unusually large spider's web.'

The demon laughed a deep, blood-curdling laugh that was mingled with derision. 'You are a respectful man; good manners are so important. Of course, I must free you.'

Without the creature even moving, the threads instantly vanished. 'Emm, now what should I do with you? It is just plain wrong to be out at this time of night, and you could attempt to rob me of my valuable goods.'

Warily, the old man regarded his companion and saw that his face was a chalky white, and his eyes were filled with the grotesque look of panic.

Amidst the turbulent depths of his terror, Leonard's thinking had become fogged, and before he knew what he was doing, he bent down to seize the knife. It was a deadly decision, as in an instant of swift motion, the stranger had drawn his sword from its sheath, stepped forward and sliced the razor-sharp blade down onto the back of Leonard's neck. A fountain of blood squirted up, his body fell to the ground and dropped to one side, and his head landed next to the torch.

John stood rigidly, not daring to breathe, too petrified to see if his friend's lips still moved. He averted his eyes. The heavyweight of the night pressed crushingly down, and he was suddenly desperate for oblivion, to be obliterated so that he would not be forced to witness any more horror. Suddenly nauseous, he violently vomited towards the stranger.

'Sorry about that. Your friend was going for that knife. I had to defend myself. There are many people envious of me who want to steal and destroy what they don't understand, but it is my rightful bequest, you see. Even wretched children have turned to thievery,' he menacingly added.

A thorn of a new type of fear pierced John's heart as suddenly he remembered Isobel, Peter, and all the other children and families taking shelter at the school.

'You and I are a perfect match. Our minds connect so well. I could see every detail of your granddaughter and her feeble companion. You could make life a great deal easier for me. You see, I am a creature of ambush. I prefer to take my victims one at a time. You could be the bait at the end of my hook. Lead the way. You can take me to the school where the fun will start.'

Avoiding the body of his friend, John walked ahead, his mind boiling with anger at the extremely ruthless savagery of the evil monster. Every creaking mechanism of his brain jolted into life as he tried to think of a way of alerting Isobel. Then he realised that this too could be dangerous, as the stranger seemed to be able to read his every thought.

When they arrived back at the school, John was commanded to go inside and bring out Isobel and Peter. On entry, the old man immediately ran into his anxious wife, Daisy.

'John! Whatever has happened to you? Your clothes are covered in blood!'

John pulled his wife close, held her tight, dropped his head into her soft grey hair, and cried. After some time, he pulled himself together and, without a word, went to the fire alarm and smashed the glass. The proceeding howling noise instantly caused chaos and a loud commotion as people awoke confused. While the torrent of panic was at its peak, John mouthed to Daisy, 'Where are Peter and Isobel?'

She whispered back, 'They are out looking for you.'

'We need to get out of here quick. Get Jeanie and the baby and hide in the church.'

Outside, Bishop Francis had thrown off his cloak and was alert. Then, his head was inundated with a thunderous cacophony, and he couldn't make out one voice from the other. He hated noise, and his hunger for destruction was activated. Every muscle in his body shook with rage, and he roared like a caged lion until the ground began to quake. As brick and mortar began to collapse around the already panicked villagers, he rose and hovered in the air. A fiery wind blew through the building, and everyone fled for their lives. Francis wouldn't allow anyone to pass, and consumed with hatred, he circled the crowds at the exits, doing everything he could to prevent their escape. One by one, he picked off his victims and slaughtered them with an array of deadly weaponry.

Chapter Twenty-two

On the previous night, after Isobel overheard the conversation between her grandfather and Leonard, she and Peter had agreed that they would track them down and explain to him their story before he headed off on his mad adventure. Only she couldn't find her granddad or her friend at the school. Eventually, she extended her search and found Peter at his abandoned home, urgently filling his father's car with food, water, camping equipment and a selection of knives. He ignored her presence, and she stood watching, a lonely spectator who was actively being excluded from her closest friend's unbearable sense of loss. She was desperate to communicate something—anything—to feel connected once again.

'Peter, please talk to me,' she pleaded.

He ignored her, unable to tear himself away from his one focus—to hunt down, seize and destroy anything he deemed responsible for the brutally painful ache, that heavy lead bullet embedded in his heart.

'Peter, we are a partnership. I am coming with you!' she shouted like a petulant child who demands to be obeyed.

'No, Isobel, you are not. I am no longer the gentle Peter, loyal to his friends and bound to care for others. I only have one thing in my mind and soul, and that is to end this ordeal by any means. I don't care if I live or die or anyone else. So, get out of my fucking way and leave me alone!' he venomously shouted.

Isobel was stunned, speechless. In all the time she had known Peter, he had never shouted at her. Feeling broken, empty and dumped, she turned her back on the torturous atmosphere and began to amble up the hill. Then she stopped, spun around and cried out to the figure that had returned to his frantic tasks.

'Well, in that case, I shall go it alone. You don't have a monopoly on hatred!'

Then she stormed off into the darkness, intending to return to the school, make up her bag of supplies, leave a note for her mother and run whilst everyone was sleeping. Her plan would then be to go and search for her grandfather and Leonard, whom she expected to find at the burial mound. A few seconds later, she heard the engine of Bill's black Rover startup, and she listened intently as it crept up behind her. Peter drew up beside Isobel and wound down the passenger window.

'You know you will get caught driving illegally,' was all she could think of saying.

'Just get in. I assume you are going the same way.'

'What has made you change your mind?'

'If you are going to get yourself killed, it might as well be alongside me. Now get in. I am in a hurry.' Peter leaned over and opened the door, and without another word, Isobel climbed inside.

'Where are you going to start looking?'

'Well, the book doesn't seem to be at the Cathedral, but someone there must know where it has been taken.'

After this, they settled back and sat in silence, both secretly glad to be united again for one purpose. When the two travellers turned out onto the main road, they were surprised to find it was deserted; they appeared to be completely alone. The landscape they were in was different from their memory; everything was either dying or overgrown. Once neat fields had been abandoned, roadside houses and businesses stood empty, and the verges were littered with discarded possessions and general rubbish.

The first part of their journey was only about seven miles, and without any traffic or obstructions, it was swift. Briefly, they stopped on the hill that overlooked the City and stared down at the magnificent Cathedral, still floodlit in a golden light, giving out its warm and welcoming invitation to anyone on a journey while withholding its dark secrets within its interior.

They parked the car by the City wall, and as they stepped out, they were swamped by a strong, acrid smell that left a metallic taste in their mouths. Furtively, they crept through deserted side streets, past mundane images of their past lives, a phone box, the theatre boarded up, and the music shop with its guitars and drums still sadly displayed in the window but looking dusty and neglected.

When they arrived at the southwest entrance, Peter instructed Isobel to wait outside until he had cleared their way. Isobel perched on the parapet of the building, feeling dwarfed by the enormous wall that stretched in all directions. Knowing that her crazed friend had not thought his actions through and that he had no specific plan made her feel extremely anxious, and she wondered if she should have tried harder to talk him out of such a foolhardy deed. She was aware of a pain twisting in her belly, and to distract herself, she played with her beads and then gazed into the eye.

'Selene, are you there?'

However, it wasn't Selene that was reflected from the gemstone but Morse's eye and spiked head. 'Morse, please! We urgently need your help.'

'I am obliged to come when you call, that is a rule of honour I must obey.'

Isobel was dumbfounded and could hardly believe that the beast was able to speak directly to her mind.

PETER IMMEDIATELY SPOTTED the two shadow figures lying in wait for him behind the pillars. They tried to ambush him, but he was ready, and with his axe in his hand, he quickly cut them down. They lay mutilated on the floor, frothing like rabid dogs. Peter approached and, taking a knife from the back pocket of his trousers, stabbed them one by one in the heart. Bloodshot up into his face, and he could taste it in his mouth, but without hesitation, he heaved up the limbless bodies and removed both their cloaks. He was not shocked or disturbed in any way and coolly slid the corpses over the smooth flagstone floor and concealed them along with two severed arms and a leg behind a tomb.

Once outside again, he whispered to Isobel. 'Here, put this on and follow me.' He threw the robe over to his companion, who followed his instruction without question.

'The plan now is to search everywhere for the book and for me to find someone I may persuade to tell us where it has gone.'

As they approached the nave, they heard remote chanting, words of an almost imperceptibly deep pitch and in an unknown language. On entering the vast space, the two intruders saw that all the pews had been removed and that the whole congregation were kneeling on the floor with their heads bowed.

'Look, Issy, they are not prepared for anything, so sure that they won't be disturbed.' Peter turned to Isobel, and she was alarmed to see that his mood was elated and that he hadn't even bothered to wipe the dots of blood from his glasses.

Then, without any prior warning, they felt the foundation beneath their feet shudder and then violently shake. Instantly, there was a thunderous roar like a million horses stampeding by and the blast of a huge wind as the air exploded through the shattered windows.

Peter and Isobel fell to the floor and bent over, trying to protect their heads. Carved masonry hammered to the floor with a dull thud, plaster crumbled off the walls, and bronze plaques dislodged and cracked marble tombs. Fractures in the stone-covered ground radiated outwards and widened, revealing the bones of the dead, and a thick, sulphurous veil of dust clouded everything from view.

When the trembling subsided, Peter and Isobel crawled together through the rubble—fragments of beautiful glass, statues and all the other wreckage of a once magnificent statement of a people's love for their God. Disappointingly, when they reached the exit, they found that it had been blocked on the outside, and no matter how much they heaved, the door would not shift. Fearing another tremor, they rushed back over the debris and through the fog of dust to the nave and the main exit where the wall had partially collapsed. Indistinguishable, dark shapes, anesthetised against any emotions, moved slowly in the same direction, un-panicked and unmoved.

It was then that it became clear that their disguise of the cloaks had not fooled anyone. The demon monks smelt humans, and when they turned, the creatures could see the fear in Isobel and Peters's faces, so they stopped in their tracks and shone their blazing, hungry eyes at the two intruders. As a small group broke away from the swaying black sea, Peter pushed Isobel behind him and held his fiery axe ready in both hands. He moved forwards, hacking fiercely at anyone who stood in their way, making a path through the whining, dismembered, and injured. The luminous blue vampire snakes slithered out of the way into the nearest cracks.

They were at the door, climbing over boulders and smelling the fresher air, so close to escaping, when their way was suddenly blocked by a winged beast that loomed up above them, hovering and leering down. There was no hiding or surrendering, so they slowly backed up, keeping their eyes fixed on the enemy.

The Bishop floated to the floor and, pushing the traitors to one side as though he was indifferent to their presence, strolled towards the pulpit. Here, he took a gleaming gold box from a bag and placed it on the lectern. He stood tall, aloof, surveying the chaos he had caused. The remains of his army were wakeful and alert and looked to their leader for instruction. The Bishop raised his hand to signal to them to listen.

'Brothers, you are not needed here anymore tonight; go back to the school. I shall finish here, and tomorrow, we will leave for our new home in the capital.'

Isobel and Peter knew that they were not included in the invitation to leave and stood rigid, petrified, both wondering what their torturer was scheming while scanning their surroundings for another way out.

'So, you have come for the book. I have been expecting to meet feeble resistance for some time, and I am happy that you are finally here on my territory so that we may reach a rational solution.' He grimaced at them, fixing their attention with his solid black eyes. 'Well, here it is, "the devil's own words", safely protected within a gold skin covered with enchanted symbols. It is absolutely beautiful, isn't it?' He didn't wait for a reply. 'The question is, who is its rightful owner—you two or I? I think the book should decide. Well, boy, if you want it, come, get it, and if it chooses you, it will grow light in your hands.'

'Peter, no, it's a trick,' Isobel whispered as she held his arm, attempting to retain him, knowing that she was no longer pleading with her once-balanced friend.

'Isobel, I have to. I could save millions.' Determined to be a hero, he shrugged her off and began to walk forward, holding his precious weapon ready above his head as it sparked and burnt with a bright glow. He hadn't gone far when, without any warning, an ancient sword flew from the shadows, severing his wrist with razor-sharp precision and his hand and the axe fell to the floor. Blood spurted uncontrollably, and Isobel saw her friend's face distort into the ugly mask of shock and pain. In the next instant, he was airborne as he was hurled across the room where he crashed into the wall opposite.

Isobel raced over to her friend, screaming hysterically, 'Peter, Peter, don't leave me.' No longer caring about her safety or the tumour of evil that was eating away at the world, she crouched down beside him and wept until she could barely see. Finding his knife, she cut off a length of the stinking black cloak and busied herself, fixing a tourniquet. Behind her, a deep voice laughed.

'It's your turn now, little girl,' he sneered and glared in her direction. 'What I suppose you are too young to understand is that I am in this position by popular demand. You inward-looking, complacent creatures want to be dominated by a dictator. It is easier for you pathetic lambs of God to follow a leader who promises you everything than it is to act individually. It's a trade-off. I take away all of a human's daily stresses of needing food and shelter, and in return, they accept my vision. What they see as the most horrendous atrocities—so long as they are counted amongst those who are exempt, special. You see the book as a destructive force, but the majority of people see that it has given them unique opportunities and understand that the population needed paring down and a simpler system put into place.'

Isobel cowered, scrunched up next to Peter, and in her state of shock and turmoil, she could quite see how the Bishop would be able to twist his words to convince the weak and suffering that his was the correct and only way to exist. In her mind, it was clear that she was defeated, that there was no way out and that Peter, in his unconscious condition, was in a better situation. The only option open to her now would be to try to grab Peter's axe and charge her diabolical oppressor, attempting to inflict as much harm as possible.

However, the Bishop was getting bored. He had planned to play with the irritating creature and pull her limbs off one by one, but now he felt like returning to his preparations for world domination. 'Still, I am rambling on, and it's getting late. I shall give you one chance to take the book. Otherwise, your only choices are to bend down at my feet in the act of devotion and take the oath or spend all of eternity counting grains of dust in the heat of hell.'

A warm wind blew through the glassless windows, and Isobel noticed that the odd fly was annoyingly buzzing around Peter's motionless body. At the same time, the Bishop heard a deep rumbling and wondered if his anger had caused a chain effect on the tectonic plates. The ground grumbled, and then there was crashing, hurling of stone as a large part of the wall by the west entrance thundered down onto the floor. Dust billowed up into an all-pervading cloud.

When everything calmed and settled, a familiar shape emerged from the fog. There stood the supremely awe-inspiring dragon. His triangle head, with its two curved symmetrical horns, the endlessly dribbling venomous saliva and the soft, glossy human-like eyes, poked through the gloom. *Morse has found me,* Isobel thought, and she could not stop shivering with amazement and delight. He moved forward, the armour of his spiked body and the long whipping tail came into view, and he placed himself between the ragged-looking girl and her adversary.

The Bishop was acutely aware that the archaic being was set on guarding the forsaken teenagers like a dog. He also appreciated that the dragon was a formidable foe, and physically, he doubted that he could overpower such a killer force.

'Your futile attempts at protecting the weak is why your kind barely exists and why you have mostly been condemned to the archives,' the Bishop spoke with a hoarse voice, trying to conceal his vulnerabilities.

The beast, without any further hesitation, stamped towards the pulpit and the Bishop, for the first time since he was a child, felt something near to fear. The dragon stood next to the book and, turning his head to one side, regarded the Bishop, who saw the wicked glint in the creature's eye and the certainty of his dominance over the heartless. Then Francis smelt his rancid meat breath.

When Morse opened his large, fanged jaws, green slime oozed out and dropped to the floor. The Bishop was helpless as the creature spread his vast wings, rose into the air and swooped over the lectern, sending Francis crashing backwards onto the flagstones. In an instant, the dragon had clasped the box in the talons of his back feet. With the surging energy of every muscle, he climbed high, almost touching the rafters, and then swooped down to Isobel's side, where he laid the treasure gently on the ground.

'Ariel! Ariel! Come quickly and bring the boy,' Francis screamed as he picked himself up from the floor, shaking the dust from his robes.

Ariel appeared from the shadows and moved gracefully towards the Bishop. The baby in her arms smiled and gurgled happily in his warm haze of innocence. The radiance of new life made Isobel think of a colourful butterfly about to be gassed and have a pin pierced through its abdomen.

'Ben! Morse, it's Ben!' Isobel cried with exasperation.

Ariel handed the baby over to Bishop Francis, who sat it awkwardly on his knee and glanced down at it with an expression of repulsion and disdain.

'Now I have something you want, and you have something I want.'

'Morse, please give the book back,' she commanded and stood up ready to take any action necessary. 'Ariel, you were once our friend. Have some pity,' she pleaded, staring at the sublimely beautiful creature with the long dark hair and emotionless white face. It was clear that she was unmoved and that it was a wasted effort trying to evoke the distant memory of compassion in one so dead. The teenager miserably argued on in a similar vein for some time, but all her begging was ignored by all sides.

Isobel wept silently, and through the mist of tears, she looked despondently into the eye, her last source of help. A mellow, tender voice came into her head, and Selene beckoned to her with a warm smile, which was reflected like a hologram from the jewel. 'Whatever happens, trust Morse. Now please follow my instructions. Even though your entire soul and love for your brother is preventing you from leaving, we all need you to do just that. Please believe me when I say you are not alone in any of this. Retrieve the axe from where it lays and then help Peter to leave with you even if you have to drag him and hide as best you can outside the City walls.' The lyrical voice filled the girl's heart with a strange feeling of restraint and peace.

'Come on, Dragon, the book! The book for the child!' the Bishop shouted, a reminder of his demands, while the dragon ignored him and continued to stand guard.

Isobel, without any trepidation, calmly stepped towards the axe that lay at the midpoint between Peter and the demon, plucked it out of the dust and pushed it under the belt of her worn jeans. She reached her arm out towards her brother and waved. 'I will be back, Ben,' she smiled, blew the baby a kiss and turned her back on her torturers.

'If you leave, your brother will die,' Francis vehemently screeched out after Isobel. The girl chose to ignore the evil words and instead, mustering up all her strength, managed to lift Peter into a standing position, wrapping his arm around her shoulder. Isobel dragged him out into the dawn that was darkening with an approaching storm.

The Bishop unfurled his wings and, erupting with a burning rage, hurled himself as high up as he could go with the baby now squirming in his arms.

'Take the book, and I will drop this revolting thing.'

Morse opened his jaws and emitted a fierce roaring, shrieking sound that shook the ruins further, then lowered his head and breathed out a line of intense flames that flared up to the ceiling and quickly spread from wall to wall, creating a barrier between the enemy and the main exit route from the building. The blaze swept back on the growing wind that came from where the entrance had once been. Before she was able to retreat, Ariel's robes were ignited, and she burned furiously. Francis looked down and saw her skin blacken and peel from her face, and he realised that it was time to retreat and find other devious means to retrieve the precious fuel of his life.

Morse grasped the gleaming gold box in his claws and heaved his body up and towards the hole in the crumbled wall and out into the tempest and freedom.

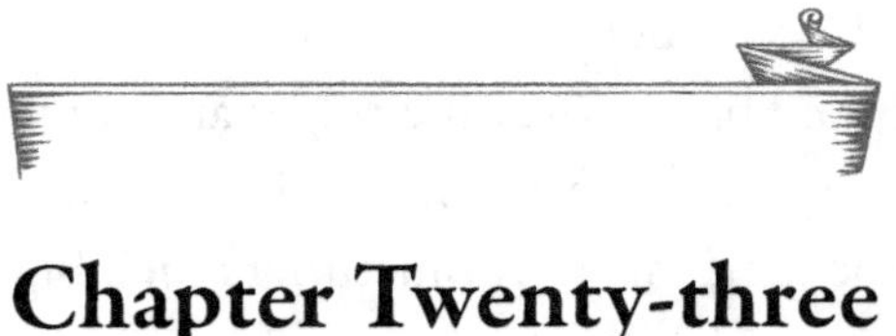

Chapter Twenty-three

Bishop Francis seethed with rage at the loss of the book. His cold heart had a limited capacity for true depth of emotion, but his aching obsession for his lost treasure was already beginning to tear him apart, and his mind was fixed on his hatred for the inhabitants of the insignificant bankrupt speck of dust where he was currently forced to reside.

Also, Francis had been obliged to hold onto the baby, which he had handed over to one of his disciples to care for. At first, a part of him had wanted to keep it as a trophy, at least for a while, but then, just as he was sneaking away from the ruins of the Cathedral and the disastrous event, the voice of the messenger, Diabolus Angelus, came boring into his head. He had demanded that an army be sent out immediately to kill the dragon and seize the book, but he went on to say that the infant had a significant role to play in the destiny of the fellowship and that it should not be destroyed.

The Bishop hid from his disciples in his chambers, situated in the old school, sitting at his desk with his head in his arms, reflecting on the messages he had gleaned from 'the book'. What infuriated him was that he had just started to decipher the last few pages, which had remained a complete mystery to the rest of the fellowship. Although in the same language, this three-dimensional text appeared to be created by a different hand and looked as though it had been added on.

Only a day before the theft, Francis had been scrutinising the book when he realised that access to the meaning of the last pages of words and symbols could only be gained by touching the original artefact. When his fingers had passed over the ridges and furrows of the words, a black pool had appeared in his mind, which quickly became crowded with moving shapes and images. Something much bigger than himself was calling him, and he felt like he was tapping into the folds of another creature's brain. It was clear that he was being given access to the unbelievable and unknowable.

His fanatical faith told him that he was on the verge of a far more important picture of everything, something that any mere human could never appreciate. Even his heart leapt when he read that 'the universe was infinitely small in the scheme of things. It was just one flickering light in a whole system of multi-verses that were constantly dying or being born. A membrane of subatomic particles divided each multiverse, which sometimes touched or could be breached with the use of the five interlocking 'Chokmah Rings.'

Francis understood that if he had read the strange words and pictures accurately, there were routes and ways to access these other dimensions for a chosen few. It spoke of the universe of 'Elohim Tsebyoth' or the eternal flame, a place of pure pleasure with an infinite energy source, whole new ways of existence and highly advanced societies.

The last few visions that bounced into his head caused him intense excitement. 'The true rulers of the universe were being held back by God's planet where the 'Malach' or ancestors of all time, with their vast knowledge, reigned. The author believed that the existing condition of peace in the Elohim Tsebyoth universe was wrong, as it prevented progress and access to the well of ultimate energy that had been discovered by the Malach. That this patch of tranquillity at the centre of one cosmos was threatening to destroy the naturally turbulent climate of the other universes and that the author's power would permanently be compromised by the still waters of peace.' The last words he heard in his head were, *I am the Devil, and I offer anyone who has read this book from beginning to end and returns the Chokmah rings, eternal life, power beyond all worlds, access to the multi-verse, infinite pleasures and limitless energy. It is we who give the orders here.'*

After this, he had seen pictures, which he assumed were maps, but he had not been able to decipher their meaning before 'the book' had been stolen.

Now the book was gone, and Francis feared that his powers would also die, and he would, in time, become nothing but an empty shell. The Bishop stood up and examined his reflection in the long mirror that was screwed to the back of the door. He wanted to reassure himself that he wasn't already transforming into some weak and feeble creature. Happily, to his eyes, he was confronted by the image of a powerful and vicious-looking monster, visual proof of his physical supremacy.

Am I mad, schizophrenic perhaps, as I have heard voices and seen visions? He vaguely considered to himself. Then, he quickly dismissed such thought as being irrelevant, as he didn't care, and it was beyond him to care. All he knew was that the race had been started, he was compelled to run and needed to ensure that he was the first and only one to reach the finishing line.

The Bishop smiled heartlessly at his likeness as he relished the memory of all those who had tried to run from him at the school and the intense satisfaction he felt when he watched people bend to his will and die. *I will continue my war on time and existence, but I can't do any of it without the book,* he contemplated. He began to pace his small cell-like room. *How could I have blown my chances? Just allow it all to be taken away. I should have fought the stupid lumbering dragon, I am mightier than he. Still, I have the child, and for a reason: the messenger wants him. At all costs, I will retrieve the Diabolus Consilium. I shall use all the cunning, trickery and cruelty at my disposal. I shall cut down anything that stands in my way of setting my hands on 'my' precious book.* Francis enjoyed the sound of his internal voice and, looking in the mirror, flicked out his viper's tongue and then snarled at his reflection like a big cat eager to make a kill.

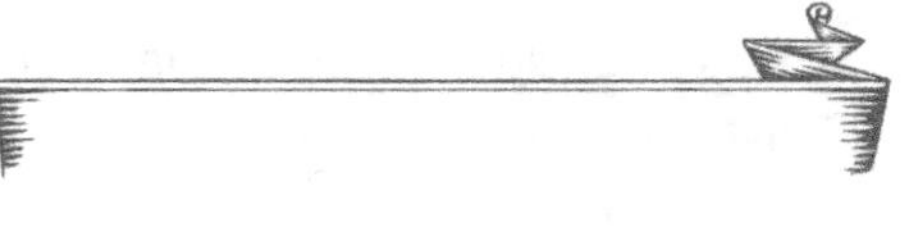

Chapter Twenty-four

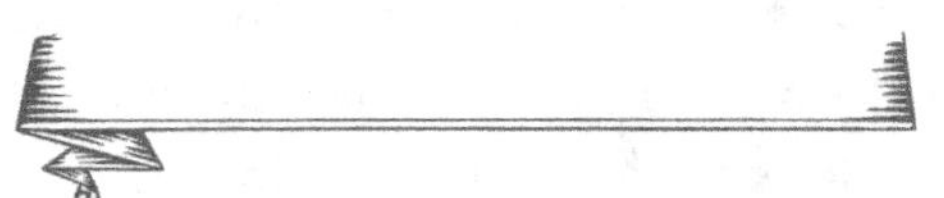

Morse bravely pushed forward through the dark, stormy skies. Below, all the details that would normally guide his way were obscured by a veil of rain. He was acutely aware that his endeavours could prove fruitless, as he understood the pure greed of humankind and their treacherous desire to destroy what they were unable to understand. Dragons were alien to the people who would soon be stirring beneath the rubble of their homes, exploring their environment, and looking to the skies for answers. Morse longed to return to his country, to the jungles on the perimeter of the Earth, to the continuity of the unbroken chain of his history and the solidarity of what remained of his noble race.

Once he had fled the Cathedral, he had exploded into the sky with all the force he could muster and flew at top speed in a frenzied flight, anxious to escape the eyes of the City where he could be spotted and shot down in a fraction of a second. However, his journey was becoming increasingly perilous with every flap of his wings. He had just crossed the boundary between the grandeur of the city and the vibrant green of the countryside when he realised that the weight of the box was increasing. After a while, progress became impossible; he was going nowhere and being dragged toward the ground. Eventually, he was forced to land.

It then became obvious to the dragon that he would have to divert from his original plan of heading north, and he could think of only one place where he might find rest, but the need to return underground sent a shiver of fear down his spine. The thought of returning to the prison that he had waited so long to be liberated from filled him with dread.

Morse crash-landed through the sheets of rain and into a sodden field. Once he managed to heave his heavy body into a standing position and had checked for damage, he uneasily surveyed his surroundings. He looked down at the glowing gold box that was completely unspoiled by the poor landing. The evil object seemed so harmless, but he understood its existence was a significant danger to the planet, and he knew that if he failed in his task, it would be at a high cost.

With a sense of solemnity, he closed his eyelids and meditated on the problem. It was then that the distant gurgling sound of a river leaked into his thoughts, and then he was aware of the lingering smell of blood mingled with wet, dense air. Summoning up the last remaining spark of strength, he managed to lift the burdensome object off the ground.

Morse had just managed to clear the bushes that lined the bank, crashed with a mighty splash into the water, and felt a sense of joy as he expected sparkling liquid to wash over his head. Instead, it felt gooey and stunk like the contents of human veins. Despite this, he was in his element, his sanctuary as the red river still flowed fast and was a lifeline that would transport him to where he needed to be. Now the box was manageable, light and powerless. The dragon's long muscular tail undulated from side to side and simultaneously acted as both a rudder and an engine that drove him forward with great speed. Beneath it, he hauled the Devil's works, not caring if it was scraped on the rocks or was damaged in any way.

The dragon passed through luscious green fields and willows that stood guard, screening him from any onlookers. When he arrived at his destination, he heaved his body out of the water and pulled the odious object up the steep bank to the doors of the tunnel that were situated at the base of the watermill. Using his thick-skinned head as a battering ram, he charged at the barrier, which broke with little resistance. Then he threw the offending box down into the darkness.

He jumped over the few steps, into the large room and as his eyes grew accustomed to the gloom, he saw the empty cages. The noise of the river had stilled, and he felt vulnerable in the eerie silence. Looking down at the Devil's book encased in its gold coffin he noticed a green light pulsating from the crack where the lid met the base and decided that he would gain no advantage by standing watch over such an entity. *He couldn't move it, and perhaps a little-known tunnel would be the place to leave it. He would return home and seek help,* he thought, knowing that really, his task was not over and that he was obliged to obey Selene's instructions.

Morse had turned his back on his prison and was heading towards liberty when he heard a noise behind him and knew something was lurking in the tunnel. Slowly, he moved his large head around, and he saw a metal man, like those who had hunted them down so long ago. He was alert but phlegmatic. He was old and wise and knew that the lump of scrap before him was no real threat. Morse thrashed out a warning with a flick of his tail, opened his large biting jaws and breathed out hot, combustible air. Then, from the mouth of the tunnel, he saw the eagle swoop down and land on the floor next to the silver-clad human. It was then that he realised that standing before him was probably the boy who had given him his freedom, so he stepped forward.

'Morse, it's me, Oswald. Please stay; we need your help with that treasure,' Oswald looked at Lance, who had perched himself on top of a cage, out of the dragon's way. 'What's he thinking, Lance?'

'He's not sure he trusts you, and besides, the box is too heavy, even for him.'

'Morse, I am not one of those fucking fanatics. I didn't take the goddamn oath even though it meant I could not stay with the living.

It's all about chance and luck, and today I am freed, as the dead have risen. All over the world, shadowy armies are climbing out of their graves. The good and bad will soon be judged.'

Morse turned and looked at the patch of extreme brightness coming from the entrance and snorted the sweet air. He wanted to return home and knew that beneath the cold garments that the boy's flesh would be enough to sustain him on his journey.

'What the hell is he thinking now, my friend?' Oswald said, directing his question towards his bird.

'He is thinking of killing you, humans are fair game since the massacres.'

Oswald was troubled by the realisation that the dragon understood that he was once again a creature of substance. *How much could the beast know the true nature of his new existence? Could he read a lie? Perhaps it would be in his best interest to slay Morse before he devoured him,* Oswald deliberated to himself. *He would not risk death when he had not long been given the opportunity to return to the future and the world of the living. Still, he was a Knight, and it was his duty to take risks.* Fearlessly, he turned back to address the brute who was dribbling acrid saliva and sniffing for the flavour of his flesh.

'You and I have a mission that must be completed. The book must go South West, to the deep caves, as master Richard instructed.'

Morse felt uneasy; the boy who had given him freedom seemed changed; perhaps it was not the same person hiding in the metal cage. However, he decided that he would not betray Selene and that his hunger would have to wait a little longer.

Clanking in the armour, which he'd found in a blanket chest in the ruins of Richard's house, and with his sword swaying at his side, Oswald moved forward and, with some difficulty, crouched down in front of the box. He took off his gauntlet, and his nimble fingers explored the surface, looking for a way to lift the lid.

'We will just take the book,' he announced to his audience. Then he took his dagger, placed it in the crack that was emitting the strange light and tried to force it open.

Morse then lowered his head, opened his mouth wide and clasped his jaws over the lid. He lifted it a little way off the ground and shook it from side to side. The weight and effort caused blood vessels to burst in his eyes. Then, summoning every ounce of energy, he heaved it high off the floor and allowed it to drop.

The box cracked, the lid sprung up, and they were all momentarily engulfed in a blue-green fog. When it finally dispersed, they looked closer. To Oswald's surprise, some kind of secret drawer had also flicked out, revealing four gold rings. He bent down and examined them more closely. They were too big to be worn on any fingers, and he wondered for what purpose they were created. Deciding that they could be significant, he dropped them into a leather purse he kept under his breastplate.

'Look, the book itself is not so heavy,' he said, holding it up to Morse. I have a mare outside. We will put it in her pannier.'

A minute later, the three of them, without looking back, headed towards the light to begin their journey towards the wilderness, aware that they could hear a rumbling in the distance.

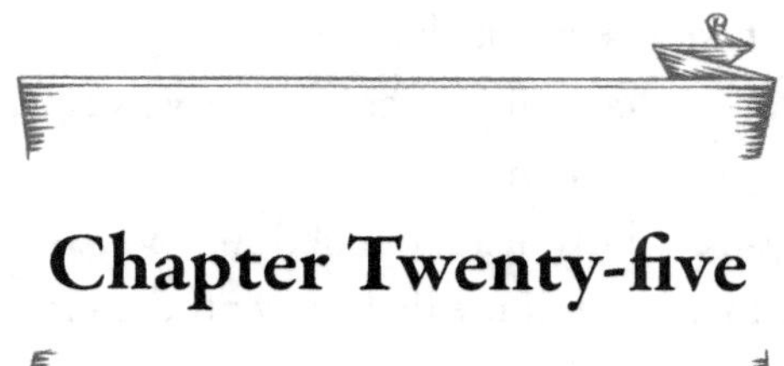

Chapter Twenty-five

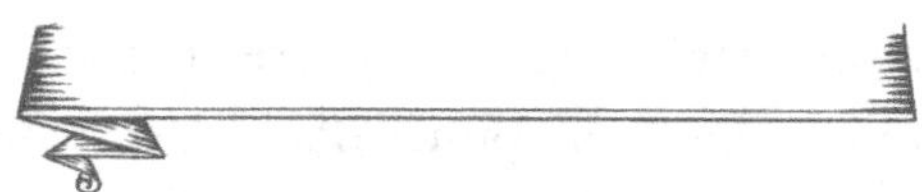

Isobel staggered forwards, bent double by Peter's weight. He was semi-conscious, and both of them were fighting the urge to cough for fear of being heard. They had left through the main archway of the cathedral grounds and emerged into a square that had once been a lively area of pubs and small independent shops. The place was deserted, crumbled and changed with piles of rubble, broken windows and clouds of dust that billowed up as they limped along. Squeezed between the taller buildings, Isobel spotted a tiny abandoned wattle and daub shop; it had stood for centuries and was still quite complete.

'Keep taking one foot forward; we are nearly there,' Isobel whispered to her friend.

The door of the shop was ajar, and Isobel pushed against the clutter of its previous existence as a place to buy cards and gifts so that they could enter. They collapsed, drunk with fatigue, into the first dark corner they could find. Peter lay on his back while Isobel squatted at his side. At last, she felt that it was safe enough to examine her patient and was horrified by what she saw in the gloom. Blood was spurting from his wrist, his lips were white, and as he stared up at her vacantly, she could see the veil of death slowly sliding over his face.

'I am sorry, Issy, I blundered, I fucking well cocked up,' he murmured.

'No, you didn't, you were a true hero. You did well.'

She saw the corner of his lip curl up as though he was trying to smile, but he coughed and spluttered instead. He wanted to raise himself off the floor but collapsed back, exhausted.

'Take my wallet out of my jeans.' Isobel did as he instructed. 'Open it.' She looked down, and glistening between the folds of leather was a golden feather. 'You had better take it and keep it with the others, where it belongs.' Tears rolled from the corners of his eyes as the girl took it and placed it in her purse with the others. Peter then sighed and fell silent.

Isobel searched around for something to use as a bandage. She felt her T-shirt and realised that it was soaked in blood and her hat and other clothes were too fibrous. Instead, she tried to re-tighten the existing tourniquet. Then, when her task was completed, she leaned forward and kissed him gently on the cheek. His face was a furnace with fever and wet with tears.

'I am not frightened of dying, I have been about to die many times. It will be a relief,' he spoke faintly.

'You're not going to die. I need you. We all need you. Just keep talking to me,' she softly pleaded, but he had already fallen quiet. Everything dropped into a profound silence, and the girl wished she could measure the distance between that moment when he was still alive and when he would die because she could no longer stay awake.

Isobel curled her body up tight against her friend, laid her head on his chest and noticed that his breathing was slow, faint, almost faded. Tears of grief and despair rushed into Isobel's eyes as she took the beads from her pocket. She held the eye tightly in her hand and, in her head, pleaded with God to turn death away. 'Please don't leave me,' she cried, 'God, I am sorry, and I repent of all my sins.' Then, unwillingly, she slipped into sleep.

In her dream, she thought she was awake, arose and found herself standing in the wide expanse of a field full of every type of wildflowers, a warm breeze blew, and a sweet peace flowed from the heavens to the ground. Isobel knew that she was at the heart of all things. She was watching a crowd of golden angels soaring freely around the sky and blowing mists of shimmering hope onto the ground. One descended and hovered before the girl, a wavering glow of loveliness. Whispering in her ear, she said. 'Go south to the moors. Your father will greet you by the rock of the giant and will take you to safety underground. Wear the dragon tear necklace with pride, for it will be your guide.' Then Isobel fell into the void of dreamlessness.

The teenagers remained huddled together and frozen in sleep for almost the whole day, but in the late afternoon, a demented wailing woke Isobel. 'Our dark lord has come for us!' and with a start, she opened her eyes, confused and not sure where she was. The first thing she was aware of was a blindingly bright shaft of light cutting through the gloom.

Anxiously, she looked down at Peter and immediately was flooded with a sense of relief. His complexion had recovered, his lips were red, his chest moved up and down with a regular motion, and the bleeding had stopped. Isobel stared dumbfounded. Was this a miracle, or just the tightness of the cloth around his arm stemming the flow? She thought and decided on the former solution. She looked down at the necklace in her hand and, remembering her vision, slipped it over her head.

With an elevated mood, the teenager was determined to brave the outside world and find them both some food and fresh clothes. Peter felt her move and awoke.

'Where are you going?'

'I am itching like mad. I think I am covered in fleas,' she said as she scratched herself through her clothes. 'I am gonna get us some new clothes and food.'

'I'll come too,' then his words broke off. 'God, what the hell's that? The sun is never that dazzling. I can barely see. Help me to the door.'

With Isobel's help and by pushing himself against the wall, Peter managed to heave himself up. Tentatively, they made their way through the debris towards the exit. Peter leaned against the doorframe.

In absolute amazement, they stared up into the firmament, and there hanging in the blue sky were seven radiant spheres. Their brilliance shone over everything, throwing all the demolished buildings into clear focus.

'What are they, Peter? Is it a sign?'

'It looks like the purity and beauty of destruction to me. The oath takers seem to believe their Dark Lord is coming to earth, or more likely, they are transfixed on the source of their destruction. Remember all those who stood mesmerised by the approaching tsunami; it was impossible for them to tear themselves away from such a magnificent sight and run.'

'Yes, I remember.'

'Look at them.'

Isobel looked down and saw groups of people standing frozen, gawking up, their hearts too cold for debate or argument, all just desperately wanting to be unquestionably led. They appeared oblivious to the stench of death that lay at their feet, the rotting carcasses, the still dying, the smoking ruins and the responsibility that emotional beings would feel about extinguishing the well-established fires that devoured the air freely.

'What do you think they are, then?'

'At a guess, they're the seven stars I was watching, but now they look like some kind of spacecraft. It's time to get as far away as we can, Issy,' Peter spoke emphatically.

'Fuck! This is such a nightmare. All those things we thought could never happen to us when we were young.'

'Those days are long gone now. We had better grab what we can as quickly as possible whilst drawing little attention. The Bishop's gonna come after us even if he has to scour the whole world.'

Together, they picked their way over piles of slippery slate tiles, past the husks of lives going through their rituals of desperation, the tumbling drunks, the tyrants and thieves. Driven by the innate instinct to survive, they all hunted for the most basic elements of life. This was now a world without any justice or compassion, and its inhabitants would strike down anyone who stood in their way.

Aware of the hostility from the other scavengers, Peter waited outside an old grocer with his axe ready in his remaining hand while Isobel nimbly picked her way through the remaining edible items. She reappeared with quite a good selection of supplies. Next, they both went into a camping shop and stole for themselves the best they could find, which included thick coats and hiking boots; the rest Peter already had in the car. Surprisingly, they met no resistance. All the rats had scurried back into their holes, and the volume of moans and groans appeared to have been turned down. Isobel looked at Peter's anguished brow.

'What's wrong?'

'Isobel, we got to get out of here, get back to the car.'

'Peter, please, we need to get you medicine and bandages, or you'll die. The chemist is just down that side street.' She pointed over the road to a small alley.

'Ok, but we must be quick.'

They crossed the empty road as briskly as they could with their burden of supplies, trying to ignore the nauseating panic that was being whipped up in their guts. The door to the shop was glass but was un-shattered. Isobel anxiously scanned their surroundings while Peter hurled his axe against the barrier. Instantly, an alarm sounded.

'Oh fuck, I wasn't expecting that.'

'Quick, quick, asthma stuff, painkillers, bandages,' Isobel said aloud to keep them focused. With frantic hands and eyes, they delved into every drawer and cupboard until they found all their desired items.

Behind the counter, Isobel tore off her old clothes and helped remove Peter's. Before they had finished dressing, they heard a loud cracking sound above the whine of the alarm. There followed a terrifying pause. Isobel squeezed her eyelids together tightly and clenched her jaws against the bangs like a child afraid of fireworks.

'It's the fellowship police. They must be shooting the looters,' Peter announced as he tried to manoeuvre his painfully injured arm into the sleeve of his coat. 'Issy, help me on with the boots.'

The girl recovered enough to follow his instructions and, bending down behind the counter, took off his old trainers and eased on the new walking shoes. There was a sudden chill, and a dark shadow was thrown into the room. Peter stood rigid, holding his breath; he could smell the rancid odour, and his skin crawled. They could hear the unfolding of wings. The roof shuddered as the creature landed above their heads.

Warily, Peter crouched down beside his friend, and they hid as well as they could beneath the overlap of the counter.

'I think it's one of the Bishop's sicko disciples,' he whispered.

They heard a stamping on the roof above them, followed by scratching and a tearing interspersed with a hollow trumpeting call like that of a rutting stag.

'He might make for the door. Is there any other way out?'

'There must be another exit, in case of fire.' Frantically they searched a back room but drew a blank. There was a momentary silence which was quickly replaced by a whimpering, yelping. Drawn by curiosity Isobel crept towards the glassless door and looked out into the alley and there she saw Umbra pinned to the ground struggling to breathe as though being crushed by some great weight. She felt pity and then alarm as she realised she was being watched. She turned and looked up and saw staring down from the roof, the crouching gargoyle-like figure of one of the Bishop's demons. All pretence at being in any way human had been abandoned, the transformation was complete. On seeing the girl, the winged devil leapt to the ground after her and, doing so, released Umbra from its grip.

Immediately, the wolf arose and, confronting the formidable beast, snarled and growled. Their muscular bodies locked together, red eyes blazing as they wrestled, black fur against black fur. Isobel stepped cautiously back and up into the shelter of the shop. Both teenagers stood wooden, hypnotised by the furious fight, at the writhing tangled ball, as lumps of flesh were torn, claws gouged, and blood spurted. Finally, Umbra's massive jaws were able to open and clasp the demon by the throat; she shook the limp body and then began to devour its soft underbelly.

'For fuck's sake, let's get the hell out of here, Issy.'

They crept around Umbra, who was intent on leaving no remains for others to pick over. They grabbed their possessions and, in a mechanical stupor, headed back out onto the main street and for their car.

The sound of the engine was like sweet music, and as they left the fallen city walls behind, they breathed a sigh of relief.

'Where to now, Issy?'

'We need to pick up Gramps, baby Ben and the others, and then we need to head South West to the ancient stones. We will be safe there.' Isobel was reluctant to explain her dream, mostly because of exhaustion, but she knew Peter would ask no questions.

Chapter Twenty-six

When Peter and Isobel's car crawled into the village, it was clear from the outset that the place had suffered considerable devastation. Buildings had tumbled, and what trees had survived the hurricane had now mostly fallen. Everything seemed to be in various states of decay.

They left the car on the boundary and together searched ruin after ruin as they worked their way inwards, peering at every distorted shape and shadow, hoping to find some friend or a familiar face. Frequently, they stopped, stood still, listened, and watched with an acute intensity, but nothing stirred, and there was not a single whisper of breath.

The silence was palpable as they wandered up the hill past the place where the school had once stood. Whenever they came across anything they recognised—toys, pictures in shattered frames, a pair of glasses, old boots—they were haunted by the images of their loved ones and the distant memory of more peaceful times. However, what was most alarming was that although they saw patches of blood, they found no remains. As they wandered over the rubble, they called out peoples' names but were fearful in case the enemy was lingering, hiding, waiting to catch any last morsel.

When their eyes momentarily left the ground and looked skywards, the sight that met them was equally harrowing. There were streaks of darkness, but the night was mostly drowned out by the brilliance of the seven stars that seemed to be growing in size by the minute. It was all disorientating, as they knew it must be nighttime, but it was more like the day.

'The place is dead. You're not gonna find what you hope for Issy. We might just as well get the hell out. Even the church has vanished.'

'Yes, but the pub's still standing. Let's check that and then we'll go.'

As the pub door creaked, open into darkness, in the flickering light of a single candle, Isobel immediately recognised a single dishevelled figure slumped over the bar. The turmoil of her emotions reached their zenith, and she rushed over to her grandfather, threw her arms around his shoulders and sobbed into his dust-covered coat. He slowly raised his head, and Issy looked into his puffy, tearful, intoxicated eyes.

'Gramps, it's me, Issy.' She watched as his face crumpled.

'Oh Issy, Issy, is it really you?' he wept in disbelief.

'It's Peter and me.'

The old man adjusted his focus and threw Peter a weak smile. The teenager nodded and smiled but saw that the man was way beyond comprehension. His hands that were clasped around a bottle of whiskey were shredded and bleeding, his face was pale with grief, and he was covered in thick dust and dirt.

'We need to leave, John, go somewhere safe.'

'Peter's right, Gramps. We have to find a way out. I know where we can shelter.'

'I am going nowhere, leave me to die,' he uncharacteristically snapped back.

'Gramps, I know where Dad is. We are going to find Dad,' Isobel gently stated, hoping to tempt the old man back to life.

'I can't leave. They are all dead, Issy, every last one,' he slobbered.

Isobel pulled out a stool, sat beside her grandfather, took his left hand from the bottle, and put it in hers. Peter heard a faint movement and anxiously walked over to the window. To his astonishment, he saw Umbra lying down outside like a guard dog. He felt a sense of security and, without saying anything, strolled back to the bar.

They both understood that trying to cajole someone into action when they were resistant was something that could not be rushed. After an hour of futile effort, Peter called Isobel to his side.

'Issy, this is the end of his world, and he is not going to move. He wants to stay with Daisy, your mother, and all of his friends.'

'I know, I know. Just give me some time to say goodbye.'

The two of them went over and sat on either side of the old man.

'Gramps pass the bottle.' He slid the bottle over, and Issy held it up. 'A toast to the best Gramps in all the universes,' she said, and then she handed it over to Peter.

'To my best mate, John.'

They all gulped down as much liquid as they could until they were bent double in fits of coughing. All three sat drunk, anaesthetised from all the horror. Then they heard Umbra howling and felt that she was signalling to them, warning them that they should leave.

'Gramps, we have to go now, but please don't give up. I shall return with Dad,' she slurred, not being used to such strong liquor.

'Go, Issy, find somewhere safe.' John paused and looked thoughtful. Solemnly, the teenagers turned to leave. 'Wait, I have something for you. A gift from a friend might bring you luck.' From the inside pocket of his coat, he took out a leather drawstring purse. 'It's a ring. Keep it safe. Too big for your finger, more of a talisman.'

Isobel took the bag. 'Thanks, Gramps. I will treasure this and give it back to you on my return.' Then she gave him one last hug and the old man lifted his drooping head and smiled.

'Thanks for understanding the wishes of an old man.'

Peter went forward, shook John's hand and patted him on the back. 'Goodbye, John.'

Chapter Twenty-seven

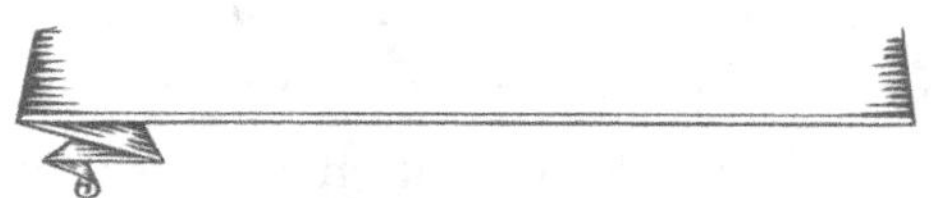

The day had come, and Lazarus, the Bishop's top scientist and professor of quantum physics, stared with anticipation out of the tall windows of the houses of Parliament. He was fascinated by the gleaming spaceship that hovered above London and felt happy that he had been caught so that he had been able to experience the most significant discoveries of all time. Other great minds had, by accident or design, been amongst the disappeared, and he was grateful to have been spared, free to follow his dreams.

Ever since Apollo 11 had touched down on the moon, he had believed that there was more to man's existence than most mortals could comprehend. At that time, he was only a young child and had been full of hope, which was followed later in life by depression, as he had feared that his considerable knowledge and skills would be wasted through a lack of funding and interest in his area of science. Then, the world went through cataclysmic changes, and his path converged with Bishop Francis, the leader of the New Order, who gave him free rein to experiment in any way he felt would advance humans into the next stage of their evolution. He understood clearly that the sacrifices had been great, but he also knew that life was a messy business and that to move forward, you had to accept collateral damage.

Today was the day: it was six in the evening, and the sky was very hot and bright for winter but so full of glorious expectations. He waited and chewed at his fingernails until they bled. He was standing on the brink of a new age, and he would have to choose which side to be on and which path to take. He had already decided that he would not hang onto the ragged coattails of the past. Lazarus desired to make sure he was on the winning side, and he was prepared to change his allegiance at any time. At the moment, the dark faith was eclipsing the light, which he could see was a good thing for life's natural progression; it was tough minds and strong convictions that fuelled progress.

Lazarus was still unsure what had brought about the collision of the two universes, but it satisfied him that his 'theory' had been correct all along. A wormhole had opened up, and the devil's subjects had managed to cross over in their vast spacecraft. However, there were a few things that concerned him: *why were they bothering to visit such a meagre planet? Would aliens be able to reveal to them the whereabouts of other similar planets in man's universe, and why was the Bishop so obviously petrified?*

Lazarus glanced over at the Bishop, who sat hunched like a vulture over his large wooden desk, his monk's cloak and hood poorly hiding his beastly appearance. Before him, the surface was covered with a forest of black candles that he had lit one by one and was watching them slowly burn down. His clawed, hairy hand was flicking a lighter. Lazarus knew not to ask him any uninvited questions and was aware that his endless thirst for warm blood made him dangerous to anyone who opposed or disturbed him in any way. The beast was surrounded by an aura of savagery, and any human who came across him sensed the threat of evil.

The door opened, and in walked the cloaked figure of a woman with a baby in her arms. Normally, the Bishop despised children, but he had plans for this captive that he had held so uneasily in his hands the day the book was stolen. The woman was relieved to be released from the loathsome burden and, with complete indifference, placed it on the floor in front of the desk. Francis watched as it crawled around curiously, exploring its surroundings. He was preparing the child to be a more significant blight on humankind than himself; it was to be his heir on the endless pathway to the stars.

A rush of warm wind suddenly howled through the city. The earth shook, and the sound of moving objects reverberated throughout the building. Then, there was a clanking and the whirring sound of machinery. Lazarus was startled, but the Bishop remained unmoved and was instead relighting the entire crowd of candles that had blown out.

Lazarus was conscious that they weren't alone in the room and turned to see a very tall figure of shimmering green and blue light. He stared mesmerised. Francis was standing and seemed to be communicating in some way.

THE BISHOP RECOGNISED the traveller from his vision and once again heard him speak directly to his mind.

'I am Diabolous Angelous, the Messenger. I have come to collect the Diabolus Conilium and the Chokmah Rings, the key to the Elohim Tsebyoth universe, where your God planet reigns, and the source of eternal energy is to be found.'

'I haven't got them with me. I have placed them in safekeeping,' Francis spoke aloud, his voice quaking. Then, as he fell silent, he heard more wrathful sounds in his head combined with images of fire, Morse the dragon and a lone knight on horseback. Then, a single word burst into his brain. 'Avernous! Avernous!' was repeated with a roar. 'You have broken your contract, failed to adhere to our divine laws.'

Bishop Francis laughed hysterically, like a lunatic. 'Do you know that you are speaking to the ruler of this whole planet? I have absolute control. I have disciples in every power base on the earth who do my bidding. I am ambitious! Lazarus here is a pure genius,' he directed his gaze to the feeble human who was longing to shrink into invisibility. 'You are but a visitor here, a stranger. But if we worked together, this world's riches could all be yours.' He squirmed, sensing that his time was up.

'Go to the window, Bishop,' the traveller commanded. Lazarus quickly moved out of the way; he wanted to speak but was lost for words.

Looking out, Francis saw balls of fire hurtling through the atmosphere and exploding on the ground. From the spaceship, a vast black cloud of winged demons swooped swiftly down, landing gently on the ground.

Francis swung around, flung his cloak to the floor, and made himself ready for whatever weapons the alien possessed.

'What does this mean?' Francis snarled with rage.

'You were unable to deliver, so there will be no reward. As you can see, you are no longer of any use. Your followers will become part of our army, and the rest of the human race will provide them with sustenance. Mass extinctions, as you have witnessed them, are necessary to the grand plan. This planet is but a speck of dust.'

Francis unfurled his vast wings, lifted his body as high up as he could go and scanned his surroundings, searching for a route to freedom.

LAZARUS STARED AGHAST, trembling with fear and hoping that the creature saw him as an asset. He then noticed tiny blue flames spontaneously flicker from the demon Bishop's bare feet. He saw the shadow of dread and torment cast over the victim's face as he tried desperately to kick off the fire. A foul smell of burning hair and flesh filled the air. At first, the fire burned slowly, and then his clothes caught alight.

There were savage shrieks of pain and a vomit of words in an unnatural tongue. The scientist wanted to block his ears and screw up his eyes against the grotesque sight, but he was rooted to the floor and scared to move even a fraction. The mercilessly hungry flames leapt higher, and Francis struggled to breathe. Eventually, all his muscles weakened, and he fell to the floor. A burning oily black mass oozing noxious liquid and a dark plume of smoke spiralling up towards the ceiling was all that remained.

In the next instant, the wavering light of the messenger had engulfed the baby, who had crawled over to the door like a dog begging to be let out. The child arose into the air as though being plucked up by invisible hands. In the blink of an eye, both the infant and stranger were gone.

Breathing out a huge sigh, Lazarus slid to the floor. He crouched on his haunches, wrapped his arms tight around his stomach, rocked back and forth and cried. Things were changing too fast, and he no longer knew where his allegiance should lie.

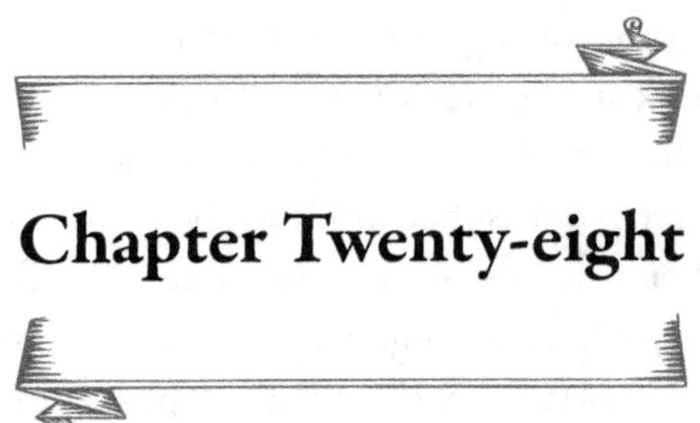

Chapter Twenty-eight

Isobel, Peter and Umbra began to cross the vast expanse of moorland, their bodies aching from the long journey. They were all pleased that at last, the agony was over. They had arrived at their destination. They strode onwards enthusiastically, sucking in the fresh chill air as though it was intoxicating liquor.

Above them, white clouds swiftly blustered over a sheet of dazzling brightness. Beneath their feet, the ground was crisp and dusted with white powdery snow. All around were steeply rolling hills and a valley draped in an early morning mist. From the dale came a symphony of sound, a gurgling, babbling river, birdsong and the whispering of a gentle breeze through the trees. On the tops of the tors jutted up frozen granite giants and scattered at their feet was a confusion of craggy boulders. In all directions, peacefully grazing ponies darted out of sight the moment Umbra stalked into view.

Isobel had learnt how to look into the depths of the eye and was able to see beyond the earthbound realms to a distant world that she could barely comprehend. They had no compass or map to guide them but followed their hearts and the wolf who strode forwards as if he was returning home.

As they silently marched on towards their sanctuary, they felt that they had entered an untouched corner of the planet, a place that continued to persist in normality. They had left so much behind, a world crying out in agony, battling against brutal invaders, and praying that they were not all taking their final breath.

Soon their vision of hope towered up before them in the form of the highest peak in the area on top of which was a tall column of precariously balanced rocks. Dwarfed by its shadow stood a lone figure.

Gooseflesh crept over Isobel's body as she realised that it was quite possibly her father who was staring down at them from the vantage point. She turned to Peter, asking, 'Do you think that's my dad?'

They stopped and faced each other. He placed his good hand on her arm looked into her deep eyes and saw that they glowed with delirious joy. Gentle tears rolled down her hot cheeks, and without thinking, he drew her close, clasping her tightly with his one arm. She in turn held on to him as her pulse quickened and he kissed her—a long tender kiss that sent every nerve ending tingling. Peter felt that he had never tasted anything so sweet and didn't want the deep warmth to end.

At last, they were connected, as one. Time moved on, and they felt compelled to release their embrace. They separated and stood smiling at each other, Isobel holding his hand not wanting the moment to end.

'Oh, Isobel Miller, I love you so, so much.' Peter was even enjoying the sound of her name. 'But yes, I think it's your father, and you had better go.'

'I love you too, Peter,' she genuinely replied.

'Go on then, run.'

'Hey, Peter, I need to give you something,' and she took her purse from her pocket and retrieving his feather handed it back to him.

'Let's stay together. We can be our own family,' Peter whispered.

She saw tears in his eyes and so turned away; these days he wouldn't want her to see him cry.

'Run Issy, run!' He shouted after her.

Peter stood watching her agile movements as she bounced over the thick, springy grass with Umbra following at her side. However, at the base of the hill, she looked around and saw that the wolf had gone and then noticed him some distance away snapping at the legs of a foal. With her chest heaving, she battled her way up the steep slope and flung herself into Jacobs's arms. They held each other tight and sobbed with both happiness and sadness.

When finally, they stood, apart they turned and watched Peter struggling up the incline, his face was pale, and his breathing constricted to the point where they thought he would collapse. Jacob went forwards and helped him to the top where Peter fell onto the grass. Isobel took the inhaler from his pocket and held it to his mouth while he sucked hard.

'We need to get you inside,' Jacob stated and helped the recovered Peter rise. He then took them around to the other side of the granite giant where there was a gap between two boulders. 'You will need to crawl through there.' Isobel could see Umbra far below devouring a poor pony.

They crawled into the opening and emerged into a large cave. Over by the far wall was a metal door.

'Everything is very sophisticated here,' Jacob said as he opened the door and they all stepped into a lift. 'What you are about to see is a secret haven, a place of safety that has been inhabited at various times throughout history. Now it has evolved into an almost completely self-sufficient system.'

As they descended deep into the crack of the Earth, they discussed with Jacob trivial everyday matters about how his soldiers took turns guarding above ground, the cleverness of the air and heating systems and how they had collected enough non-perishable food to last them years. Somehow, they had all silently agreed to put on a brave face and pretend that nothing had changed, that life was proceeding as usual. Isobel found it too difficult to share the lead weight of grief and loss that lay at the centre of her being, and her father knew by their absence that most of his family had perished. Peter also feared confronting the fact that he was an orphan as touching the memory of his lost parents was still too painful to bear; and besides, it would pollute his current state of absolute happiness.

After about twenty minutes, they stepped into a wide passage carved through the grey stone and lit with soft blue lights. An emerald stream rippled like a vein through the centre and stalagmites and stalactites grew decoratively down from the ceiling or up from the floor.

When they opened the next door, a cacophony of noise and crowds of people milling around blasted their ears.

'This is the heart of the place, where we hold meetings, eat and try to communicate with other resistance groups around the world,' Jacob explained. Then they were shown down another passage. 'This is our kitchen, pretty good, isn't it?' They nodded their agreement as they were introduced to a cook. 'Bedrooms, oh and this is the most important room of the entire building, the science lab.' He held the door ajar, and they glanced in and saw an immaculate modern-looking room that resembled nothing else in the cave.

'Selene, where's Selene?' Isobel enquired.

'That is where I am taking you now; she requested to see you both the moment you arrived.'

They walked on to the furthest end of the tunnel and went into a small softly lit room. In the centre was a glass cage with a transparent door at the side. Selene sat in the centre on a stool. The two teenagers stood staring, their eyes firmly fixed on their host. The angel beckoned them to come closer.

'I am sorry you have to meet me like this, but your human diseases are no more on my planet, so I have no immunity,' she explained in a lyrical voice.

Jacob quietly left the room.

Isobel and Peter couldn't speak and continued to gaze at her wide-eyed, mesmerised by her beauty. The angel at the burial mound had glowed brightly whereas Selene looked dull in comparison. It was evident that something was wrong. The golden hue of her skin seemed faded, and tarnished, her long hair and wings looked brittle with colours ranging from brown, yellow, and red, like autumn leaves. The angel's head was bowed slightly, and she seemed despondent.

'The Diabolus Conilium is not with you, nor the Chokmah Rings,' she sighed tragically.

'If you mean the book, it is safe. Morse the dragon took it that day, and I have a ring that my grandfather gave me,' Isobel bravely replied.

'She is right, the book is safe,' Peter added.

'I am glad you are here. You have come on a long journey and gained vast knowledge, but I must speak, for there is little time. I want you both to know that you are not alone and never have been. We are always with you even if you are not able to see us in an expected way. Our essence lives in your brain and heart. In your way of perceiving things, I am only able to explain it by saying science and religion are one. Within your, DNA are particles too small to be seen, sub-atomic particles, or intelligent particles. The only evidence that it exists is in how it affects and directs your heart and soul and the finite choices you make in life. It is like an umbilical cord that connects you to the Divine. As you grow and learn, you feed this essence until it becomes something unique but still connected to our universe. Your body is but a vessel. You are privileged.

'However, there is a multitude of universes which take on numerous forms, and just as we seek knowledge and enlightenment, others seek power and control. We have reaped the rewards of seeking wisdom, and there are those who desire to steal from our well of eternal energy. They would not be able to locate us without a particular map that was brought to your earth when it was still young when there was hope before evil stamped us out and we retreated. Even if they found us, they would need the keys that were lost to us all those centuries ago when Christ walked the Earth, to break our shield. We need to prevent access and destroy the Diabolus Conilium, or our universe will be annihilated.'

Then without warning, the lights in the room flickered and within seconds extinguished.

'There is a superstorm coming,' Selene murmured.

'What do you mean?' Peter asked feeling confused and panicked.

'There is no time, they are coming, and Umbra is howling, warning us.'

The two teenagers couldn't hear the wolf but felt a trembling beneath their feet so rushed from the room. In the corridor, they heard the wailing of alarms and everyone was rushing in and out of rooms in a state of panic and hyper-vigilance. Jacob suddenly appeared from nowhere and grabbed Isobel's arm, leading them both into the central meeting area.

'What's happening?' Peter asked in a panicked tone.

'Someone is approaching. Perhaps you know who they are or maybe they followed you. They might be safe because the boy is with a member of the monster race.'

'Dad. Dad, it's ok. They are our friends. It's Oswald and Morse, and they have the book with them, the one thing that will stop all of this.'

Jacob turned around and addressed the anxious audience.

'It's okay. This could be what we have been waiting for. We might be about to receive the book of hell which shall be buried in the depths of the earth, so bringing an end to all the destruction. If a few demons accompany it, we shall be ready.'

Everyone seemed relieved by Jacob's words of optimism and huddled together in excited groups. This could be the final day, and soon their war could be over.

'You and Peter had better go back up and greet your visitors. Myself and a couple of the soldiers will join you.' He smiled, glad to, at last, have soldiers that he could lead into an attack against those demons who had committed so much slaughter against his previous unit but inside he was far less confident that their victory was indeed, imminent.

By the time, they emerged back out onto the windy peak, the visitors were already at the base of the hill. Oswald was riding on a horse, his face concealed by a metal helmet, but the teenagers knew it was him, as high above circled Lance and at his side was the enormous black form of the dragon.

The light from the sky was dazzling, and Peter stood, shielding his eyes with his arm. Isobel peered down and saw Umbra snarling and growling uneasily at the knight's horse.

Peter's eyes adjusted to the brightness and he scanned the horizon as though he was looking for something.

'Can you hear that noise?' he uttered with a disquieting awareness that something was wrong.

'What noise?' Isobel replied.

The small group of soldiers, Jacob, Isobel, and Peter, fell silent and listened intently. Then there was no mistaking the source of the humming, as over the brow of a distant hill was a cloud blacker than any darkness they had ever seen, and it was heading towards them. The swarm was in both the sky and the ground. Soon it was thundering towards them like a tidal wave. They all froze, the dangerous force held all their attention, and for a moment they were unable to respond.

Finally, Jacob gave the order. 'Men, retreat, Isobel and Peter you must join them, and I shall remain here to greet our guests. Go, go back into the cave, and enforce total lockdown. Don't open the doors for anything.' The men vanished in seconds, but the teenagers refused to leave.

'You must go underground. It is safe down there. That is an order,' Jacob bellowed, exasperated by Isobel and Peter's stubbornness and blindness to the urgency of the situation.

'We need to go and save Oswald, and we believe he is bringing the book to us,' Peter explained, as he focused his attention on the small group below. With a heavy heart, Jacob conceded and remained by their side; believing that the next time he and his daughter met would be when they were being welcomed by their dead ancestors.

Peter was agitated by a sense of urgency as his lifelong pent-up emotions bubbled to the surface. He was desperate to save his friend, remembering all the times he had defended him against school bullies in the distant past. 'Ozzy, Ozzy, run! Run!' There was no response. It was as though he could not hear beneath the hood of metal.

However, Morse unfurled his wings and moving to a better location, swept high into the air and perched on a nearby tor. There he stood mightily, throwing flames up into the sky and down onto the ground trying to prevent the advance of the opposing force. Many tumbled to Earth but the numbers were limitless, and his efforts had a little overall effect.

They all watched as Oswald climbed from his horse, lifted his visor and looked up towards Peter and Isobel and smiled.

'Run, Ozzy, run!' they screamed in unison.

Then, caught up in his personal damnation and without a second thought, Peter launched himself down the hill. Never had he run that fast.

The demonic army was gaining ground when they suddenly came to an abrupt halt.

Peter stood in front of his friend and their eyes met.

'Oswald, look behind you. You must come with me. You are in great danger.'

'I am not who you think I am. That day at the Cathedral my sister Ariel came to me and explained all this great knowledge to me. As she spoke, I felt as though I had some residual memory of her and so I listened to what she had to tell me. She reminded me that I had once lived as her brother that I had promised never to desert her and how I had drowned in a tragic accident. She told me if I took the oath that, I would live forever as a solid creature made of flesh and blood. Eventually, I chose life.'

'When I left the ancient building, I felt anxious and had a desire to speak with Richard. I was scared that I would no longer be able to see him, so I rushed back to the castle. As I walked down Hollow End Street my vision grew misty, I felt as though I was looking at my surroundings through transparent skin. Not too far in front of me, I saw three men standing next to Jane Lacy's grave. They were covering a pile of boulders with soil and laughing as they went about their business. I heard one of them say, 'We have got rid of Lord Langley, dispatched the girl, the foolish old monk hangs from a gibbet, and now all we need to do is find the boy.'

'I rushed to Richard's house sure that he would have left me a message. There in an old chest, I found some papers that revealed that Jane was my mother and Langley, my father. Being illegitimate, I was given into the care of the Monk Richard Long. With all those, I love gone, my heart turned to stone, and I realised with absolute clarity that our world had belonged to the Devil all along.'

'Then I came, to understand that it was my duty to return the book to its rightful owner. You are the traitor Peter. It is you who should not be here.'

'Oswald, you have friends. You are Oswald Hunt, not a Langley. Please, I beg you to come with me now. There is no time we can't fight a whole army together.'

As Isobel and Jacob looked down, they could read the signs that not all was well, that the atmosphere was wrong.

'Peter, leave him, come back. We must go,' they both screamed.

'It is you who don't understand, it is you who is a spy and a traitor. They come for you not me,' Oswald added.

Peter could see from his friend's eyes that he was looking at a stranger and turned to leave, to return to the safety of the sanctuary. From afar, the onlookers saw the glint of a dagger in Oswald's hand. Peter felt a sharp pain between his shoulder blades.

'No! No! Oswald stop!' he screamed.

The knight did not stop. He was fulfilling his duty and continued his savage attack until Peter's body fell limp to the ground.

Oswald turned around, and before him, a green and blue figure materialised. They communicated in some foreign tongue. He then went up to his horse and took an object from the pannier. The girl with the broken heart saw that it was the book. He held it out to Diabolus Angelus, the messenger who took it from him. Then he took from his pocket a drawstring purse and held it up.

In an instant, the observers understood what was happening.

'No! No! This is all wrong!' Isobel yelled out as loud as she could.

The messenger once more addressed Oswald, 'you have done well young warrior the Diabolus Consilum, and the Chokmah Rings shall be returned to their rightful owner. I will leave you to lead our army into battle against all the beasts of this world. We will meet again.' In the next instance, Diabolus Angelus was gone.

Oswald crouched down over Peter's blood-soaked body, took from his belt the angel axe, climbed back on his horse, and raised his hand to signal to his forces to advance.

About the Author

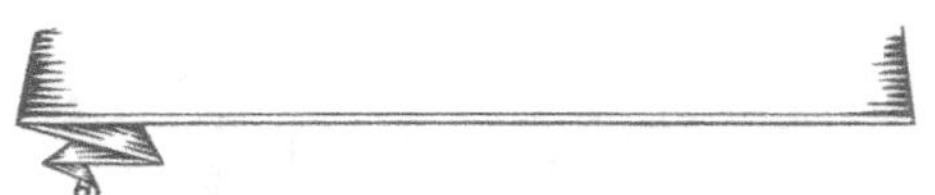

Elizabeth Wixley was born in Hertfordshire in the United Kingdom but has moved many times during her childhood. She attended the Camberwell Art School and joined a design studio in Convent Garden. Moving to Bristol, some years later, she worked full-time for the Local Education Authority, supporting children suffering from emotional and behavioural problems while ensuring that the transition into a mainstream school was done in a supportive and nurturing manner. While providing children with a haven for learning, she raised two sons as a single parent while studying for a degree in education at the University of the West of England.

Her love of fiction started at the age of six when Elizabeth's grandmother died of cancer and to ensure that the rest of the family was safe, she would spend the nights roaming the house looking for the "C" monster to make sure that he did not claim any more victims.

One sunny bright day, her sister told her that fork lightning would come and strike her down, after which she would spend her days hiding in the garage and when she heard that the sun was falling out of the sky, well, needless to say, she very seldom ventured out.

With trial and error, Elizabeth soon realized that to fight her foes, she had to stare them straight in the eye, explore them, and conquer the inner demons to stand righteous. This helped fuel her love of horror and the many mysteries of the world, creating a why and what-if scenario that runs prominently in her fascinating fiction.

Throughout Elizabeth's life, creative arts have been her passion, whether it is visiting galleries, painting, or writing. She enjoys nothing more than sharing a compelling horror story with others and holding the sanity of her readers in the palm of her hand.

Other Books by E. M. G. Wixley
Adam's Cross: Witchfinder Series
Kane's Cross
Devil's Cross
Zach's Cross
In the Devil's Own Words: Cathedral Chronicles
Blood Borne
Reflections
The Tethered Unicorn: Living Dreams
The Warning
Secrets and Shadow of the Missing
Traitor Sun: Earth's End
Vengeful Earth

SIMULATION GAME
Alfie's Treasure Hunt
Looking for Life
Email: liz1949@hotmail.co.uk
If you enjoyed this book, please leave a review. Thank you!

Don't miss out!

Visit the website below and you can sign up to receive emails whenever E.M.G Wixley publishes a new book. There's no charge and no obligation.

https://books2read.com/r/B-A-IMIE-VOHBB

BOOKS2READ

Connecting independent readers to independent writers.

9 798224 191833